"Packed . . . with plenty of humor, heart and true-to-life dialogue."

—Shelf Awareness

"In *How to Party With an Infant*, Kaui Hart Hemmings has struck on the perfect recipe for a delicious, hilarious read about motherhood, love, loss, and Lululemon.

"With the irreverent raunch of Amy Schumer, the unsentimental maternal insight of Ayelet Waldman, and the culinary ebullience of Julia Child, protagonist Mele Bart skewers an anxious, overthinking tribe of San Francisco mommies who run in a 'momtourage,' worship at the barre, and subject one another to 'catty scans' daily.

"Anyone who has ever considered jumping from a window during a nursery school tour or longed for a pot brownie during a playdate will feel validated and hugely entertained by this quirky, occasionally bitter, occasionally sweet, and wholly original novel."

—Wednesday Martin, *New York Times* bestselling author
of *Primates of Park Avenue*

"*How to Party With an Infant* is about moms—and a few good (and not so good) dads—but parenthood is by no means a prerequisite for loving this funny, honest and occasionally heartbreaking story of friends who earn the privilege of family. Kaui Hart Hemmings reminds us that we all feel like observers on the playground of life; the trick is to find someone fun to sit next to on the park bench. As they get to know each other, her characters endure all the stages of parenthood, from idealism to judgment to surrender. Their journey through the competitive, tech-rich San Francisco preschool scene is as treacherous as a ride down Lombard Street on a skateboard, and every bit as exhilarating."

—Elisabeth Egan, author of *A Window Opens*

"Kaui Hart Hemmings is the master of heartfelt unsentimentality. Her third novel looks unflinchingly at the rewards and pitfalls of single motherdom in a culture obsessed with sanctimonious parenting. By her first Brazilian wax, you'll be rooting for the unscrupulous heroine to emerge victorious (and bushy!) from the Mommy Wars."

—Courtney Maum, author of *I Am Having So Much Fun Here Without You*

HOW TO PARTY WITH AN INFANT

KAUI HART HEMMINGS

SIMON & SCHUSTER PAPERBACKS

New York London Toronto Sydney New Delhi

Simon & Schuster Paperbacks
An Imprint of Simon & Schuster, Inc.
1230 Avenue of the Americas
New York, NY 10020

First Simon & Schuster trade paperback edition August 2017

For information about special discounts for bulk purchases, please contact Simon & Schuster Special Sales at 1-866-506-1949 or business@simonandschuster.com.

The Simon & Schuster Speakers Bureau can bring authors to your live event. For more information or to book an event contact the Simon & Schuster Speakers Bureau at 1-866-248-3049 or visit our website at www.simonspeakers.com.

Manufactured in the United States of America

1 3 5 7 9 10 8 6 4 2

Library of Congress has cataloged the hardcover edition as follows:
Names: Hemmings, Kaui Hart, author.
Title: How to party with an infant / Kaui Hart Hemmings.
Description: First Simon & Schuster hardcover edition. | New York, NY : Simon & Schuster, 2016.
Identifier: LCCN 2015042738|

Subjects: | BISAC: FICTION / Literary. | FICTION / Contemporary Women. |FICTION / Family Life.
Classification: LCC PS3608.E477 H69 2016 | DDC 813/.6—dc23 LC record available at http://lccn.loc.gov/2015042738

ISBN 978-1-5011-0079-6
ISBN: 978-1-5011-0082-6 (pbk)
ISBN 978-1-5011-0083-3 (ebook)

For my Ellie

HOW TO
PARTY WITH
AN INFANT

My twenty-two-month-old toddler was shoved facedown from the top of the slide at Cow Hollow Playground by a three-year-old, non-English-speaking bully. The parents don't speak English, nor do the kids. I think they are some sort of Eastern European or maybe Chinese. There were three other children, who were all throwing rocks and the parents didn't care! When I tried to talk to the parents about the rocks, they just smiled and said, "Is not okay?" I know there's a cultural element to such behavior, but it can be maddeningly frustrating. What can the cops do about this? Should I call Immigration Services???

—Renee Grune, Post sent to the San Francisco Mother's Club

COOKING A BOOK

The afternoon holds the beautiful promise that it will soon be over. A rusty gold light falls through the clouds, the cold air has an even sharper edge, and white halogen headlights from cars on Fell and Oak make the little playground light up like a stage. Mele Bart eats cashews from a Dora cup and watches her daughter play on the purple slides.

Ellie, a wonderful mistake, is two and a half years old. Amazing. Mele remembers bringing her home from the hospital, her little head not yet fitting in the support cushion of the car seat. Mele kept looking back in disbelief. Two days prior she had left her apartment without a baby and now she was returning with one.

There were times in those first weeks, when Ellie cried and cried, her face always shaking to the right, that Mele wanted to throw her out the window. She would cry alongside her baby, wondering what was to become of her life as a single mom, the love of her life having knocked her up, then run back to the love of his life. But now, when she looks at her daughter, she wonders what was even good about life before her. What did she have? What did she do with all that time?

Movies, brunch, writing short stories. Cooking for women who had dinner parties for women they didn't seem to like very much.

Still, that doesn't make her less angry at her lying-sack-of-skin exboyfriend.

Ellie is talking to herself on the tire swing—she is quite bossy in her make-believe. In Mele's prior life she'd never be doing this: sitting at a playground and filling out a questionnaire for the San Francisco Mother's Club Cookbook Competition. She would never have predicted even joining a mother's club in the first place, but after just a few months of being with her baby all the time, she'd known she had to find some life beyond their apartment walls, for her sake and her infant's.

She smiles to herself, remembering those early days, when she was one of those friendless parents—the ones that smile too eagerly at other moms and apologize if their babies sneeze. The ones who use lame pickup lines like "I like your burp cloth" or "How do you like your Britax Roundabout?"

Mele would hit up all the hot spots—Gymboree, Day One, Music Together, playgrounds, parks, and museums—hoping to meet someone. She'd see other mothers in groups, laughing on polka-dot throw mats and think: Where do I find them? And how do I act once I do?

She imagined approaching a table of mothers with her lunch tray and asking if she could sit. She imagined the mothers telling her she had to chug a six-pack, spin around twenty times, then change a diaper in one minute flat. She kept at it—flirting, mixing and mingling, hoping to meet parents she clicked with or who at least didn't bug the shit out of her. She remembers pushing her Peg Perego up to a cool-looking mom, about to strike up a conversation. She was proud of her baby, proud of her stroller. She could fit this mama mold. It really eliminated a lot of bullshit in her life, frankly. The mom looked at them and said, "Your stroller brake's not on," then turned back to her friend, and Mele went from mother to twenty-eight-year-old single slut in an instant.

When Ellie was six months old Mele gave in and joined SFMC, the San Francisco Mother's Club, which promised to find her a playgroup that would be a perfect match. She would go ahead and pay dues for friendship. Though at first she was totally mismatched—she was like Goldilocks, trying out moms—some were too DIY, others too do-nothing-yourselves, total outsourcers. There were the design moms who looked like they walked out of *Dwell* and always seemed to have three names, like Gabrielle Muir Blake. They had husbands who all looked alike—glasses, tight black T-shirts, like something assembled: IKEA men.

There were Pac Heights moms—the kind of women who don't seem to see you—they were like Range Rovers coming down a sidewalk, expecting everyone to scatter like pigeons.

There were the article moms—who have read every book and essay on parenting and look at you like you're certifiable if you're feeding your baby with a plastic spoon instead of from your mouth to boost her immune system (like the premastication article suggested).

But finally, she has found her fit: Annie, Georgia, Barrett, and Henry. She loves the way they talk—the clip and rhythm of it. An afternoon with them can make her feel warm and invincible. She knows they aren't that original. Like the blues, parents all over the place use the same words, same chords, but it's so great to be able to synchronize with people postchildren. It's a joy, a relief, and really, a key component to happiness.

How serendipitous that at three thirty in the afternoon they all did the same thing: migrated here, to the Panhandle park. They eventually worked up the courage to talk to one another and move past the banal chitchat. Soon they found themselves laughing, shit-talking, texting, even talking on the phone! They became an unofficial playgroup, then later (this was Barrett's idea) an official SFMC playgroup, thereby able to receive the benefits: SFMC Online Forum, meetings with lecturers (free wine), and discounts at the Gap and the San Francisco Zoo. Now she catches other parents looking at them with longing and sometimes has the perverse desire to tell them their stroller brakes aren't on. She isn't completely happy, after all.

Mele looks over a few of her answers on the questionnaire, every now and then glancing up at Ellie—her adorable, pink floral baby doll dress over thick brown tights, a brown velvet coat. Children can wear period costumes from every era.

Mele has gotten a little carried away with the questionnaire, but figures she can pare it down later. She can pare it way, way down. Or maybe this is what the committee is looking for—honest first responses that jump off the page. Something wild and raw, zany and unplugged. The anti-cookbook cookbook. They are in San Francisco after all—progressive, provocative! Strippers probably breast-feed onstage! But no, things are not that cutting edge. Harvey Milk and Jerry Garcia are dead, moms shop cute boutiques in the Castro, and the mother's club of San Francisco has its very own political climate. If she is going to impress the committee, then her hobbies will have to include DIY potato stamps and cardboard sewing cards shaped like polar bears and cacti. Who fuckin' does that! Cookbook contest entrants, that's who.

In any case, the process is therapeutic; cathartic and cleansing, like a juice detox or an enema, and she's going with it. Maybe everyone should answer interview questions, even if the answers are never to be published or aired. It's comforting to be able to explain yourself, or to be asked anything at all . . .

The San Francisco Mother's Club Cookbook Competition

The annual SFMC Cookbook Competition is on! We are calling all moms who want to share their recipes and feelings on food, friends, and motherhood! From appetizers to desserts to everything in between, any type of cook has an opportunity to win. All San Francisco Mother's Club parents are eligible to enter. You'll need to fill out this questionnaire—be thorough!—and provide three recipe examples. We will then narrow down the competition and invite our five unique finalists to cook for some Very Important Moms, our fellow members Rachel Kawashima of Chopsticks Publishing Group and Lyndsey Price, head chef at Boulevard. Ever wanted to publish your own cookbook? Who knows? This could be your big break, Yummy Mummy!

We are looking for originality, variety, thoroughness, clarity, overall appeal of the recipes. The winner will win a culinary trip for two to Napa, an oven from Sears, and perhaps a book contract!* Good luck, ladies! Bon appétit!

*A book contract is at the sole discretion of an outside party and not an official prize of this contest.

SFMC Questionnaire

The purpose of this questionnaire is to let the Steering Committee know more about you, your cookbook, and your writing style, so please be as detailed as possible. Through your questionnaire we are hoping to "meet" you and your world. Since the book should include vignettes on motherhood and your playgroup friendships, we will be looking for an original and clear voice. Have fun with it! Whet our palates!

Name: *Mele Bart*

Three possible titles for your cookbook:

>*Bread to My Butter*
>*Hungry Woman*
>*How to Party with an Infant*

What are your interests, avocations, and hobbies?

I love to read and write and take long walks while I listen to music and rehearse answers to a pretend Barbara Walters interview. I should say, I *used* to like writing, reading, and taking long walks. I used to like my looks, too, keeping them up. Now I rarely look in the mirror.

I used to like going to movies, having sex, shopping, but now, as you know, I have a baby. My current interests are crosswords, heavy snacking in front of the television after Ellie goes to bed, thinking of possible *Saturday Night Live* skits, hunting for the best soda fridges in town, strolling in grocery stores, ogling food at the Embarcadero Farmers' Market, and making fusion gum (this is where I put a piece of fruit-flavored gum in my mouth, then about a minute later, a mint-flavored gum). I am also interested in television and not in an ironic way. Certain shows on Bravo make me say out loud: "My God, I love America."

Bobby, my ex-boyfriend and father of my child, would only tolerate a reality show about motorcycle mechanics, couldn't stand when I watched entertainment news.

"They just spent fifteen minutes telling us some actress put a quarter into a parking meter," he'd say.

He liked looking at motorcycles and pizza ovens on Craigslist. He'd browse for hours, perhaps shopping for his other life out of the city that I didn't know about: things for his garage, his house, and alas, for his fiancée, a cheese maker in Petaluma. When he first told me about her I envisioned a country woman milking goats, her jeans pulled up to her nipples, but she isn't like that at all. She's finely assembled, chic and classic. She has a perfect ponytail, big teeth, and high cheekbones—that alien look of models. She knows how to sail, make cheese, ride horses, and she's marrying the man I thought I'd be with for the rest of my life.

What do you do for a living?

Right now not much. My mom and stepdad help me out. They don't think people should have babies out of wedlock, yet are total pro-lifers, so it's a mixed message. They're also not "kid people," something I already knew, having been their kid. They live in Hawaii, a place I jammed out of as soon as I got my diploma. I miss the house, of course, my bedroom and its sliding glass door with wood trim. Every morning I would wake to the sound of chattering birds and the looming greenness of the mountain range upon which battles between tribes were fought. On my four-poster bed I'd inhale the scent of tiare through the wooden jalousies, then I'd walk to the kitchen, where a woman named Lehua would be making me breakfast, both of us ashamed and feeling sorry for one another.

My stepdad is an overdeveloper on Oahu. He has a Tesla and chest hair. Howard. He purports that his buildings reflect the Hawaiian spirit, but imports everything from Italy and caters to high-end Chinese. If there's any Hawaiian spirit it's because the buildings probably sit on ancient burial grounds.

My real dad (a kind of Hawaiian spirit) left when I was two, which was fine with my mom because all he did was fish and smoke pot. She needed essentials like a BMW and white leather pants. She was twenty-one and over the slumming-it stage.

He called me on some birthdays—my eighth, tenth, and thirteenth. Since age six I have only seen him twice. He's like a whale that way. Our conversations were very abbreviated, for me because I didn't know what to say; for him because he spoke pidgin English. I recall very little (though there is little to recall):

Him: What grade you in now?
Me: Third.
   Cut to two years later.
Him: Did you get da kine jean jacket I sent?
Me: Yes. But it's a size five. It's like a crop top. We can't show our midriffs in school, and I wouldn't want to anyway.
   Three years later.
Him: What grade you stay?
Me: Seventh.
Him: Shoots. I'll send you some Yellowman CDs. You like 'em.
Me: Can I visit?
Him: Nah.
Me: Why not?
Him: Uh . . . we remodeling, das why.

End scene. That's it. I'm done with those chapters. Ellie is my family. I think of my mom and stepdad as sponsors. I will wear their clothes, advertising from a distance that they're a decent company.

I used to work for a place called Wheelbarrows, where I'd make and deliver meals to people who could afford not to cook. I was also a menu consultant. Now Ellie is my job and I still have my recipe blog, which pays fairly well with sponsors like Tyson chicken, Epicurious, Whine and Dine, and Freecreditscore.com.

If you read the directions in the posted recipes you'll notice I'll slip in little anecdotes about my day, my interactions with other moms and the things I've overheard. For example, yesterday at SF Gymnastics I overheard a conversation where mothers were offering advice to a mom whose baby was so cute everyone wanted to touch her and she needed ways to politely say no.

One mother offered this advice: "People who touch babies are creepy. Everyone wanted to touch Janey, especially when she was neutropenic and had no white cells. This made her look like an ivory doll and strangers just pawed at her. Tell them to back off, or to touch her toes."

Another said this: "It's because there are no children here. They're like Birkin bags. I'd just avoid crowded public places and neighborhoods like the Mission with high immigrant populations."

The last mom contributed this: "My daughter gets touched all the time. It's what happens when they're pretty. The other day this bum-like person kept trying to remove her hand socks and smell her! And she's an old people magnet. I keep antibacterial wipes ready and wipe her hands immediately after contact with anyone. Even the nonelderly."

You can find this exchange under "Ancho Chili Steaks." I could add that to my list of hobbies: overhearing. I listen to everything. It's something to do when you're at playgrounds or kid classes. I've heard some crazy things, said in the most earnest way. People really care about stuff! My intention with these asides isn't to be a mean girl, soaking in the candid chitchat then turning around and enlarging it for the sake of entertainment and enhanced self-worth . . . but sometimes that ends up happening. People like it though. I get comments like "Those women make me want to shoot myself" or "When people ask to touch my baby I just say, 'She bites!' Jesus Christ."

Or I get total misinterpretations.

Take this mother at an SFMC meeting who happened to read my blog post on sake-steamed halibut and separation anxiety.

"Thank God someone's talking about babies sucking the life right out of you," she said.

"Um," I said. "That's not really . . . I was just writing about fish and soba—"

"Your life is gone. Just gone," she said, looking off into the distance; then she rubbed her hands together and said, "You are so bad!"

People like it when other people are bad. It lets them off the hook. But I'm not bad. I'm just listening and looking around. I hope, when Ellie starts school, I can find a way to put this to use. While my parents won't let us go hungry, I want to do something with my life—I want to raise Ellie well and I want her to have a mom who does more than raise her. I went to grad school to be a writer, and I guess I still want now what I wanted then: to write about my woes, yet use structures and plots and characters that make them your woes as well. I want to reveal something true. I want you to turn the page.

What inspired you to work on an SFMC cookbook? What will make it different from other cookbooks?

When I heard about the competition, I thought, How lame, and then: How lame if someone else won and got a book contract out of this! And so I thought I'd give it a go and try to come up with an original angle.

It happened that the very day I decided to embark upon this culinary journey my ex, Bobby Morton, was coming over to see Ellie (for the first time in two weeks) and so I thought I'd go ahead and freshen up a little. I'd clean the apartment, blow out my hair, put on some lipstick, and, um, go out and wax my privates. I had never done this before.

Within one minute of meeting my waxer I was on a bed, naked from the waist down, and her hand was on my parts. She had a thick head of hair and red lips and smelled like a scratch-and-sniff sticker. I was trying to think of something to say, but all that came to mind was "So, have you seen any good ones lately?"

She took me seriously and told me who she knows, who she waxes—I guess there wasn't client-waxer privilege. She was telling me what was "in" these days, which made me think of women requesting long layers or a bob, but I didn't really hear what she was saying because she poured the burning wax onto my skin, and holy fuckface, all thoughts disappeared. She placed a strip on my (God I hate this word) labia and pulled—rip!—and holy Whitney Houston I was angry at this woman! I wanted retro bush to be "in" so she'd be shit out of a job! Why do people regularly subject themselves to this? Why was I torturing myself for Bobby? He left me, and even if he hadn't, he never needed incentive. In fact, to avoid pregnancy I should have gotten myself a reverse Brazilian. What would that be? A Greek? An Armenian?

I was in so much pain. I almost told her to stop, but it was too late because then I'd look like I had mange.

"Should I keep a strip, make a triangle, or take it all off?" she asked.

"Take it all," I whimpered, not because I'm stoic or anything, but because I don't get the little landing strip thing. Can you imagine if we shaved our armpits but left a strip of hair? Or shaved our legs but left a hairy triangle?

Before I went in, I asked the moms in my playgroup, "Why do people get this done?"

"Who knows?" Barrett said. "To feel clean? Gary's lucky if I bathe. He doesn't care."

"Maybe it's like getting a haircut or highlights," Georgia said. "You're taking care of yourself. But I guess you can't really show everyone the results as you would with highlights."

"It's not like a haircut," Annie said. "My hairdresser doesn't tell me to hold my butt cheek while she waxes my asshole. You do it for the guys. They like it for the same reason they like you to swallow. It's porno. It's that special thing."

"I don't know," Georgia said. "I go to Supercuts."

The waxer took another pull from the top. Tears welled in my eyes. I was writing my will in my head and wondering why I ever agreed to let this stranger touch and hurt me so. Bobby was engaged. It was over. The last time he had seen my vagina a head was coming out of it and I had pooed on the table. I'm sure these images could not be superseded. I began to really tear up then, but of course my "stylist" thought this was in reaction to her yanking out my pubic hair.

"You're doing real good," she said, even though I wasn't doing anything, just lying there, my legs in second position. She told me about her last two clients. One yelled "motherfucker" after each tug. One prayed. I could just hear it: "Please, Lord, give me the strength to withstand the pain of hair being pulled off of my privates so that I can go forth into this day with a clean, porno va-jj. Amen. Oh yes, and bless those in Darfur."

Finally, she was done. I took a quick peek and was horrified. It looked like that hairless cat, Mr. Bigglesworth. It looked cold and lonely. I hated it! I hated my privates! I hated Bobby. I didn't have a witness—no one to commiserate with, no one to love my daughter with. Not having a dad around was such an unfair strike against her. I didn't want to raise a hitter, a biter, or a child so scarred by abandonment she'd shake on the sidelines while other kids laughed and lobbed balls at one another. And then she'd get older and sleep with everyone and experiment with tons of drugs, like me. On the waxer's table I thought, How could he bear to be without her? She has a fantastic sense of humor. She can be dramatically sour and fiery, then moments later gooey warm and sweet. She's like Thai food. She's my little Eggplant Pad Ma Coeur.

I came home and cooked that very dish, feeling good, like a mother, a single, determined, capable mother with a sexy pelvis and a beautiful daughter, and I thought: These feelings equal Eggplant Pad Ma Coeur. And this dish came from a story about vaginal waxing.

What else? What are some more of life's little word problems? Because this—the eggplant was yielding and vibrant—this I could do. This I could solve. This was making a shitty thing into something damn right delicious.

I've decided to come up with recipes inspired by my friends in my playgroup. My angle: What kinds of culinary creations do they inspire? Barrett, Annie, Georgia, and Henry. I'll take moments from their everyday lives—moments that define their issues somehow, and come up with the food equivalents. I will make a difficult moment in their lives a little more palatable.

What are your contributions to SFMC and our motherhood community? What have you "brought to the table"?

I don't know what you're talking about . . .

Mele looks up to find her daughter. Ellie's still on the slide, climbing to the top. Another mother is telling her boy, "Excuse me, Branson, we go down the slide, we don't climb up," but Mele couldn't give a fuck if Ellie goes up. Who cares? The more rules you have, the more you have to enforce them, and Mele likes the option of sitting on her ass sometimes.

The answers felt good to write, and read. She's surprised by the emotions the process produced: anger, jealousy, but also, a moving appreciation for the life she has. Sometimes you have to trudge through the muck to experience one of the best things in the world: gratitude. She knows this feeling could pass so she holds on to it like it's a coin, something small and hard and pocketable. She is a single mom. She's not dead. This is good. Ellie is healthy and happy and almost worn out, and in a few hours Mele will bathe her and feed her and read to her and tell her about the sand crab and tell her she loves her more, and then she'll sit on the couch and watch *The Real Housewives of Wherever*. Soon her friends will be here and she'll begin her new venture. Georgia, Henry, Barrett, and Annie will each have a turn to tell her a story.

Renee—I am very sympathetic to your desires to keep your child safe. Safety is nonnegotiable. I understand that you are outraged, but your insinuations are inappropriate, bigoted, insensitive, and racist. Please don't mistake concern for your child for bigotry against other ethnic groups. If you believe calling USCIS will "solve" your problem, then the real problem is much larger than this discussion forum. Best of luck.

—Beth Nelson

I can't imagine having an affair. That would mean having to have sex with *two* people!

—Overheard at Quince restaurant

CARVING A WIFE

er friends have taken over the back corner table at the Panhandle playground. They're all drinking a cheap Shiraz from red plastic cups and watching Gabe, Georgia's almost three-year-old son, sitting in the sandbox, swatting his tongue, and screaming. Today Georgia looks like one of those women in Theraflu commercials, yet without the luxury of being in bed under clean, cool sheets. Zoë, her newborn mistake, is sucking on her left boob.

"You better win this thing," Annie says. "It better not be that woman who's always posting links to her cupcakes. Aren't people sick of crazy cupcakes? Red Velvet Pudding Pop with Grenache, Quinoa, and Pop Rocks."

It's funny being sandwiched by these ladies: Annie on her right, the ends of her blond hair dyed blue, a Batman tattoo on her left shoulder; Barrett on her left, her blond hair in a stringent bob. As a parent you're friends with people you never thought you'd be friends with.

"What is it you're doing again?" Henry asks.

He's the only man in the group. He's a forty-five-year-old retiree (he sold his company to Microsoft) who owns a beautiful home in Pacific Heights but avoids playgrounds in that area because he sees those people enough as it is and he likes to slum it whenever possible.

"The moms only talk about fund-raisers and redecorating, the men all talk about investments and who's 'killing it,'" he has said to Mele.

His wife is the daughter of a prominent family, who actually refer to themselves as scions of San Francisco.

"Old money," he told her. "They're even weirder. Her mom has a wall made out of peacocks."

Mele doesn't think he's very happy.

Sometimes Henry meets the group here without his four-year-old even though there's a sign on the front gate that says, ADULTS MUST BE ACCOMPANIED BY CHILDREN.

"I'm entering the cookbook competition," Mele says with a flourish to disguise embarrassment. It's always a tad humiliating to admit you're trying to accomplish something, and a *mother's club* competition sounds like such hogwash. What is hogwash anyway? She imagines little piggies getting scrubbed down with a loofah, their tiny tails in erect spirals.

"What you'll do is tell me some kind of anecdote, something personal." She says in a lowered voice to the ladies: "Remember when I told you I turned my Brazilian wax into Thai food?"

"Has it grown back yet?" Barrett asks.

Mele wiggles on the bench as her answer.

Barrett gets up, most likely to tell her daughter, who's in a face-off by the tire swing, that hands are not for hitting.

"What are you guys talking about?" Henry asks, moving down the bench toward Mele.

"Nothing," Georgia says.

"Mele's going to take your despair and turn it into cupcakes," Annie says.

He glances at Mele, and she looks down. She's always a little shy around him. They have this innocent flirtation going on, but now that he's having marital problems, the innocence isn't stained necessarily, but is taking on a different hue.

"Despair into cupcakes," he says.

He seems off today, sullen and pensive, like he's deciding on whom to fire.

"You'll tell me a story," Mele says, "and I'll create a suitable recipe. If that makes any sense."

"I tell you stories all the time," he says, and it's true. It's something they all do, something Mele has always had a knack for: drawing people out, unraveling them. When she first met Bobby, who was reticent and mysterious, she asked him about his regrets, past girlfriends, his first memory, what he was like in high school. She watched him open up. He was intricate origami, undoing the folds, showing her how he was made. It was so simple. Ask questions, then listen.

"Tell me why you're so lost in thought," Mele says to Henry.

Observe people. Notice them. Ask what they're dying to tell you anyway.

She watches Barrett's daughter push down on Gabe's head as if he were a jack-in-the-box. Gabe-in-the-box raises his fleshy fists in anger. Mele squints, pretends she's watching midget wrestling.

"You know you're not supposed to say *midget* anymore?" she says.

"What do you win again?" Annie asks, and Mele knows that what she's really asking is, Why are you wasting your time with a cookbook competition?

"A trip to Napa," Mele says. "I don't know, it's just something to do. I do it anyway, basically. Maybe it can be a real book one day." She laughs so they know she isn't serious, but she is so very serious. She wants to publish a book, to make her dream come true, but she doesn't want to say she wants this—she just wants it to happen and then say that she wanted it. Her other motivations are too difficult to express. Single motherhood, Bobby, no real career, the love she has for her child, the guilt she has about her impatience, laziness, and sometimes utter boredom with being a mother. She has no interest in seeing Ellie play with blocks. None.

She needs something tangible to work on, and immersing herself in food and other people's stories should keep sadness out of sight, simmering. She needs some tiny accomplishment to shove up Bobby's ass and an excuse to cook, something she didn't enjoy that much at work, but at home, in her own tiny kitchen, cooking with music and a glass of wine, little Ellie flipping through a book or watching *Barney*—this is the best part of her day.

She's entering the contest because vacancies should be filled, hunger should be satiated, and Bobby called the other day and had the audacity to invite her to his wedding.

"We'd like Ellie to be the flower girl," he said.

We. Meaning him and the big cheese.

Mele looked out her living room window, dazed. She could hear Ellie behind her pressing the buttons on her musical frog. *Five minutes to night-night.* And then a song came on, a mournful waltz. Mele's eyes came to focus on someone trying to parallel-park, holding up a row of cars. She felt united with this driver—different problems but that same feeling of panic and inadequacy. She wanted to put her life in park, lean over the steering wheel, and sob.

"I'll call you right back." She settled into the armchair in the living room, as if a show was about to begin. Ellie had the plush frog in her lap, and its lament filled the living room. Mele felt a deep shame and guilt, wanting her child all to herself. How happy it would make Ellie to be a flower girl, to don a princess dress and walk down the aisle, but at that moment she'd rather Ellie feel rejected or without. There was a new challenge to parenting just then—it was hard to do it on your own, but harder to maintain a generous spirit while parenting with someone who hurt you. A good mother lets go. A good mother hides her sadness.

She called him back, and yes, Ellie would be the flower girl, but as for Mele coming to the wedding, she would have to think about it.

She's been looking for a dress ever since.

"I could use something to focus on," she says. She catches Annie rolling her eyes. They all knew about the invitation to the wedding, and some were more supportive than others.

"Here," Annie says. "Here's some inspiration." She looks at her phone. Mele knows she's going to read them an email from the SFMC group. They're all obsessed right now with the posts from a mom threatening to call Immigration for playground roughhousing.

"She says she understands bullying is a cultural element, but that doesn't mean her son has to fall victim to hate crimes."

Annie starts to type.

"What are you doing?" Mele asks.

"I'm posting." She reads while she types: "I totally agree. The Chinese love mu shu pork and rock throwing, but it doesn't mean they have to do it at our playgrounds!"

"Doesn't your email show up?" Mele asks.

"No, I have a fake one just for this purpose. I sign off using A.L., West Portal. Ooh this next one's good. So this woman needs a stucco consultant, and she had to say, 'for my three-story, seven-bedroom Gold Coast home.' These ladies always have to slip in their square footage."

Henry sits up on the green bench. "She went behind my back. Again."

"Who?" Mele asks, not knowing what he's talking about.

"Kate," he says. "My wife. That's who wrote that post. I told her we didn't need a stucco consultant. We don't need a thing for our house. It's perfectly fine."

Tommy, his four-year-old, jumps onto his lap, and he winces. Mele wonders what he meant by *again*. She imagines his wife sneaking into a room full of undercover consultants.

"Ouch," his son says from his lap.

"Sorry," Henry says, and he loosens his grip on Tommy's thigh.

"That was your *wife's* post?" Annie asks.

"You have a three-story, seven-bedroom home?" Georgia asks.

"It's not what you think," he says. "It's way the fuck beyond. Oops. Sorry, son."

Tommy squirms off his lap, then runs toward the tire swing. "See you later, fuckers!" he says.

"Oops," Henry says, watching his son run off in what seems to be a wistful, desperate way, as if he has an urge to yell: "Good luck out there!" He looks over at Mele and seems to shake himself off after coming up for air.

"The other night," he says just for Mele to hear, "I overheard my daughter saying to her brother and his friends, 'You'll either cry or laugh your ass off.' Something like that. I had no idea what she was talking about, but that's it. That sums everything up right now. I'm ready to tell you what's on my mind."

Mele moves closer to him, her hand near his and the graffiti that's etched into the bench: MY DICK. Someone came here and took the time to write that. What a poor, lost soul.

Georgia and Annie walk away to join Barrett by the kids, and it's nice—witnessing this migration toward their young. A hard light shoots through the fencing. She can hear the guys behind her at the basketball court. One of them yells, "Move off me, son! That's what I'm talking about!"

"Ready when you are," Mele says. She has trouble looking him in the eye. She can speak boldly and candidly, but always looks ahead, a light smile on her face. He sinks down, assuming his usual position on the green bench, his legs far apart so that he looks like he's in a dugout, waiting to hit it out of the park.

HENRY AND THE GIRL

enry has been drinking, but doesn't think the boys can tell. Maybe they can. They're sixteen, after all, and he knows they're considered good-looking and popular. He isn't sure what makes one popular these days—it must vary from place to place, school to school. At his son's school, he imagines money has something to do with it. Money, yet a cool, false dismissal of it. Trendy tattered clothing, friends on scholarships, going green. He has known these boys from the time they were in preschool together. God. That was a long time ago.

Henry supposes the kids might be drunk as well. When he and Kate got back from dinner he found them all in the kitchen, devouring chips and cold pizza, quesadillas, the kinds of foods you want after drinking. Maybe they're stoned. They've either stacked their potato chips on top of their pizzas or rolled them into their tortillas. His son has a huge bowl of ice cream with a jar of chocolate sauce in front of him, something he wouldn't normally eat. He moves a chip toward the ice cream, then changes his mind and puts it in his mouth, plain. He's so stoned.

Is Henry supposed to say something? "Are you high?" "Are you drunk?" "Do I care?" He realizes they're all looking up at him and remembers he's been telling them a story.

"Where was I?" He holds the counter and looks at the one, two, three boys. He hears a toilet flush. Four boys. Four boys are waiting for him to tell them about girls.

Ross comes out of the bathroom, wiping his hands on his pants. Tim Tupper, Tupp, they call him, punches Ross in the leg, and Ross says, "What was that for?" and Tupp shrugs.

"Where was I?" Henry asks.

"You were telling us to forget about the cheerleaders," Shipley says.

Henry wishes his name wasn't Shipley. He's known him the longest. He had sex with Shipley's mother, but that was way back when she had brown hair and smoked cloves. She drank dirty martinis in public, Zima in private. Now she's blond and always looks like she's going to a ballet class. She probably doesn't drink at all anymore. She probably does nothing but collect art. Unfortunate the way time ravages us, he thinks.

"The thing is," Shipley says. "Cheerleaders aren't cool now anyway."

"Well, you know what I mean," Henry says. "The ones you're supposed to want." He pictures Kate and thinks of the playground she goes to (she wouldn't dare go to the Panhandle, his favorite). Just as dogs resemble their owners, people resemble their playgrounds. Alta Plaza is freshly remodeled with a nicely manicured layout and top-of-the-line structures. It's in an expensive neighborhood, at the top of a hill, looking down upon the city of San Francisco. It's clean, safe, and pristine.

Kate has straight brown hair, cropped and professional as if she had a job. She has a manicured body, top-of-the-line bone structure. She carries herself easily and never has problems knowing what to do with her hands when standing in groups. She never adjusts her clothes. She holds her head high, looking down upon the city of San Francisco. Kate is very pretty.

"The pretty girls," Henry says. "That's who I mean. Stay away from them. They have short shelf lives, believe me. If your purpose is to get laid, go for the rebels, the sarcastic ones. The prissy, pretty ones, they'll tear your heart in two and it's not worth it. The girls in black, the ones with combat boots. That's where it's at."

A few of the boys chuckle. Shipley says, "Can you imagine getting with Carla? Freak show. She'd bite your pecker off."

"You're the only one around here with a pecker, Ship," Tupp says. "The rest of us have dicks."

The boys laugh, then appraise Henry's reaction, but he's absorbed in his own advice, which he knows would have been completely different if he were talking to these kids a year ago. Still, he decides to stay the course. So what if he says the wrong things and so what if he's saying them because he's angry with Kate? They shouldn't be listening to him anyway. You're not supposed to listen to fathers.

"I don't care if Sophia Jagger's shelf life is short," Tupp says. "She's Sophia Jagger. I don't care what she looks like in ten years. Even five. She's hot now. That's all that matters."

The boys grumble their consensus, and Henry feels his authority slipping away. "Yeah, but will Sophia Jagger sleep with you?" he asks. His question seems to put them into a philosophical and possibly erotic daydream.

"She's going out with Austin," his son says.

"And who was she going out with before that?" Henry asks.

Ross raises his hand. "Me."

"For how long?" Henry asks.

"Seven months."

"Did she sleep with you?" He really shouldn't be talking like this.

"No," Ross says.

"See?" Henry says. "She goes out with boys. She has long and mean-ingful relationships. She's not going to screw around. The girls you boys are neglecting—the skaters, the loners—they'll screw around. I'm telling you."

Henry looks at his son's ice cream and wishes he could have a bowl, but he can feel the fat on his face when he jogs. He used to be able to eat anything he wanted to. He wishes he could slip into his son's body for a day to eat and talk to girls in high school. They were so attentive back then! Boys were their life! Why didn't anyone tell him it would never be like that again? He wishes he and his son could crash into each other like in the movies when the kid and the parent switch roles. His son is lithe and always tan. His son uses big words and knows what they mean. His son looks nothing like him, or at least how he looked when he was his age. When he was younger, Henry had an earring in his left ear and a beard that made him look scary. He was scary, or could be. When he shaved off the beard he noticed people started smiling at him, which in turn made him nicer.

On prom night a few months back, his son and his friends and their dates were over at the house and Henry saw his son give his date this look—his mouth sort of made this chewing motion and he winked slightly, as if by accident, and this took Henry back because it was the same sort of thing he'd do at The Shoe when he'd spot Kate across the room. They were twenty-two and had solidified their relationship quickly by sleeping together the first night they met. He liked that they went to bars and she didn't hang all over him. She'd talk to other people, she'd flirt and dance, but their gazes would always find each other and he'd give her that look—something he didn't even realize he did until she pointed it out to him.

How long has it been since he's given Kate that look? Earlier to-night he just watched her blankly as she and Nadine gossiped about their work on some committee. He found himself getting angry. She made the same segues, the same jokes and speeches of concern. He couldn't stand her voice, or the ways she tried to get him into the conversation; one way was by a firm kick in the shin during the first small-plates course of bitter greens. Why would anyone eat bitter greens? He can't stand mesclun and endive or radicchio, or that spidery, throat-itching green that makes him feel he is chewing on a tumbleweed that just rolled out of a Western, but when the salad came everyone lit up and proclaimed it "gorgeous." It had some pear in it, some kind of cheese, and some kind of nut. Big deal. Of course it wasn't described that way. On the menu it was something like Bodega Bay arugula, Stinson goat cheese, house-cured ham made from pigs that only eat water chestnuts.

Henry thought of the salad he and Kate always got at Original Joe's. A wedge of iceberg lettuce with blue cheese dressing. That's it. She loved it then, so why is she too good for it now? He almost asked her why right there at the table in front of their friends. He also almost asked, "Why are we pretending to love each other? What happened last weekend? Just tell me," but he knew she wouldn't tell him. He had already asked, and she claimed there was nothing to tell.

Henry looks at the boys' snacks. He hates small plates! He hates them! He opens the fridge and takes out the mayonnaise and turkey. He's going to make himself a sandwich.

"What kind of girl was Mom?" his son asks.

"What do you mean?" Henry says.

"Was she a weirdo or was she like Sophia?"

Henry thinks of the party in Russian Hill they'd attended the previous weekend. He'd seen her talking to a friend of theirs, a married friend who is quite famous in the city for being the son of someone rich. He goes to parties and gets photographed. That's his job, basically. The man's wife and Kate are on Neighborhood Watch together, which Henry thinks is a joke. They live in a diverse, cosmopolitan city, though in a part of the city where you may as well be in a suburb. Suspicious activity simply means a minority who doesn't work for you is in front of your house. When he drives down Pacific he often sees the other man's wife in the window with a phone in her hand, gazing worriedly at the construction workers in front of a neighboring home. Actually, he drives down Pacific hoping to see her in the window, hoping to see her fear.

But the party. Some party for some fashion designer. This man and Kate had been talking to one another much more frequently at other parties, group dinners, fund-raisers. But Henry wasn't suspicious until this night, where something seemed different. They weren't talking that much, but when they did, they did so very close, almost nervously. The entire time she looked embarrassed by whatever he was saying.

At one point in the evening Henry lost sight of them and he went on a search. He found them in a hallway. She and the man were standing close together. They both looked drunk and almost angry. During the car ride home he said, "What was that all about?" but she just said, "What was what all about? What are you talking about?"

Henry puts mayonnaise on both slices of bread.

"Dad," his son says. "I asked what kind of girl Mom was."

"Mom was cool," Henry says. "She was, you know, a popular girl. I met her after college though. The categories don't apply. All girls sleep around after college."

The boys perk up at this.

"Didn't you just get back from dinner?" his son asks.

"You don't eat when you go out to dinner," Henry says. "You order small plates. You take a bite and it's over. I probably took seven bites the whole night."

Henry layers chips over the turkey and cheese.

"You'll also never have fun when you go out to eat," he says. "Where do you guys go? To a taqueria? Or a fast-food joint? Your best times are probably there, right? You joke around, talk about what went down, you're loud and obnoxious, you throw shit, you maybe even get into fights." Henry remembers wrestling in a McDonald's with a guy named Steve-o. "Well, not anymore. Now you just sit there and eat lame food and talk about lame food and about what was in so-and-so's chicken recipe the other weekend. And if the people you're with happen to have had a baby recently, then forget it. You'll just talk about the baby's sleeping patterns and that's it."

"What else?" Ross asks.

"What else what?" Henry takes a bite of his amazing sandwich. "Ah," he says.

"What else happens to you?" Ross asks.

"What else sucks when you get old?" Tupp says. He throws an apple against the fridge.

"What the hell?" Henry says.

"It was rotten," Tupp says.

Henry looks at the boy. He's a buff kid, though stubby, low to the ground. Henry notices dandruff in his eyebrows.

"Well," Henry says, ignoring the apple, "the other day I picked a pillow off the floor and I grunted. Every time you get up from the couch or your chair you'll feel it in your ankles. You don't have sex, but you guys are used to that."

He wants to say, "You won't be madly in love with the woman you thought you'd be madly in love with forever. And she won't be madly in love with you. She'll just be mad. And, one day, you'll come home not knowing what she's just done to you. It will make you furious and you'll yell at the dog for no reason. You'll gaze at your sleeping toddler for company. Your sleeping toddler will be your best friend. You'll tell him: "I love your mother, but only because another man might."

"Getting old," Henry says, looking at these boys, who can run fast, jump high, eat like shit. "It will be a shocker." He may be upsetting the boys. They look worried as they chew their food. Tupp cleans up the fridge. The apple.

"It's got some perks, though," Henry says, but he knows he doesn't sound convincing.

Shipley cuts in. "I hear you should go for the softball girls and tell them everyone thinks they're lesbians and then they'll do it with you to prove they're not."

"But what if they are?" his son asks.

"Then it's still a score 'cause you get to do it with a lesbian."

Ross falls off the edge of his stool, and everyone laughs then looks around nervously, and then Henry really knows that they've been drinking. Ross grins and smooths his black hair back, returns to his chair.

"You can't drink," Henry says. The boys all look down. His son's face flushes—he has that same giveaway skin. "I mean, when you're old. When I was in college I could really knock 'em back—me and my buddy, Chavez—we'd drink a case of Bud Light every night. A case each. Every single night. No way could I do that now."

The boys all smile except for Shipley, who opens his mouth and after a pause lets out a belch that sounds like a foghorn. His son still seems a little nervous, and Henry wonders if it's in response to "Chavez." Who's Chavez? he must be wondering. The thing is, when it comes down to it, he and Chavez would have kicked his son's ass if his son had been, say, in a McDonald's one night and he happened to look at them the wrong way. Henry grew up in Concord. He didn't like city boys like his son, with their private schools and preppy clothes and longish hair. His son skis and drives a brand-new Escalade. His ass would have been demolished. But he loves him now, of course, as an adult. It's just that his kids, the way they live, it's all just a little foreign to him. The apple fell far, far away from the tree. Then smashed into a Sub-Zero.

He supposes his eighteen-year-old daughter isn't as conventional. He passed her room the other day and heard her friend Jillian say, "Did you see what she was wearing? It was camouflage, but purple, and I went up to her and was all, 'That's cute.'"

"Glamouflage," he heard his daughter say in an annoyed voice. "That's what it's called. And who the fuck cares?"

Her spirit reminded him of Kate's when he first met her.

His son is eyeing him, and he wonders if he knows he and his mom are having problems. If he can feel the tension between them.

"What else, Dad?" his son asks. "What else is wrong with your life?"

Yeah. He knows.

"Nothing. I'm just shooting the bull."

"So were you a player or something?" Shipley asks.

Henry thinks of Shipley's mother, her rich brown hair like a desk in a banker's office. They grew apart, he endured her more than liked her, and then she introduced him to Kate. Kate had good taste in music. That's what he liked about her immediately. She was funny, too. Sharp. He remembers she'd get so wasted on this nasty pink wine and he'd have to carry her from the car to the bed, up those damn steps off Fillmore. She was light, though a bit heavier when she was drunk. It made him feel like she trusted him with all of her weight.

"I guess I kind of was a player," Henry says. "But I was a good guy." He gives the boys a sarcastic smile. "I loved 'em all."

He takes another bite of his sandwich and sees Kate in the doorway looking at him. His confidence in front of the boys whittles down to a splinter. He can never be someone else in front of her.

"You loved them all, huh?" She has her arms crossed over her chest as she always does these days. The boys look in her direction, then focus on putting the food into their mouths as soberly as possible. Except for Tupp, who says, "Hi, Mrs. Hale. Mr. Hale here was just giving us some fatherly advice."

33

"Oh?" She's drunk as well. They're all drunk in the kitchen. Henry can feel mayonnaise in the corner of his mouth and he decides to leave it there. Fuck it.

"What kind of advice?" she asks.

"Advice on girls," Tom says.

Kate laughs that kind of hateful laugh meant to shrink his balls. Henry wants to push her. He actually wants to harm her because of this laugh, but then he realizes what he really wants to do is take her into his arms and say, "Let's laugh for real! Remember we used to do that?" But then he catches her eye and doesn't want to hold her anymore. He's right back to his abusive thoughts.

"So, what's the advice? What gems has my husband handed to you tonight?"

"Stay away from the cheerleaders," Shipley says.

"Go for the ugly ones," Tupp says. "They'll put out."

"I did not say that."

"Are you eating?" Kate asks. "You just ate."

"I did not just eat. What we did was not called eating."

"The punks, the rebels," Shipley continues. "The loners."

"You're teaching them how to get laid?"

Henry can feel his son staring at him, a sad, sharp stare. He remembers when his son was preschool age he liked to eat his dinner on Henry's lap. This would bother him, but after a few beers he'd like it, especially if they were out with other families. A few beers would make most annoying things endearing, and he suspects that's a parenting tool no one really gives a lot of credit to. Beer.

"You want to know what to do?" Kate says.

The boys laugh weakly, like an old lady has just made a knock-knock joke, and then the room is silent. Henry thought it was always silent, but now that the chewing and munching has stopped, it really is. Kate walks up to Ross, the quietest of the boys, the most handsome as well. Everyone in the room knows it. He has mahogany skin and all the things girls like on boys: long lashes, water polo physique, thick head of hair, crater-size dimples, the works. Ross is basically set for life. Kate stands in front of him. She's wearing her pajamas, which are fitted cotton pants and a matching shirt. Her hair is pulled back with a headband, and she looks girlish and confident, like a tennis player.

"You tell her how hot she is," Kate says. "Not beautiful, or pretty, or nice, but sexy. You tell her she's driving you up the wall. You can even be lewd. Try to hold her, touch her. It will make her feel good, and after a while you know what will happen? She'll fantasize about you."

"Yeah," Tupp says. "Yeah, right."

"Listen," Kate says. "Boys. You're all we think about. We have grand fantasies about kissing you and walking with you and being held by you in public. You bring us flowers in front of all our girlfriends, you hold our hands, you drive our cars. We think about this when we go to bed at night, trying to force it into our dreams. We want you as much as you want us. Trust me."

Ross moves back on his chair, and closes his legs.

"So," Kate says. "When the girl walks into class, say out loud, 'Oh my God, what are you doing to me?' Embarrass the girl, draw attention to her."

Henry watches them hanging on every word. His son has stopped eating his sundae. Tupp and Shipley keep glancing at each other and grinning. Ross looks down as though being chastised.

"Then after a week or so, slowly turn your attention away," Kate says. "Look at another girl. Flirt with her, but don't say the same things you said to the first girl, just turn your attention a bit, but stay friendly, stay nice. Act like you tried, but failed."

"But what if it works right away?" Tupp asks. "I mean what if she's good to go?"

"Yeah," Henry says. He wants to tell them that he hadn't had to do any of these things to get Kate in bed. She was in it just a few hours after meeting him. They had flirted with each other all night. When she brought him to her apartment, he tried to think of things to say that would impress her, but she just lunged at him. He didn't have to say a word. Afterward she said she moved so swiftly because the more a guy spoke the less she liked him and she didn't want that to happen with Henry.

"She won't be good to go," Kate says. "She's a good girl. A pretty, popular girl. The stakes are raised with this one. She has a lot to lose. You must build the foundation."

"Jesus, Kate," Henry says.

She ignores him and slurs on. "Then," she says. "Are you ready? Are you with me?"

The boys nod.

"Give it to me, Mrs. Hale!" Shipley says. "Let me hear it!"

"We're with you," Henry says. "What does the boy do next? Say they're at a party in Russian Hill. There are plenty of rooms. Hallways. What happens next, Kate?"

She looks at Henry, but not with a scorching glare. Her gaze is soft and unreadable, supple—it could be saying either this or that. She turns away and faces Shipley, but she seems different now. Slow, distracted and sad.

"Then, once you've given her attention and backed off, try to be at the same party as her. See that she's having a good time. Perhaps engage in casual conversation. Be chipper and occupied. Have identical interactions with other girls. Run into her every now and then, but be busy, have fun. Believe me. She'll be watching you."

"Then what?" his son asks. His eyes are watery as if he's been in front of a campfire all night. He acts pissed off when he's mortified. "Then what do you do, Mom?"

Henry sees her caught off guard a little, perhaps by his tone, or because she's forgotten he's here, her son is here, her baby boy, who used to eat on Dad's lap. She looks at Henry, then around at everyone, as if at once realizing all eyes are on her. But they usually are anyway. She's beautiful, polished, thin, too thin. Every now and then she gets a pimple on her chin, right in the same spot. This has happened for as long as he's known her, and now he looks forward to its appearance— the only thing about her that's stayed the same.

"Then you're going to notice that this girl is looking for you, you know, talking to her friends in a way that you know is a performance. A show for you. A show that says, *I'm having a great time.* But you'll be able to see through this. In fact, she may look a bit disappointed, a little unhappy. She misses your attention. She misses you. That's when you make your move. Maybe the girl's at the bar getting another drink, or by the keg, or whatever."

Ross raises his eyebrows.

"Oh, please," she says. "Like I don't know."

"Or," Tupp says. "Say she's getting some fresh air because she drank too many root beer floats. That's what we usually drink, Mrs. Hale."

"Okay," Kate says. "So, she's getting fresh air. Though it's okay if she's with other people. Talking to a group of friends. It's more eventful this way, and then when people ask, 'What was that all about?' she'll have a secret and she'll love this secret because it gives her something to think about. Something different than the things she thinks about every single day."

Henry clears his throat. "Kate, I think we should head upstairs. I think we should go," but she talks right over him:

"Approach the girl and take her hand unexpectedly," she says. "Without saying anything lead her down a hallway. She'll laugh. She'll say, 'What's going on?' but don't answer. Don't say a word. Then, when you've found a place away from the group, stop walking. Face the girl.

37

Hold her shoulders. She'll know what's happening. Move her against the wall, and without hesitating, kiss her. The girl will kiss you back. I promise you. Don't kiss her kindly. Don't be delicate. Bump your teeth against hers, make her mouth stretch. Kiss her violently, desperately, like what's meant to happen is finally, finally happening. Try to swallow her whole. Touch the sides of her body. Move your hands up and down. Hook her leg around your body and press yourself in. Let her feel you."

"Jesus Christ, Mom!" his son says.

And Kate blinks. It's like watching someone come about of hypnosis.

"Is that how it's done?" Henry asks.

"Yes," his wife says. "That's how it's done."

He can see the boys' chests moving up and down.

"So, then what?" Henry asks. "What happens now?" He remembers her flushed face in the hallway, her silence during the car ride home. She gazed out the window the entire time with an expression of grief except for one moment when she smiled quickly to herself.

"After the boy has conned her into thinking she's special, what will the girl do?" he asks. "What is she willing to do?"

"Forget it," his son says. He stands, and his chair falls to the floor. He startles, then picks it back up. His body is rigid, on edge, but his face is wilted and lost. He has chocolate on his cheek. His friends look at him anxiously, as if they know he could blow their already blown cover. His son swaggers to the fridge. The other boys try not to laugh. Henry could care less. They should be drinking. It's what you should do at this age. At least this is something his childhood could have in common with his son's. Poor kids, rich kids, they all like to get lit.

"Forget all this," his son says. "I don't want to deal with that bullshit anyway. Fuck girls. I've got everything I need."

"Yeah," Ross says, quietly. "Your hand and your shower."

The boys laugh. Tupp punches Ross's leg and says, "May the force be with you, Hands Solo."

Kate looks like she hasn't even heard what the boys are saying.

"But I want to know," Henry says. "I want to know what the girl will do. The story isn't over yet."

They all look at Henry's wife, her cool skin, her sharp eyes. She's a fortress, standing there. She looks like a stranger. The woman before him is not his wife.

"The girl will do anything," she says. "Because she's never felt so wanted. It's not about the boy. It's about the boy showing her it's not too late. She can be anything, anyone. She's still alive."

"So does she fuck him?" Henry asks.

"Whoa!" Shipley says.

"Whoa!" his son yells. "Whoa, whoa, fuckin' whoa!"

"Whoa!" his daughter yells. She has just appeared in the doorway. She hangs her car keys on the hook. Henry thinks she has been drinking because she looks really happy.

"What's going on here?" She looks around the room at the boys. "What's up, losers?"

"S'up," Shipley says.

She's only two years older than they are, a freshman in college. The boys are looking at her legs in the skirt, slung low on her hips. Her T-shirt reads, LOOK ME IN THE EYE, ASSHOLE, and Henry notices their eyes dart from her chest to her face. Her hair seems damp, and black eyeliner smudges the skin below her eyes.

Henry tries to catch Kate's eye. *This is what you were like, remember?* But she's looking at her two children with worry.

"Why do you look damp?" Kate asks their daughter.

"I was at a concert."

"Which one?" Tupp asks.

"Anti-Flag."

"Oh, I love them."

"Please," his daughter says. "You probably don't even know their first album was released in 'ninety-six."

"I do now, killer," Tupp says.

"You missed out," his son says. "Mom and Dad are telling us how to get laid. It seems they have different approaches."

Henry can feel his face tensing. He wants to hear the end of the story. This isn't a big joke to him.

"You don't have to convince a girl to do it," his daughter says. "Just convince her you won't tell. Believe me, they want to do it as much as you. They'll even make playlists of songs you can do it to." She opens the freezer and unwraps an ice cream sandwich. "On second thought. You guys hang with those prissy bitches. They won't give it up unless you buy them all kinds of shit, and they'll be all stupid about everything. They'll own you, basically. Go for the punk girls. They're still sensitive, but they won't let you know."

"That's what I said," Henry says. "What did I tell you?"

His wife seems crestfallen that no one's paying attention to her anymore. But that's what happens, right? The boy paid attention, made her feel special, she revealed herself, and now he is gone. It was a trick. She was tricked. Henry feels he knows the end of the story. The girl got pressed against the wall. The girl was happy for a while, the good feeling still pulsing between her legs, until she realized it was over, not the relationship—that's not what she mourned—but the feeling, the possibility. That was over, and here she is, back where she started. A husband, two teenagers, and a toddler sleeping upstairs. She can't be anything, anyone. It's too late. Or is it?

Henry walks toward his wife. "The girl really did it, didn't she?" he says quietly.

The boys aren't listening anyway. They're busy with the girl in the room, asking about her night, asking about her friends, trying to impress her by throwing another apple at the fridge. Henry's wife turns and walks out of the kitchen unnoticed by all of the boys.

She hasn't yet reached the stairs, so Henry knows she wanted to be caught up to.

Her back is to him. Her shoulders are slumped, and the back of her neck looks fragile and thin. He quickens his steps, and when he gets behind her he turns her toward him. She's crying, but her expression isn't angry. It looks defeated, or maybe just tired. He holds her shoulders, and he moves her against the wall right outside of the kitchen. He almost leans in for a teeth-to-teeth kiss, but it would be a ridiculous thing to do. She sniffles, and then to his surprise she raises her arms and he walks into her embrace. It feels like a final embrace, but most likely they will embrace again, no matter what the outcome of all of this is. He holds her hair. He thinks about pulling.

"What's happened to us?" she asks.

"You cheated on me with Greg Dorsey," Henry says. *His name rhymes with* horsey. "That's what's happened. In a nutshell."

"And now?" she says.

He resents her not denying it, even if honesty is the entire point of the evening. Now that it's out there he'd like a little room to hide in. He wonders if this is how people feel after they remodel to an open floor plan with floor-to-ceiling doors and windows.

"I'm very tired," he says. "Aren't you? Aren't you just . . . tired?"

The question seems to devastate her. A grave diagnosis.

"I'm going to bed," he says. "I think that's what we should do for now." He lets go of her hair, then walks up the stairs; a chorus of laughter comes from the kitchen. When he wakes up, his marriage may be over. It will be over.

He trudges on.

He strains to hear the voices of the children—it's like a song, exiting music.

"You don't even want to know," he hears his daughter say. "Like for real it will make you cry. Cry or laugh your ass off."

"I doubt it," he hears his son say.

"I'm telling you," his daughter says. "It will."

I'm not hatin' on them because they don't speak English. I am not racist. FYI I have *tons* of foreign friends. My favorite person in the world is German, my other favorite is Venezuelan. They love me and I love them. I was furious yesterday because my son flew facefirst down the slide. He was hurt. I saw the whole thing because I watch—not like those other parents. If they are living here illegally and I threaten to call the authorities on them, maybe they'll avoid me and my problem is solved.

—Renee Grune

Renee—you have every right to be upset when someone, English-speaking or not, unjustly bullies your child. However, the language you have used in your grievance is quite disgusting. Perhaps an overview of bullying philosophy might be helpful. Powerful nations have used their military to bully other nations (including their children) for hundreds and thousands of years. Some English-speaking armies are bullying quite a few non-English-speaking people around the world right now. To what extent are you complicit in that? I suggest the following books, with all sincerity:

A Theory of Justice by John Rawls,
Enemy Pie by Derek Munson, and
Understanding Power by Noam Chomsky.

—Marina Willis, A non-English-speaking U.S. citizen

I also suggest you read *Marley and Me* and *Bedding the Wrong Brother*.

—A.L., West Portal

Please list any awards you've won in your life, or accomplishments. What are your strengths?

Tonight I was awarded by a very tired child who expressed her fatigue with actual words. I was lucky. Gabe left the park howling, poor Georgia, tense though calm like a nurse getting a drug addict through a bad trip.

We left a bit later than usual—I was talking with Henry, listening to his story while imagining and inventing the details. It's exhausting sometimes—I feel like a medium—and I don't know if I'm a better or worse listener because of it. Do I tune in more clearly, squeezing out the juice? Or do I insert myself into things, missing the point? Whatever it is, it's something I've always done and I'm not sure if I'd call it a strength. It could be a useless portal. Even now I'm still thinking about Henry, trying to imagine his home, his stairs, his kitchen. I can see him in that space, licking mayonnaise from the corner of his mouth. Sorry. You don't know what the sauce I'm talking about.

Awards: none. There are no pictures of me in magazines crouched on my knees and looking up into the lens like it's a hand offering kibble. As I've mentioned, I wanted very badly to be a writer—I even went to school for it and wrote about things like immigrants struggling to save their families by selling tropical fruit in a marketplace. I thought I was going to be around rebels. Visions of hunting, drinking, and traipsing through Paris danced in my head, but instead I found myself at parties with cheap wine, SUV-size blocks of cheese, and boys talking about their latest accomplishments, like being published in the *Higgleytown Reader* or the *Chugachoochoo Review*. In class they'd keep telling me to earn things—my endings, my beginnings, my metaphors. Then they'd look at the professor. See, the main goal in a writing workshop is to say something that makes the professor nod emphatically. If the professor didn't nod, I'd look at my classmates and think, Earn this, losers. But alas, I never made it. I succumbed to rejection emails, telling me that "at this time we don't have a space for this story." But I'm back at it, I guess, in cookbook form.

I don't feel particularly accomplished from the job I had last. I was a menu writer—that's how I met Bobby, head chef at one of those old, manly steak houses in Union Square whose menu used excessive blurbs to sell different parts of a cow: "Mouthwaterin'!" "Whoppin' huge!" and so on. I suggested less punctuation. I suggested the sides have more description. Instead of "creamed spinach," why not 'Sonoma creamed spinach with a dash of nutmeg"?

Bobby suggested a booth and a Bordeaux. We dated for almost a year. I fell in love with him. He was mouthwaterin' and yes, whoppin' huge. Four months into the relationship he opened his own restaurant out in Sonoma, using all of the ideas we had gone over—huge windows, a hot young butcher, open kitchen, a whimsical menu, a communal table, and using only local foods because when you put "Local" on a menu people come in hordes, feel great about themselves, and are willing to dish out forty bucks for a chicken wing. Ten months into our relationship I got pregnant. Oh, the stories I wrote, the movies I made in my head. My mind was on fire. I would be more than a chef's wife, I'd be a partner, creating a restaurant of substance. After establishing a cult following, I'd create a cookbook that was surprisingly popular with millennials—Alice Waters, French Laundry—that was their mothers' thing. They liked the lady with the radish tattoo (or perhaps a little pig). We'd have a beautiful home in the valley, rolling hills, regal oaks, a pool, and a detached office/studio, and a place where I could write, both fiction and non. A studio of my own. My profile in *Gourmet Magazine* would be brilliant. I'd wear makeup that didn't look like I was wearing makeup. My baby would be six weeks old, and the interviewer would exclaim: "You don't even look like you've had a baby!"

"It's the breast feeding," I'd say.

But then the scene cut to Bobby, his expression when I broke the news. I was radiating hope and confidence and pure love. Sure, I made room for worry and fear, bewilderment. But we had talked about what we'd name our children. We had long postcoital conversations about dream houses and vacations. We had gone snowboarding with each other. I knew he had a special uncle who died when he was twelve. We had reached the gas-passing phase with one another. We were there! I had even told him what I wanted to do in my life—the embarrass-ing I-want-to-be-a-writer admission. When a man says "I love you" and "I love what we have," I don't think to question it, and so I never predicted his reaction or his words:

"I'm kind of already engaged."

So, no. No major accomplishments for me, per se, though I sup-pose I helped create a restaurant, I've supported local farmers—I've practically married one off. My other accomplishments for this week include reading Ellie the whole series of princess stories without skip-ping ahead or stopping to insert my views on the princesses' hopeless futures—cleaning, breeding, and endless blow-jobbing. This week I've pushed back my cocktail hour to five thirty, and this evening, I came up with a dish after having talked to Henry.

Seems like his already troubled marriage reached a new low. I knew something was going on. He was looking so dazed and slumped where he usually sits up straight or moves around the park as though he were at a cocktail party. The nannies light up when he opens the gate, except for one named Hilda, who wouldn't light up unless you set her on fire.

He told me that his wife finally admitted to what he'd been suspect-ing for a while. She was having an affair with another man. It shocked me to think that women do this. Men get horny. I can see that, but as a woman with a baby, it's the last thing I'd want to do. It would be so much work.

Henry looked confused versus angry: stupefied. Twenty-one years of marriage. You keep building this tower together and then someone decides to knock it down. My tower was only a year's worth of work. But maybe Henry will rebuild. His wife seems to like remodeling. Yes, they could build an even better tower. Not that I know what he'll do or that I care. I mean, I care. I'd support him either way. God, I sound like Bobby after I told him I was pregnant.

"It's your decision," he said. "I'll support you with whatever you choose," all the while I imagined he was chanting to himself: *abort, abort, abort*, as though Ellie and I were a mission gone wrong.

"I'm so sorry," I said to Henry today. We hadn't made eye contact. The closest I got was looking at his leg next to mine.

"Yeah," he said. "I guess you . . . you've dealt with this. You're dealing with this. Though it's different, I'm sure."

He refilled my plastic cup, and for a second I had a feeling of nostalgia for something I've never known: a husband refilling my glass of wine. I often joke and make light about the single life, forgetting that it's something that may last forever, that it might not just be a stage like teething.

"It's different," I said, though I'd be hard-pressed to choose between the two blows. There's no catalog of pain where we can choose our hurt, but if there was I wonder what mine would cost compared to Henry's.

"At least we have each other!" I finally looked at him. I meant the humor in my voice to mask the truth of the matter, the feeling that Henry's misfortune had somewhat depleted a bit of my own and that we were in on something together. I wanted to give him a hug, but in a friendly way. "You are my friend!" I wanted to say. "Perhaps my best friend lately. I don't have friends like this. And neither do you." He has told me that his so-called friends actually seek advice on what to wear and how and whom to entertain. "We are unexpected! I love you!"

I felt guilty that his misery had given me sustenance, and I kind of bowed my head.

"I'm sorry," I said again. His hand was on the bench, and I patted it once. He looked down, acknowledging my gesture, though I don't know how he felt about it.

Henry is so simple, in the best of ways. It takes very little to make him happy—a day at the park, a sandwich, things that are what they seem.

I thought of effortless salads, straightforward foods, late-night sandwiches, comfort and love. Blue Cheese Greens, a crisp salad to refresh. A Croque Monsieur sandwich with butter on both sides of the bread; a side of Bud Light to keep things light. I looked at him, then quickly looked away. I felt it. A nervousness, a crisp tang like tarragon vinegar on iceberg lettuce. A life without Bobby could be possible.

"What are you going to do?" I asked, and maybe like Bobby I was chanting the answer I wanted to hear. We've always flirted from the safe realm of impossibility. But now . . . But now nothing. I was thinking illogically, selfishly. Now I had a friend who needed some support.

"I don't know," he said. "What are you going to do about Bobby?" He was lightening up, his habitual expression was back—amused, present, mischievous.

"I'm going to look great at his wedding," I said.

"Attagirl," he said. "Let me know if you need some arm candy."

I didn't know if he was joking, and it seemed like he didn't know either. We both got quiet and had slightly puzzled faces. Before I could respond, Tommy ran back to the bench.

"I have power," he said, cupping something in his hands. "I got some under there in that hole."

"Good job, son," Henry said. "Power's good. Go and get some more. Get some for me and Mele."

I suppose for a minute we looked married, the parents of Tommy and Ellie. We sat in silence for a while until Ellie came and got me, for the first time asking to go home. It was late, I realized. I could smell people's dinners wafting out of apartment windows. Henry got up, moving a hand through his thick brown hair. He walked toward his son. "Let's hit it, all right, kiddo?"

I've never seen him rush or panic, or hurry his child by counting to three. He tricks the eye. Sometimes he looks like a boss, an overseer, other times he looks like he chops down trees for a living. He has steely green eyes, a boyish face, an athletic build—you can tell by the way his clothes hang. I felt a little guilty for bringing it all out of him, but he looked better than when he first got there. I feel like our talk was a kind of triumph.

"See you guys," I called out to everyone. "We're heading out."

He looked back at me leaving and smiled that true smile that takes up so much of his face.

When Ellie and I got home and she pushed her tricycle into its spot in the basement so that it was just so, I made Henry a Croque Monsieur, which translates into "crispy mister." Just a ham and cheese sandwich, but béchamel's the opposable thumb of the meal, making a primitive thing into something deliciously evolved. I got into it, also making a Croque Madame, placing a fried egg on top of the sandwich, then decided on two eggs and called it a Croque Second Wife. I created a Croque Enfant for Ellie, placing apple slices on top. She ate all of it. I can't tell you how proud I feel when my child eats everything I put in front of her, when I can sit down with my baby and talk and sip wine at a leisurely pace and not have to scream: "Eat!"

These are my accomplishments.

Renee—that's great you have foreign friends; however, the issue is your proposal that calling the police is an appropriate response. So your kid gets pushed and the solution is the family goes to immigration jail?

—Beth Nelson

Has your husband ever asked you to use your breast pump just for fun? Like, in a foreplay kind of way? I wasn't sure how to respond to this and pretended like I had "bowel issues," but I don't know how long I can keep using this excuse. Is this *a thing* guys like or . . .

—Anonymous, please reply to general forum

Now *that's* special. Never got that request before! There's a dairy farm in Vallejo if he wants to check it out and get his milking fix. It's organic!

—A.L., West Portal

Does your husband cook? How do you divvy up the responsibilities?

Way to rub it in my face, you sick, kitten-heel-wearing bitches. The only thing your husbands cook is probably the books. I bet you complain he doesn't do enough. He doesn't pick up the kids. They're driving you crazy. You're trying to post something about your miracle cleanse and they're fighting with one another over the iPad again. You need to post about the cleanse this minute and how you know exactly what you're putting into your body and you're so happy and healthy! You need to Instagram your body Before and After! You need help from your husband—he works too much, he doesn't treat you the way you should be treated. He didn't notice your highlights. He didn't notice your pedicure. You have eggplant toes, god damn it! The It color!

So, I'm a little off this week. The Big Day is three weeks away, same time this book's due, and I'm anxious and depressed. Annie is adamant that I don't go, but I can't help but want to. I want to see what he's choosing. I want to see this life I'm somehow a part of.

Today I browsed through Bobby's registry, scanning for appropriate gifts—carafes of shit or a set of silverware—the latter already purchased by the Mittwegs. How greedy to ask for a punch bowl when he has a toddler! He should register for preschool tuition or princess dresses. He should register for wine and therapy for the mother of his child.

I'm at my desk, which is in the living room. Ellie is banging on her little piano, which isn't helping my hangover. I swear motherhood leads to alcoholism. I never used to drink like this.

Last night, Annie, Georgia, Barrett, and I confessed we had a drink every night of the week. I don't think it's that untypical for women to have a couple glasses of wine with dinner every night, but I guess it was our seemingly dire need for it that was interesting.

We were at Barrett's house, sitting in her living room, drinking wine, civilly.

"After a day it just sounds so good," she said.

"And it makes it seem like your child is behaving better," I said. "You're charmed versus pissed."

"It's sort of like an award at the end of the day," Annie said. "Like, good job. You can clock out and relax now."

"Except you can't," Barrett said. "It's like the Hotel California." We continued our conversation, moving on to margaritas and tequila. I stayed with wine. Doesn't make me a better person. I'm just neurotic about sugar, and citrus makes me sweat. Our kids were racing around until ten, and we were all like, "Fuck it. Cheers. Man Pie. What the hell is man pie? Oooh, I love this song. What is this? Sir Mix-A-Lot? Oh my God, look at you in that picture. You looked so young! Where are our husbands? Who cares! Screw the husbands! Or wait, don't screw them! Hahaha."

It was practically Dionysian, like some mother binge. Barrett was slurring and swerving in place. She tried to sober up, but we found out she had just switched to watered-down tequila. Her husband swooped in to the rescue, making her say good night. How I yearned to be put to bed.

I know you're judging me, just as I judge you most likely, but sometimes I think we should all vow to back off. As a mom, you should be able to be a pill-popping shoplifter and not garner scorn for all the crap you have to do, and I'm saying this as a person with a decent child, something not all of you have. Some moms have boys! That's like having hyenas! What was great about last night's binge was the relief everyone felt that we could be open about everything—thinking you have to uphold this Mother-of-the-Year image is tragic and sad, lonely.

"Wine is my savior," Georgia said, completely sincere. I thought she was going to make out with her glass.

I could never see men getting together and talking about beer this way. It's standard that a man needs a beer at the end of the day. It's American. It's deserved. Beer ads only target men, and their messages are: You're strong, you have a big truck, girls in bikinis like to randomly rub up against you, and your wife looks at you like you're handsome and don't have butt acne.

Does my husband cook? That was the question. Bobby used to cook, the most simple things since it would usually be late at night. Pasta with garlic and olive oil, fresh basil, anchovies. We'd eat and watch late-night TV, my feet in his lap. Those noodle and cigarette days are over. I can't imagine Ellie waddling into that scene with binkie in mouth, blankie in tow. I can't imagine her with a stepmother either, and the idea of this makes my blood swell—I imagine it having currents and barrels. Some surfer could win a trophy on my rage. This was never part of the life I imagined. She will have a stepmother with blond hair, someone who looks stunning in rubber boots and turtlenecks, someone who can say, "I'm just a simple cheese maker," a.k.a. the daughter of a winery owner who is privileged enough to say to herself, "I should just go and do something artisan, organic, and fashiony on all that land we don't use."

We definitely don't divide the responsibilities. I am responsible for Ellie, but I guess I want it to be this way.

He came to the city yesterday morning, as he sometimes does on Sundays when they close the roads in Golden Gate Park. We strolled around with Ellie on her tricycle with the push handle and I pretended we're a real family. We liked to watch the Rollerbladers who disco. Or, we liked to watch Ellie watching them.

"Pedal. Use your legs," he said to Ellie for the ninth time. I was counting. It boggles my mind when he can get frustrated with her in the first half hour when he hasn't seen her for weeks, knowing that he's just going to take off again.

"Is it really that big a deal?" I asked, pushing her with the steering handle while she sat without pedaling—I used the bike more as a stroller than an actual bike.

A swarm of runners went past us, and we had to sidestep some staggering toddlers.

"It's a transition bike," he said. "And she's never going to learn to move it herself if you keep using the steering bar. I told you to get her one of those balance bikes. Then you can bypass training wheels."

His brow was furrowed. This was an actual issue for him—Ellie's tricycle-riding skills. I felt a mixture of annoyance and contentment. He cared at least. And it was fun to hear those words come from his mouth—*transition bike, training wheels*. He looked like all the other swagger-free dads at the park, no hint of his old self, the man who'd come in late at night, walk purposefully to me as if I were on fire, and without saying a word, strip off my clothes and take me wherever I happened to be sitting, standing, or lying down.

"I'm not really worried about her bike-riding skills," I said. "That's really the least of my worries."

"You need to stop feeling sorry for yourself," he said.

"Do I though?" I said and stopped walking.

He pushed my back to keep me moving. "Don't be dramatic."

I walked and talked quietly, my jaw tense, words barely seeping out. "I think I can feel sorry for myself and be dramatic and any number of things."

"Okay." He shrugged. "Whatever it is you need."

"God, you're such an asshole," I said.

He shrugged again, as if that was something obvious, like telling him he had black hair and wide shoulders, and a coy, seductive smile, god damn it.

"Stop!" Ellie said, and we stopped on the bridge by the de Young museum to watch the swing dancers. She was entranced by their synchronized movements. I was entranced by their bliss, the fact that they were dancing like this in a public park, in daylight, without alcohol. To do this you had to be incredibly fulfilled.

Bobby smiled at the scene, but in a way that seemed to say, *Look at this nerd herd.*

I watched an older couple dancing as if in a trance, a moving meditation. The man touched the rim of his hat while she twirled, and I wondered if he did that every time and for how many years.

"What does she think about you being here with us?" I asked. It took him a moment to understand.

"She's fine," he said.

It pissed me off that the cheese artisan was fine, that I wasn't someone who rattled her. He never gave me details when I asked how she managed to forgive him. He always just said, "We worked it out."

I decided to push it. "You got another woman pregnant while you were engaged. She sure is a forgiving lady."

He looked down at me. "Do you want me to hurt you more? Admit that yes, she is forgiving, yes, we worked it out. You always bait me into saying something that will just upset you. We didn't get married when we were supposed to a year ago. But yes, we worked it out and now it's wonderful."

"Can we go to the duck pond?" Ellie asked, and we moved on, thank goodness. The love and joyfulness around me was making it hard to breathe. I wiped tears from my eyes.

"I just can't believe it, I guess."

Bobby walked with his hands in his pockets. I pushed the handle of the bike, enabling our daughter.

"She can't have children," Bobby said. "So she thinks this is good, in a way. She found a bright side to all of this."

My breath was sucked out of me, like I got hit with a ball in the stomach.

"She's happy that I have a kid," he said. "And now, she does, too. She always said that down the road she'd consider adoption, but now . . ."

I picked up the pace. I wanted to roar. I wanted to run, but it was too hard with this bike. Ellie's legs were already circling too fast. She looked back like this was a thrilling ride. She's the child that will save them all the hassle of adoption? She's the clasp to their almost finished circle? I've given them both a gift. I'm like a surrogate mom! And now they want me to give them a punch bowl?

"Slow down," Bobby said. "You asked."

I slowed down, turned off the main road to the path that runs through the tree fern dell. I needed shade, cooler air, plants that hovered over us. Whenever I'm overwhelmed I come here. I like it better than the Conservatory of Flowers across the street, the rows so orderly. I prefer this chaotic feast of green, the wildness, the sound of birds. Everything will be okay because Ellie is here with me and the ferns are regal and gigantic.

"Is it okay if I bring someone to the wedding?" I asked.

Bobby blinked really fast while smiling, something he does sometimes when he doesn't know the answer to something and another guy does.

"Of course," he said. "Like a girlfriend?"

"No," I said.

More blinking. I was beginning to feel better.

"Sure," he said. "Sounds great. That's great." He reached out and plucked a leaf. "What's his name? So I can fill out a seating thing."

The ferns were so bold and elegant. Ellie unbuckled herself and ran toward the lily pond.

"Henry Hale," I said.

Now I'm in a bit of a bind, but I like the bind—and the three-week deadline. It gives me something to solve. The task makes me nervous, but puts a spring in my step.

I forgot to really answer the question though.

Yes, my child's father cooks, but for another woman, and I ended up getting them a cheese grater and a set of knives.

Beth. I will include a summary of everyone who appreciates what I said, excluding names. I saw you on LinkedIn and notice you change companies about every other year. I will file a complaint at your latest workplace if you continue to respond. My attorney friends are too busy to harass people like you did to me today.

—Renee Grune

Do people still really use LinkedIn?

—A.L., West Portal

My elimination specialist's "potty party" totally backfired. Silas was yelling "No potty!" then went on to have a total sleep regression, waking up and asking to be rocked like a baby. Now when he has to go he just stands there naked and demands his diaper. When I don't put one on he flaps his arms and bulges his eyes and won't speak. I need to hire someone new.

—Overheard at Julius Kahn Playground

DINING WITH
DELINQUENTS

M ele drives to the daycare in the Inner Richmond to pick up
Ellie. It's always kind of like driving to an abusive husband.
How will your child treat you? Will she make it to the car
without making a scene?

When Mele gets out of the car and goes into the small railroad
apartment that smells of urinals and clay, Ellie runs to her right away!
They say good-bye to Mary and the other children, and then her child
gets into the car! No meltdowns, no stalling, no stipulations or nego-
tiations. If only kids could figure out that when things go smoothly,
your parents don't dread being with you.

Morning drop-off was easy, too, but it was because of the new departure method that would have to be updated. Ever since Ellie started
to go to daycare twice a week, Mele has had to create little routines,
but they always have to get updated, like Adobe or Windows. What
worked then (sitting down with Little E at breakfast with the other
kids and departing after she got her "milk kiss") doesn't work now. So

Mele started to read her a story before she left and then she'd wave at the gate. It worked at times, but still there were days when Ellie clung to her and cried, then howled with her face pressed between the bars of the gate, making Mele feel like the biggest asshole as she left to grab coffee and check Facebook.

But then one day, Ellie seemed to create her own routine, her own solution, which was to have a story, walk Mele to the gate, give her a hug, and then kiss her butt. Not just a peck, but a full-on, long kiss, like the kisses in old movies. Lots of head movement, no tongue, thank God. 'Cause that would be weird. This transition trick, the butt kiss, was created months ago, and it has stuck, and so every day Ellie walks to the gate with her face pushed into Mele's ass.

"Ha ha," Mele says when it happens and looks around nervously. Ellie just looks like she's hugging her from behind, so she can get away with it most days, but sometimes Ellie will yell with crazed glee, "I'm going to kiss you on the butt!"

Mele has vowed to make it stop, but it works so well. When Ellie starts to cry, she whispers, "Come on, you can kiss my butt."

This morning a parent overheard her and Mele imagined the woman calling Social Services. What parent tells her child to kiss her ass? They need a new routine. There are so many reasons Ellie should be sent away to Child and Family Services, Mele really doesn't need another.

They drive down Fulton toward the Panhandle.

"We need to think of something else to do in the morning," Mele says to Ellie in the backseat. "Maybe kiss my cheek or elbow."

"Or butt!" Ellie says.

"Or my mouth. Why can't you just kiss me on the lips like the other kids?"

"The other kids don't kiss you on the lips."

"Well, you should."

"I should kiss your butt!"

"Or my belly, or my foot."

"A foot is dirty!" Ellie says.

"So is a butt," Mele counters.

"But a butt has clothes on it."

"Right," Mele says. "Anyway, you shouldn't do it anymore, okay?"

"But I just want to kiss your butt all the time!"

Mele thinks about this. "I understand," she says. "It is something people ought to want to do."

It is settled then. Her daughter made a good argument. She often does, and sometimes it makes Mele really proud. Other times she wishes Ellie were one of those dumb kids she sees all the time—malleable and silent.

"Want to go to the park?" Mele asks. Why did she ask that! She needed to state: We're going to the park. No choices. Please say yes. She wants to see Henry. She has been telling herself all day that she didn't want to see Henry—she just wanted to go to the park, like always, but why lie to herself? It's impossible, and it's such a better feeling than wanting to see Bobby. Plus, Georgia said she had a story for her.

"The park!" Ellie says.

"The park!" Mele says. Everything has been so easy. And yet, there are many more hours left in the day. Mele always pencils in "some kind of conflict" into her mental calendar, so that she's not disappointed if it comes. It's expected, a fact of life. It's right there in the calendar.

The Panhandle is not a dreamy playground. The equipment is old and somewhat dangerous. The wooden structure with the slides has a sign on it that says, WASH HANDS. WOOD CONTAINS ARSENIC. Parents are always finding cigarette butts in the dirty, gritty, not-really-sand sand. Georgia once found a Bud Light bottle cap in Gabe's mouth, Gabe, who just the other day made an unfortunate voyage into the bushes, where he stepped into a pile of shit that (because of the corn) was most likely human. Mele sees Georgia on the bench.

"Hey," Mele says, looking around to see who else is here.

"Hi there," Georgia says. Her nose is red and she looks like she's in a sitting savasana—dead man's pose. Ellie runs to play with Gabe. Mele puts a sweater on over her sweater. Clouds and a chill usually hover above the Panhandle as though it's an ogre's castle.

"Cold," Georgia says. "I don't know why we come here."

Georgia lives near Dolores Park but likes the playground's proximity to Ben & Jerry's and a little organic market where she buys things she can't afford. She carries her produce in her hands and the crook of her arm, showing off her squash and bitter melons.

"Here you are," Georgia says, pulling down her shirt to nurse, not her newborn, who is swaddled in the stroller, but Gabe, her almost three-year-old son.

"Oh God," Mele mumbles. It disturbs Mele to see a little boy nurse when he's able to walk and talk, too. Gabe is tall enough that he could probably stand to nurse if Georgia sat down and leaned over. It's like she's the water boy on the sidelines, or that person in a boxing ring that squirts water into the fighter's mouth. The poor gal seems constantly overwhelmed. Her life is stuffed in the lower compartment of Zoë's stroller. And three kids, boy. That's just asking for it. Although, Henry has three kids. Mele recalculates: three kids + no money = asking for it.

"Is anyone else coming today?" Mele asks. It's always a bit awkward with just Georgia. They never seem to have a lot to talk about.

"I think so," Georgia says. "It's early." Gabe wipes his mouth and heads back out to play.

"George," Mele says and gestures to Georgia's huge, hard breast she forgot to fully tuck back in.

"Oh!" she says, then plucks Zoë out of her stroller. "While it's out . . ."

She presses her daughter's mouth to her breast, which still has fuel in it. She kisses her baby on the top of her head while Zoë pulls at her nipple.

"So something happened the other day?" Georgia says. "I thought you could make a recipe out of it."

"Great," Mele says. "Ready when you are." She has no idea what Georgia inspires or what a woman like her needs. She's never negative. She never gossips or says bad things about people, which is a barrier to them truly becoming good friends. Maybe pound cake? Basic and pure. Mele smiles, feeling guilty. Georgia is nice, and Mele needs to start valuing niceness even though it bores her so.

Georgia begins some story about dropping off her older son at Leroy's house in San Bruno. She talks about what time it was, what street they were on, all this pointlessness. The story's accents are clearly in all the wrong places, but Mele watches her daughter on the purple slides while patiently wading through the junk, thinking of stews and other sludge-like recipes, and is startled when Georgia leads her to this: "And then I had to pick him up in jail all the way down in San Jose."

"Jail!" Mele says. *Bread and water. Bruschetta!*

Zoë begins to cry, and Georgia tucks her into a sling. She stands, bounces, and begins to hum. When Zoë settles, Georgia sits back down and Mele looks away and listens.

GEORGIA'S WAR BABY

They are almost to their destination. Georgia tries to find a song on the radio that matches her mood, which is nearing elation. She and her two children have made it from point A to point B without traffic, tantrums, or barf. She finds a tune, but it's fading out. The DJ comes on and makes a joke about teenage sexting and then gang initiations, which Georgia doesn't find amusing at all. In the past few months men have been clubbing unsuspecting women with pillowcases filled with jars of artichoke hearts. The media always says "unsuspecting," as if any woman out there would suspect she'd get clubbed with marinated vegetables. It is truly bizarre, and a most undignified way to go to a hospital or a grave.

She hopes to God Chris isn't involved in a gang, but that seems too ambitious for him. Even sexting would require too much energy for a seventeen-year-old boy whose only passion seems to be sitting on the couch, watching *Wheel of Fortune,* and yelling things at the contestants like "Can I get a 'Who fuckin' cares?'"

"Chris trash can?" Gabe asks. Georgia takes a quick glance back at him and his sister. His car seat straps seem a little loose.

"No," Georgia says. "He's at a police station. Police keep people safe. They're keeping Chris safe."

"Tickle me homo?"

"No. Not that."

"Okay!" he sings. "Okay!"

She should try to find out what he means by *tickle me homo* but doesn't want to intimidate him or do anything that would restrict his imagination or keep him from talking. He's two and nine months and hardly says anything that makes sense.

"We're almost there!" Georgia says. "Can you believe it? Are you doing okay back there, Zoë?"

She turns onto a wide road lined with trees. The sky is slowly darkening. Men and women are walking out of what seems to be a courthouse. They're all looking at their phones, every single one of them—they're doing something important. When Chris was a baby everyone who walked out of workplaces would light up a cigarette, now it's phones. She can't imagine her husband, Eric, walking out of a building, holding a briefcase, wearing a suit. God, she would love that. She'd take a picture. Annie complains that her husband is always working, but how Georgia longs for that. She's thankful he's not here, even if he's at the Kabuki film festival, from which he will come home angry and jealous of all the other filmmakers who use "conformist plots" and "unadventurous structures."

She will keep this a secret from him, not so much because it would create a greater distance between father and son but because Eric would try to draw a correlation between her son's experience and the sorry state of California's public school system. Ever since quitting his job in sales for 24/7 Alarm, he has had way too much time to complain, mope, and focus on his "shorts"—abstract little films with close-ups of things like a fly in a glass of milk, which is somehow supposed to illustrate the conflict between North and

South Korea. Georgia very much wants this to be about her son and nothing else. She envisions the problem as a real thing, a small flame in her belly—not necessarily a negative image: a flame. She is sustaining something, keeping it lit. What is she doing that gives this flame life? How can she convert this fire into a more productive form of energy?

She takes a right onto another wide boulevard and sees the squat building lit up like a small casino.

"We're here!" she sings and pulls into the parking lot, quickly choosing a spot and smiling to herself. It feels good to park so quickly. Whenever she's without Eric or Chris, or any adult, she can make decisions, but if someone else had been in the car she would have driven around, trying to divine somehow where her passenger would like her to park. She realizes this about herself and for the first time understands it to be an irritating versus a thoughtful quality.

She gets out, puts Zoë in her sling, then takes Gabe out of his car seat and holds his hand. Zoë looks up at her and stares, wide-eyed, and Georgia knows she's pooping.

They walk toward the entrance, and she tightens her grip on Gabe's hand. "We can't run around in here, okay? Do you think you can calm your body? Perhaps play and run around in your mind?"

He tries to squirm away. "I have candy," she says. "I have candy to give to good boys."

"Gabe want," he says.

"If you're good in here then I will give you one."

"Want now!" he says, then jerks his body away from her. When she reaches for him, he arches his back and wails.

"I know," she says. "You're upset because you want a piece of chocolate. You're upset because this isn't part of our routine."

She doesn't know how "talking him through" can help if he can't hear what she's saying. She feels her body heating up. Gabe's red face is wet and blotchy. When he tantrums, two red dots bloom on his forehead.

"You look like the devil," she says because he's crying too hard to hear, and then she says loudly: "Crying is not the best action, Gabe. Try to find a better action!"

More crying, arching, glaring through fat, pulpy tears.

She sifts through her purse and gives him the damn chocolate.

After Georgia posts Chris's bail, hugs him, cries, is admonished for hugging him and crying and acting like a "freak," she and her children walk back to the car, and once everyone is buckled in she drives out of the lot. She says nothing. She waits for Chris to make the first move. This requires so much self-restraint that she keeps shifting in her seat and fake-yawning.

"What's your problem?" Chris says. "Do you have a hemorrhoid or something?"

"No," she says and refrains from telling him that his father does. "I think I have a hemorrhoid," he said last night during *Dateline*.

"They're pretty common," she says. "Nothing wrong with it."

She can feel him looking at her. Eric has beady ferret eyes that Chris fortunately didn't inherit and thin little lips that he did. Zoë coos, and Georgia remembers her soiled diaper, but doesn't want to stop, especially since Gabe has fallen asleep. She looks in the rearview mirror and sees him with his pacie in his mouth, his filthy blue blanket over his legs. Chris looks back at his sister. "You're dumber than knuckles," he says.

"That's not a nice thing to say."

"I don't mean anything bad by it," he says. "She was playing with this toy the other day. I took it away and she didn't even notice it was gone. Then I put a mirror in her face and she didn't know it was her own reflection. Babies are funny. You can totally mess with 'em."

Georgia holds the steering wheel tightly. She takes a deep breath. "Why?" she says. "What?" She doesn't know what to ask. An officer told her that he was arrested for third-degree burglary. She gasped, but then he explained that Chris walked onto someone else's property with the intent to burglarize—that's what constituted the burglary.

"Why did you go onto this person's property?" she asks. "And who's Leroy? I had no idea you had a friend named Leroy."

"It's pronounced *Lee*roy. He's not frickin' French."

Chris puts his foot on the dash and plucks off dried clumps of dirt from his boot. "This guy stole Leroy's jacket. We know him! His name's Dumb Todd. So we went to his house to get it back and he called the cops like a little bitch. You can't steal your own threads. It's a bullshit charge. Don't worry about it."

He fusses with the stations on the radio, then stops on what Georgia thinks is Brazilian music. She waits for him to change it, but he doesn't.

"Well, I am worried about it," she says. "I'm very worried about it. About you."

"Don't worry about me," Chris says. "I'm the least . . ." He looks up at the ceiling and crosses his arms over his chest. She isn't sure if she should take 280 or 101. She slows down hoping he'll indicate which way he'd like to go.

"Oh, wait, stop," he says. "Turn in to there. Can we get In-N-Out? I'm starving."

"What's In-N-Out?"

"You're kidding me? Are you serious right now? Are you for real?" She doesn't answer.

"It's fast food," he says. "Hamburgers."

"Oh," she says, noticing he didn't say "It's fast food, God!" because everything he usually says to her is constructed that way: "Do you want dinner?" "Yes, Mom. God!" "Are you ready for school?" "Like ten minutes ago, God!" Sometimes when he speaks this way she wants to shake him and ask, "Don't you remember how much you loved and needed me? You used to hold my face and repeat 'Mommy' in the sweetest voice that made me feel like we were in on something together. Something small. Something tremendous."

She turns in to the strip mall, then takes a deep breath. "Do you remember going to the playground with me?" she asks. "Do you remember all that time we spent together? Do you remember holding my face?"

"Are you having a stroke or something?" he asks.

"Maybe," she says, giving up.

She drives to the end of the lot toward the neon lights sparkling like a refuge. Zoë makes a frustrated whimper. Georgia wishes the other two weren't here, that it was just her and Chris. She glances back at Gabe. His pacifier has fallen on his lap and sits there like a severed thumb.

"How have you not heard of this place?" Chris asks. "You and Dad are so disconnected or something."

"We like that Thai place on Masonic," she says, remembering that when Chris was little they used to get takeout from there every Friday. They called it Thai Day Friday. Eric always got number 42, and it was sort of an unspoken agreement that they'd make love that night. They'd do a position she called Thai Me Up, which was really just missionary position, but it was fun to say, and she was really into themes back then. Then Thai Day Friday turned into every other Friday. Then it disappeared. She misses it—the food: green curry and prawns with chili paste, that soft, squishy eggplant she's never been able to re-create. They still have sex occasionally, though she really has to give herself pep talks or trick herself into attraction. If she squints her eyes when

Eric's on top of her, he kind of looks like Eliot Spitzer, so that helps. It helps a lot.

"Is this where I go?" she asks, turning in to the narrow passage.

"Yes, Mom. You look at the menu? Then order?"

She used to go to drive-throughs all the time, but it seems so different now.

"Just order me a cheeseburger, fries, and a shake," he says.

"Could I order a cheeseburger?" she says to the neon sign.

"Not here!" he yells. "You need to pull up, God!"

She pulls up toward the window.

"Stop!" he yells.

She slams on the brakes and sees a metal box. Someone says something out of the box.

"Hello? Okay. Well, my son says he would like—"

"Don't introduce it," Chris says. "Just say the order. Just say it!"

"Oh, well. We would like a cheeseburger, fries, and a shake."

"What kind of shake?" the voice asks.

"Whatever," Chris says.

Her face burns. "Well, I don't know."

"Just pick one," Chris says.

"Chocolate, vanilla, or strawberry," the voice says.

"Which one would you like?" she asks Chris.

"It doesn't matter! Just pick one!"

"I suppose the chocolate then. Or could you do a Neapolitan?"

"A what?" the voice says.

"Nothing. Chocolate. Chocolate's fine." She glances around, feeling as though a lot of people are laughing at her or waiting for her to parallel-park.

"Anything else?" the voice asks.

"I don't think—I suppose a Coke or something. Or maybe I'll have a chocolate shake, too."

Silence.

"You need to say 'I'd like a chocolate shake,'" Chris says. "Not 'maybe I'll have one.' She takes orders, not wonders."

"I'll have a shake then," she says. "Chocolate. Okay. That's that."

"Anything to eat?"

"Well, maybe—"

"Just double the order!" Chris yells, leaning over her. "Two of everything!" He goes back to his side. "God!" he says. "Sometimes you can just, like, kill events. You make things so unnecessarily difficult." He flicks his hand forward. "Pull up."

Georgia does as she's told.

Driving on 280 she feels protected by the rolling hills and the silence of the cool night. With the light of the moon on the hills the ride feels almost romantic.

"If you're having any trouble you can tell me, you know."

"I'm not having any trouble," Chris says.

"But I just picked you up in jail."

"All I did was get a goddamn jacket, then I'm in some ghetto holding cell stripping in front of a guard who could have butt-raped me if he wanted to."

"I still think something is going on—"

"I just explained!"

"You're not . . . you're not in a gang or anything, are you? I've heard about these initiations—"

"With the artichokes! Oh my God, that is so messed up. Where did they even come up with that?"

"So you're not—"

"No, I'm not psychotic! That's like *Clockwork Orange* shit. Scary." He looks back at Zoë with what seems like concern.

"Well, you do get detention a lot," she continues. "That's trouble."

"That's nothing, too. Just a bunch of bullshit. I was in there last time for not running. Big deal."

"What do you mean?" she asks.

He looks up at the ceiling. "In our timed mile I hid behind this blue mat. The mat people land on after they leap over a pole with a pole. What's that called again?"

"Pole vaulting," she says, happy not only to know the answer but that her brain had transmitted this knowledge so quickly.

"Why the cock do people do that?" Chris asks. "Who even came up with that? I mean, for reals. So I hid behind the pole-vaulting mat, then joined in on the last lap. Curt, a total vagina, ratted me out."

"Why did you just run?"

"Because it's a ridiculous thing to do," he says. "People need to compete all the time. Coach Ron is standing there with his clipboard. Coach Jon is recording our times. Why? What's the point? People eat spiders and roll around in bat feces to win something. I'm not going to put on little shorts and *jog* so I can beat my record."

He needs a role model, Georgia knows, and yet Eric is proving to be a bad one. Chris doesn't respect him—his art, his mind, and his "alert approach" to living. If only he could relate to him somehow, to both of them.

"Your father thinks running is ridiculous, too," she says.

"Yeah, but he has no problem putting spandex on every Saturday morning and riding down hills on a bicycle with his asshole in the air. I don't see why they all have to wear those tights. You can bike in normal clothes, you know."

"Your father was in the army," she says, having no idea why she would say such a thing and what it's supposed to accomplish. She was watching something about Navy SEALs on the *Today* show and they seemed so stoic and wise, not to mention incredibly sculpted.

She supposes she wants him to envision his father moving through a swamp with a cigarette dangling from his mouth. There he is in the jungle or the desert, squinting in the hot sun. He's had a hard day, lost one of his best friends in a surprise attack. He holds a letter to the friend's wife that says, "If you get this it means I'm gone, my love." Eric looks up at the sky and shouts. The other men look away, uncomfortable with his savage grief. He'd cheer up later that day after receiving the letter from Georgia, telling him she was pregnant with his son, a war baby.

"He was not in the army," Chris says. "Are you kidding me?"

It's a horrible lie, and what did she expect to get from it?

"I think he was," she says. "Just a little stint—to pay for his education."

"Big deal," Chris says. "And if he was he sure doesn't act like it. At that barbecue he had to scrape the grill because bacon touched it! It's like someone's done a 187 on his manhood."

She remembers Eric scraping the bacon essence. She caught her friends exchanging looks, Mele mouthing, *Oh my God.*

"He has allergies," she lies.

"Bullshit." He coughs.

"I wish you wouldn't talk like that," Georgia says. "Your brother and sister are susceptible. They're like sponges."

"Yeah, right," Chris says. "Gabe can hardly talk. Kids are supposed to talk by now. *Gabe want milk. Gabe make peepee.*" Chris laughs.

Georgia experiences a shock of humiliation and guilt. She has a faulty child, and it isn't a manufacturing problem. It has to do with care and maintenance. She fills Gabe with juice and candy. She lets him watch hours upon hours of toons, and the toon he loves happens to be about a bunch of kid scientists who, quite frankly, behave as though there's no chance in hell that they could be scientists. She gets too tired to make lunch for him and gives him Lunchables instead, which make his fingers puffy. She wonders why Chris isn't eating. The burgers smell sweet and smoky.

"Kids are all different," she says. "They all move at different speeds. Gabe excels in other things." She tries to think of the other things, but when she measures his abilities against those of the Panhandle bunch, Gabe comes out a dwarf. He doesn't have milestones. He has centimeterstones.

Zoë begins to make her hungry cry, and Georgia speeds up. She doesn't want to have to nurse her in front of Chris. The absolute worst thing would be if Gabe woke up and wanted to nurse—*Gabe want boobie!*—fussing with her breast like a kitten with a ball of yarn. She has kept it a secret from Chris and Eric that he still breast-feeds.

"Hush, Zoë," Chris says. His voice isn't soft, but it's kind. He always speaks to Zoë as though she's an adult. "I bought you a blanket," he says. "It's pink. You'll love it. Don't cry."

"You got her a blanket?" Georgia asks.

"Yeah," he says.

"Where?"

"Giggle."

Georgia has never gone in there—that fancy Marina baby store with modern baby furniture and poison-free plastics.

"The saleswoman said some celebrity has the same blanket. She said to a customer, 'If they have an ugly baby, just get it some gorgeous clothes!' She sucked."

It occurs to Georgia that her son is the only one in their household earning a paycheck.

"That was nice of you," she says.

"I know," he says.

They wind down the freeway toward the south of the city. A blanket of light rolls out before her. She feels this way about her son, too—that he's rolling out before her.

75

"I want you to know that if you need help I'm here," she says. "If you're doing drugs you can tell me."

"I'm doing drugs," he says.

"Oh," she says.

"Just weed," he says. "Like, socially. I'm not a hermit or anything toking day and night and talking crap about *reality, man.* That's probably what you did back in the day. Actually, you and Dad probably weren't even doing that."

"Well, I think it's natural to experiment, and I appreciate your honesty, but you need to make sure you're safe. In fact, you shouldn't—"

"Have you?" Chris asks. "Have you done drugs?"

She hasn't. Nothing. Some grass in high school, but she never liked it. She'd take fake hits, then dance in her peasant skirts, pretending to be high and enlightened.

"Yes," she says.

Chris laughs as though he doesn't believe her. "Like what?"

"I don't know," she says. "Grass."

"Grass." He laughs. "Rad."

"And acid." She quickly checks his face and hopes he won't ask her what acid looks like. "And I've snorted cocaine."

"What!" Chris says. "Nuh-uh." She smiles because he seems so proud of her.

"I was a real cokehead," she says. "So was Dad," she adds. "That's how we met. I mean, that's how we bonded."

Chris stares, his mouth agape. He's envisioning his father as a smoker, a fighter. They both tripped out and did white lines. Perhaps he sees Eric tucking a wad of cash into her bra and saying, "Go get yourself some cocaine. It's on me." Perhaps he's imagining his beautiful mother tottering off on platform heels.

"But then I overdosed," she says. "And we sobered up. Together." There she is convulsing on the floor of a bathroom, blood running out of her nose. Eric hoists her over his shoulder and smokes a cigarette as he carries her to the hospital. He could drive, but it's a nice night, warm and humid like Kuwait. "You hang in there, sweetcakes," he says every now and then while gently patting her bottom.

Chris looks amused, yet confused, like he's listening to a comedian that he hadn't planned on liking. Georgia's a bit afraid of her son's gaze. She knows this small thread of respect could unravel in an instant, but she settles her shoulders, leans back, and lounges in the deceit.

"Wow," he says. "Well, all right."

They drive in silence, and Georgia knows that he's thinking he's wrong about her, and that she's an interesting person. Zoë starts to make little whimpers—little accusations. They clash with the Brazilian woman's throaty whimpers, which sound like she's enjoying something delicious.

"Aren't you going to eat your burger?" Georgia asks.

He takes a sip of his shake. "We can pull over if you want," he says. "If you want to eat, too. Or just wait till home or whatever. I was just going to wait. I don't like eating in motion."

"Neither do I," she says, slowing before the next exit, her heart racing. "So should we pull over or can you wait?"

"Up to you," he says.

It's not a life-or-death decision, she reminds herself. Just make a decision. Just veer off course. She takes the exit.

The dirt lot at the top of the hill overlooks Pacifica.

"This is such an odd parking lot," she says.

"It's probably for maintenance people," Chris says, nodding toward something near the entrance that looks like a water heater. She parks so that they can look out at the ocean, black and rippling like oil. Houses are huddled together by the expanse of forest and ocean, a little, bright patch of life. She can see Target, the telltale bull's-eye, and thinks of toilet paper. She forgot to get some this afternoon, which reminds her of Zoë's full diaper. Zoë has gone back to sleep. Chris hands her a bag of loose fries and a burger wrapped in wax paper.

"I hate when they don't give you enough ketchup," he says.

"You hate a lot of things," she says.

"You should try it sometime." He takes a bite of his burger. "Ah," he says. "It's good to be out of jail."

She laughs, realizing her son is funny. She has a funny child, and for the first time she considers it's something to be proud of, that funny is an intelligent and hard thing to be. She unwraps the burger, and the paper fills her with warm nostalgia. She takes a bite. The bun is soft on her tongue and it melts into her teeth and onto the roof of her mouth. Everything collides and becomes one—bun, patty, sauce. She puts a fry in her mouth just to employ everything equally, and the dense concoction is heavenly. She has never felt so centered, so content.

Except.

She wishes there were a bathroom. Her breasts are full and hard and she can feel them growing. She's worried Zoë will make a sound triggering the downpour of milk, which feels like raining needles. She wishes she could squeeze her breasts over a sink or even outside on the dirt. Chris catches her eye, and they both look away from each other with full mouths. They come back though. They chew and their eyes meet again.

"Bomb, isn't it?" Chris says.

She nods. Yes. Bomb. She tries to think of the other fake things she did when she was a girl. What kinds of things would he appreciate?

"Vanna White sure looks good still," she says.

"Yeah, but she's got those hard boobs that are everywhere now." He chews and looks like he's contemplating something significant. "It will be weird when these ladies get superold, but their boobs will be the same. Their boobs will be like the old perv who still tries to look young and hang with the kids. They'll be perv boobs." He takes a loud sip of his shake. "I don't how Vanna can do that job for so long."

She pictures Vanna clapping her hands in a way that allows her to keep every other part of her body still. It's very easy for Georgia to see how Vanna can still do what she does. Same reason she can be with Eric for so long, or can let her son speak to her the way he does. Same reason she hasn't weaned or potty-trained Gabe. People get stuck, and not a good kind of stuck, like Vanna. Some people just don't have what it takes to be anything else. Lose a turn, sorry, too bad. It's a thing, a place, a person. Can you solve it? What would you like to do now, Georgia?

"I used to model," she says.

She sees a flicker in Chris's eye, something wanting.

"Is that how you got into coke?" he asks after chewing down a fry.

She hadn't put that together. "Yes," she says.

"That's awesome."

"I didn't like it though," she says. "The modeling. I just wanted to travel. I went to India. That's where I learned yoga and why we live so . . . minimally."

She thinks of Eric and his joke of an art, likes that she can source their failure in spirituality. She can do anything she wants. She takes another bite of her burger.

"I just want you to have a chance to see the world like I did. I want you to be able to make mistakes, but have the education and support to lessen the effects of mistakes. Cocaine didn't kill me, but it could have if I hadn't come from a good family and done well in school."

She has never expressed herself so well. She did horribly in school. Her mother and father were alcoholics. Her dad worked as a teller at a bank in a wealthy neighborhood and would come home, drink his gin, then have conversations with imaginary customers. "Yes, Mrs. Rich

Bitch," he'd say. "Is there anything else?" At dinner he'd look under the table and yell, "Are you under there, Mrs. Rich Bitch?"

When she was little she actually thought this was a real woman.

Chris nods as he chews. Georgia looks over the ocean; the music is low on the radio. She is beautiful, well traveled, deep, experienced. She's a mother eating fast food with her son. They should do this more often. Come up here, hang out, talk. What are his goals, his dreams? What are hers? She's about to ask. She'll just come out and say: "What do you want, Chris? What do I want?" but just then Zoë issues a sharp wail that stabs their beautiful bubble. It's an awful, awful sound, and her breasts respond to it immediately, like servants. Wetness blooms on her blue shirt. Two round wet circles, one bigger than the other.

"I need to feed her," she says. Chris looks at her shirt and stops chewing.

She passes him her food, then turns to get on her knees and move over the console. She unbuckles Zoë and brings her to the front so Gabe won't wake up and see them. Zoë makes frantic movements, butting her mouth into Georgia's shirt.

"Hold her," she says, and Chris looks down at his hands, then places everything on the floor and takes his sister.

Georgia sits back down in front, then unbuttons her shirt and pulls down her bra. She has never bought one of those nursing bras with the flaps. She just pulls one side down and it stays underneath her boob. "Okay," she says.

He hands her to Georgia, but positions his body so that he faces forward.

Her exposed breast is spraying milk all the way to the dash. It's like an old-fashioned hose-end sprinkler. Zoë latches on and sucks desperately, and Georgia's unused breast drips. Zoë pops off, takes a few breaths, then goes back.

Chris looks out the right of the car, then reaches down for his shake. He sucks on the straw, then stops. He turns the radio's volume up a little louder, looks down at the baby, then looks away. She knows she has lost him. He sees her for what she is, for the only thing she can be. The beautiful woman and the soldier are gone. He gets shot in the head. She breaks her neck somehow. Everything has vanished.

And now Gabe is awake, in tears, his face red and critical. He makes the sign to be fed over and over again. *Gabe want milk. Gabe want milk.* All of her children are always so hungry.

"Use your words," Georgia says, but Gabe keeps signing. She doesn't know why she ever taught him such a thing.

"You're not an ape!" she yells. "Use your words! Just say what you want! Just speak like everyone else!"

"Mom," Chris says.

"What?" Georgia yells. "What, Chris?"

Georgia has ripped Zoë off her nipple, and her depleted breast hangs like a sock. Zoë roots around her chest like a little pig looking for truffles. The woman's voice on the radio does a kind of ethnic yodel, and all Georgia can think is that this woman seems terribly, terribly free.

"Just ignore it," Chris says. "Let's just get home." He takes Zoë from her arms, then gets out of the car to put her back in the seat. Does he even know how to buckle a car seat? Does she care? She fixes her bra and her shirt. Gabe screams and continues to make signs.

"Stop that," she says forcefully. "Stop making those signs or the bad men are going to get you. The gang is going to get you." Gabe takes a pause, looks at her searchingly, then howls. When Chris opens the door to put Zoë in, he says something to his younger brother, but she's not sure what. She faces forward, looks out at the lights below. Gabe is suddenly quiet. She glances back, and he has his pacifier in his mouth, his lids heavy with what looks like bliss.

Chris walks back to his side, and as he's getting in, the car brightens with someone's headlights and for a second she sees them all lit up as if onstage. Two cars come into the lot, rolling in slowly over the gravel.

"What if it's them?" she says. "The gang with the artichokes."

"Yeah, right," Chris says, in a way that's not at all convinced. He holds his burger on his lap. "Let's go," he says. "We can finish at home."

She starts the car. The other cars seem to be waiting for her to leave. She reverses, then drives forward. One of the cars also moves forward, toward her left. Chris stares straight ahead. When the car gets closer to them it slows, then comes to a stop.

"Just keep going," Chris says, but she thinks this could be the wrong move to make. In fact, even thinking about moves is the wrong move. These are probably just teenagers or maintenance men, or someone who's lost. She stops and puts her window down. "What are you doing?" Chris says through clenched teeth. He shifts in his seat, putting a foot on the dash, then putting it back down.

The driver of the car grins at her. He's small—compact and ropy. His car is a honey brown that glistens.

"You're not waiting for us, right?" he asks.

"I don't think so," Georgia says. Two guys in the back of the car laugh, and the driver nods as though she's said something wise. He looks into his rearview mirror, and Georgia looks ahead at the car behind him, which is somewhat blocking the exit. On the other side of the exit is a patch of trees and a Dumpster.

"You sure you're not waiting for us?" the driver says, and his passengers laugh again, though less so this time.

"Just go," Chris says, and she realizes her son isn't nearly as bad as he'd like to be, that jail was just a fluke, a stroke of bad luck, something he's probably proud of.

Chris is afraid. He thinks they are going to die, and for some reason this gives Georgia a small thump of joy. She is his mommy.

"Hey, you're listening to the same song as us," the driver says. He reaches forward to turn his volume up, and she hears the woman on both radios. Her cries are insistent, firm taps. They blend with the drums, simmering like flavors, building toward something exquisite and exotic yet entirely expected.

"Nice," Georgia says. "Like a duet." The driver bobs his head, then says something to the others in Spanish. She doesn't understand why she isn't frightened. Maybe residual adrenaline has morphed her anger with Gabe into something like courage or something like apathy or something like hope. She loves when days don't go as planned, when she's not on a playground bench staring into space, when she's not at home watching other people on television making love, drinking pretty cocktails, fighting wars, or asking Pat for a *T*, please. She loves that her son is afraid and that she isn't.

She feels the cold air blow through her wet shirt. The driver looks at her again, nodding to the music and tapping his fingers against his lips.

"Good-bye," she says, but the driver just nods.

"I *was* waiting for you," she wants to say to the little man. "I've been waiting for you my whole life."

"Go," Chris says, and Georgia goes on.

Has anyone tried Julie's Method? We've done the diaper countdown, telling her that now no more diapers exist in the world. My husband and I have committed and gone cold turkey. However, we'd like to revisit diapers at night to avoid doing so much laundry, and also we have a wedding this weekend and we're not sure if the babysitter can handle this. I feel like we would break our contract, but what do you do for night and special occasions?

—Carrie Lee

Yes, I've done Julie's Method. Do not put a diaper back on! That's the whole point of Julie's Method. We created a potty song, loaded our daughter up on juice boxes. She was in heaven! We practiced for three days, never leaving the apartment. I strapped the portable to me and shadowed her. I was totally committed. By day three she got it. She poops, she pees, she loves it.

—Amanda Fuller

I agree. Julie's Method works. The biggest barrier sounds like you. I would wait until you are ready. Kids get things, and if you aren't 100% into it, the kid will know and will work it. Like Amanda, I was committed. I was pregnant and did not want to be wiping two butts. Dude, poop is terrible. It's so liberating for the child to have that control over their body. It's easy. Good luck. I really hope for planet earth and your child that you do it!

—Johanna Weller

The Pant-less Method worked for us, except there were skid marks all over the house.

—A.L., West Portal

What was the last thing you ate?

Thanks to Georgia, the last thing I ate was a burger from In-N-Out.

She told me a story that left me stunned and humbled. You never know what's behind a person. For a moment she lied her way into another life, so tired she was of her own, and I admired her lies, the way they revealed the truth.

"I don't know how you do it," I said to her, thinking of her three children.

"I don't," Georgia said.

"But you do. You are."

"I envy you," Georgia said, and I spit out a laugh. "I'm serious. You're free."

"I'm not that free," I said and stopped there. She could pour her heart out, but I wasn't about to say: "I'm afraid and hurt and a tad desperate. The thought of being with a man sickens me, but sometimes I feel this pathetic need for one."

Also, by saying that I was free, I think she was talking about her marriage, the way it confines and limits her.

Henry had come into the park during part of her story, and he was pushing Tommy on the swings. He did so much with his kids. I couldn't imagine leaving someone who cared so much about my child. I couldn't imagine leaving anyone who looked like Henry. I know he must be devastated about his wife, but he had to be unhappy before. Why would he spend so much time getting away from her and everyone in his circle?

"Imagine growing up in a neighborhood and never leaving it for the rest of your life," Henry once said. "That's what these people do. They go to the same schools, live in the same places, use the same designers, fight the same fights, go to the same parties, none of which are really parties. Then they have their kids replicate their steps under the impression that they're making their own choices."

Henry was here, making his own choices.

"Are you ready for the wedding?" Georgia asked, and it took me a moment to jump onto another line of thought. "Yes," I said. "I mean, no."

"I think it's good you're going." Georgia got up to gather her things.

"You do? Annie thinks I'm crazy."

"Ellie's the flower girl. You have to be there. Just to watch her."

Georgia scanned the playground for Gabe, found him, check, and then she turned back to me. "Just have fun with her."

"And the vows, the kiss, the dancing? Feeding each other cake." I was beginning to think Annie was right.

"You'll make it," Georgia said.

I sighed and sank a little, thinking about a dish for Georgia. Perhaps Thai-spiced burgers with French fries—creative, exotic fries, because Georgia, and so many parents, needs to be transported. An artichoke dish, of course, and mini–milk shakes. Neapolitan to avoid having to make a choice. Sometimes there were too many choices. Just let Georgia have it all.

"Thank you," I said to Georgia.

At the wedding, during those hard parts, I'll lie my way into another life. I'll transport myself. I'll watch my daughter and pretend we're all extras in a movie, something utterly unreal.

"Did you ever tell Eric?" I asked.

Georgia smiled. "No. I think Chris really likes the secret. Things have been good with us." She looked out, content, some private thought changing the normal structure of her face. She looked at peace.

Secrets and lies, so healthy sometimes.

She got up and walked over to the sandbox to take something out of Gabe's mouth. I walked to Ellie at the play structure next to the swings.

"What's up?" I called to Henry, all cool and casual. I leaned against the metal bar and promptly slipped off of it.

"Howdy," he said, something I had never heard him say before, and he seemed a bit embarrassed by it. He crinkled his nose and shook his head as if he was disappointed. Henry has one of those faces where you know, absolutely, that he was very good-looking when he was younger. This isn't to say he's not very good-looking now—dark hair, with a few wisps of gray on the sides, dark eyebrows, green eyes, a strong build, but not an uptight triathlete build, more like the accidental strength that surfers or skateboarders have—it just comes with the job. I could tell he was a star once, and yet I never liked the stars, and the stars looked at the other stars—like Kate. I don't believe in luck. I believe in timing. We could only be friends at the ages we are now. That went for all of us.

A drunk homeless person was standing by the playground gates screaming to Ellie that she was wearing the cutest hat. Ellie screamed back in delight, smiling at this man who looked like he had scurvy. I picked her up and kissed the top of her head, a reflex. She needed a bath. Her hair smelled like expensive mushrooms. I put her in the other swing next to Tommy, and Henry and I pushed their small backs.

"She had a really good story," I said.

"Better than mine?" he said. "Adultery?"

"Different problems," I said. "So how are things with you?" I faced Ellie's back as I said this. It had been almost a week since he told me his story.

"She's not staying at home right now." He faced the back of his child. There we were in parallel play.

"Mommy's on a work trip," Tommy said, which must have hurt Henry—the lie of it, how he will have to lie to this boy for so long, perhaps forever. Children are always listening.

I thought of Georgia and her yearning for something, anything. I found myself pushing so softly, Ellie was barely swinging. The metal squeaked, making a rhythm with a nearby bouncing ball and a distant bongo drum.

I wondered if Henry would be like Bobby's fiancée: forgiving because he'll get something out of it.

"Nice afternoon," I said, so lame, but it was clear and crisp, promising something. But what? It was almost dark and I'd go back to my small apartment. He'd go back to his wifeless, big house. Or.

"I'm craving In-N-Out," I said, stepping to the edge of the diving board. If I could ask for this, I could eventually ask for more in life. Bobby was right. I needed to stop feeling sorry for myself. Ellie wasn't a baby anymore, and I was still reacting versus living. It's just that these years went by so darn fast.

"Want to go on a field trip?" I bit my lower lip.

"Sure," Henry said, his voice energetic, though that's probably how all men respond to burger proposals.

Thank you, Georgia, I thought.

And so we took our separate cars to the south of the city, enduring traffic and hungry children and a glitch in our very set routine.

The last thing I ate was a hamburger with tomato and onion and a root beer. I ate it in a booth with a married man and our two children, who had sword fights with their French fries. We didn't talk about anything significant. The kids were there and we were sitting in the moment. I was planning on bringing up the wedding, asking if he was serious about being my guest. I had a speech, so as to assure him he'd be there as a prop, not as a date or anything, of course. He'd save me from a bit of humiliation. He'd make Bobby jealous. He'd make me feel less awkward and alone, but none of this sounded good or right to say. The speech highlighted my insecurity and made me rethink asking him at all. His presence would be proof that I hadn't moved on.

"Wow," Henry said at our table, pushing away the rest of his fries. "That was something. Thanks for asking us along." He ruffled Tommy's hair. "Say thank you, champ. This place is a national treasure."

"Thank you," Tommy said, grinning at his father with a fry in his front teeth.

"Say thank you to Mele, not me." Henry looked across at me. I tucked my hair behind my ear.

"But you bought it." Tommy shook a ketchup bottle.

"Yes, but good ideas are harder to come by."

"Thank you, Tommy's dad!" Ellie said.

"Thank you, Ellie's mom," Tommy said.

Think back to when you were young. You're walking with some big guy on campus, and while you're exhilarated in the moment, content with just him, you're also looking around, hoping other people are seeing you, cementing the image of the two (or four) of you. That's what it felt like being there with Henry and our kids. There was no better place to be, and I wished everyone could see.

Of course you should provide food. Do you want your babysitter or nanny to be hungry? I don't know about you, but
when I'm hungry I become irritable. So who suffers? Your
children.

　—SFMC response to "Should you provide food for the
　nanny?"

I say no. You'll get stuck in a cycle. We should have never
provided food for our nanny in the first place. She is such
a large woman. We finally had to sit her down and tell her
that tonight would be her last supper.

　—SFMC response

I just leave my credit card by the phone and a variety of
take-out menus. It's a simple solution versus a selfish one.

　—Tabor Boyard

BAKE THE BABYSITTER

Henry isn't at the park today, and Mele feels a bit silly about her outfit. She's wearing fitted jeans—very fitted, and a V-neck cashmere sweater. Even though her breasts have gone from melons to oranges and seem to be further transforming into week-old tangerines, they're still respectable, edible.

"Would you ever get a boob job?" she asks Annie, who is sitting next to her.

"Nope," she says. "But I'm, you know . . ."

"Married," Mele says.

"Plus implants kind of scream, 'I just turned forty!'"

"That's true," Mele says.

"And you're only thirty. That's insane." Annie lays Max down on the bench and proceeds to change his diaper. It's gross, but Mele can't stop looking at his bare bottom, his little balls like spoiled grapes, his legs kicking in the air. She feels fortunate to have a little girl—vaginas are so much cuter.

"How are your recipes coming along?" Annie asks.

Mele hears a bit of ridicule in the question. Maybe *ridicule* isn't the right word though. Pity. That's what she hears.

"Good," she says. And it is good. She's always loved that about writing—how it gives you an excuse to know something better, or know someone.

"I want you to do my babysitter story," Annie says. "I inspire Sloppy Joes. Or something spiked."

Mele laughs. Annie is such a character. Funny and tough, punk rock. She has a deep need to keep in touch with the person she once was ("Are you there, old self?" she imagines her friend asking her reflection. "It's me, watered down."). Yes, Annie has told her a lot of stories from her prior life. She thrived off a semiprecious list of youthful antics: heavy drinking, jail (just one night), promiscuous yucky sex, stealing, flashing, having keg parties in her nice suburban home when her mother was the president of the local MADD, the usual, and while all these things are now as distant as a tiny village in Nova Scotia, Annie has a hard time turning her back on the self she has outgrown.

Mele thinks she has a hard time letting it go because then she'd just be "Mom." She'd be like Georgia, Mele, and Barrett, people who in her prior life, she would have growled at.

She thinks of the incident that happened almost a year ago. That would require something reckless or irreverent, something you wouldn't think could taste good. Squid—ribboned to look like noodles with butter and garlic and shichimi togarashi. Something like that? Or is that just gross?

"You haven't heard anything from that babysitter, have you?" Mele asks.

"No," Annie says. "Looks like I'm in the clear."

"Jeez," Mele says. "She sure riled you up."

"Exercise class. That's all I really wanted. I wanted to have normal fun."

"There's nothing wrong with Sloppy Joes," Mele says. "Everyone loves them. Embrace it. Be a Sloppy Joe."

"Are you trying to find something I inspire or that you think I need?"

"Both."

Ellie runs up to them, her hand grasping her crotch. "I need to go potty."

"Are you sure?" Mele asks. She hates when Ellie needs to pee at the park, but during potty training you have to stop, drop, and pee on your child's whim. Mele has caught on to the pee lies, a technique Ellie uses to get out of the gates and play in the disgusting bathroom, which usually has no toilet paper and a moaning homeless person. She sits on the potty forever while Mele stands in the cramped stall, arms crossed.

Ellie wiggles and really digs in as her answer. "I do."

"Quickly," Mele says.

"Real fast. I'll pee, pee, all fast."

"I'll be back in five hours," Mele says to Annie. "I'll think about you and your babysitter."

She leaves her friend and notices her discomfort. There's a group of mothers on the other end of the playground, all laughing at something Annie would probably think isn't funny at all. Mele can at least blend a bit, but with tattooed arms and blue hair and a Porta Potti mouth, Annie can't quite merge, despite the fact she is similar to them at the core. Mele catches her friend briefly smiling at the other moms while passing by with Max. Baby steps. Annie is trying.

ANNIE'S FUN

During an awkward employer-employee lull, Annie asked her son's babysitter what she did for fun.

"Um," Jenny said. "Hang out with friends?"

Jenny then asked Annie what *she* did for fun, and for some inane reason Annie has been thinking about the question ever since. It's like the question was a firm shake, an inquiry not just into pastimes but into life itself. *What did she do? What did she want? How long could she take her husband working so much? Why couldn't she have a little fun without him? Who was she?*

Brian had been in Palo Alto for four nights in a row—last week it was three nights, in a trial representing Fletcher Webber IV—some hedge fund manager being sued for . . . something bad. Annie always tried to listen when Brian filled her in, but he had a low, monotone voice, and her mind always drifted—he was like a white-noise machine. Besides, his client's name was Fletcher. Of course he was guilty, especially with the Roman numeral in his name. Warren Buffett said to give your kids enough to do something, but not so much that they could do nothing. Annie would add: "Don't name your kid after yourself unless you want them to be a total douche."

But back to the fun. The fun! Where was it? At the time all she could think of was dessert. For fun she makes cookies, tarts, bars, muffins, and dense gooey hybrids—brownie puddings, pies with oatmeal cookie crusts. She's especially fond of using alcohol in her recipes. It doesn't do anything, buzz-wise, yet it gives her comfort knowing it's there. What else? she wondered before answering Jenny. Wine, yoga, dishwashing . . . for a real treat, when Max is all squared away, she'll smoke half a joint and read interior decorating magazines. Or whatever. Weed is insurance for anything. And so she gave the babysitter an honest answer, saying, "I bake," though this seemed so unsatisfactory—was that all? Ever since she has been constantly foraging.

"What do *you* do for fun?" she asks Mele, who has just strapped Ellie into Max's high chair and given her a wafer to suck. She has stopped over for a walk that they probably won't take. The sky looks inhospitable and their legs seem to prefer to be left unmoving. Plus, Jenny would be here, and Annie's on a cleaning roll, eradicating crumbs, grounds, and things unseen.

"I watch TV," Mele says. "I eavesdrop."

"I can't imagine what Jenny does. She's a good girl."

"So what if she's a good girl?" Mele says. "A mother wants a dork."

"But it's awkward. It's weird," Annie says, thinking of Jenny, the Hello Kitty width of her face, her perfect painted nails, glassy white like grocery bags. She finds a new patch of counter to wipe with her killer sponge. She read about the sponge on a mom's blog, thought the mom was getting a little hysterical over a cleaning product, vowed to never be a mom who cared about such things, and now feels she could be the sponge's goddamn spokesperson.

"What's in this sponge?" she wonders aloud.

"I don't know, but you look like you're on coke," Mele says, which feels true. Annie wants to swipe new surfaces, find new things to clean, absolutely euphoric until the power runs out.

"God, what a horrible drug," Annie says. "I remember being in bars and snorting the stuff off of toilet lids, then going back out and having these involved conversations with idiots, rubbing up against boners, swigging straight gin like it was Juicy Juice. I must have been Jenny's age." She stops cleaning, finding this unfathomable. "She watches Lifetime," Annie says, to prove a point. "While Max naps. I have TiVo, cable, Netflix, Amazon Prime, and still she watches Lifetime. And she can never sit for me Fridays. Ever, and that was part of the deal."

Max starts to baa—he alternates between sheep and horse sounds—and she takes him out of the ExerSaucer and sets him down on the floor. He leapfrogs on his butt toward the cupboard, still not crawling at twelve months. Instead he straddles his legs wide open and scoots himself across both soft and hard surfaces. He's gotten so good and fast that it takes Annie by surprise when he flies past her. It's like getting passed by a legless skier.

"You should say something to her," Mele says. "You're clearly peeved. And you're making me nervous. Sit down or something."

"She'll be here any minute," Annie says.

"So? Give her the sponge. Give her a dustpan."

"She sits for Tabor Boyard," Annie says. "Can you imagine going there, then coming here?" She looks around the kitchen, making sure she got everything. She has put away her Wu-Tang and Mos Def CDs. On the fridge she took down the coupon from a Korean restaurant for FREE MAN DOO. Frickin' hilarious. In the bathroom off the kitchen she has a bottle of lotion that once said MOREY BUTTER until Brian rubbed out the *y* and the *er*, so that it says, MORE BUTT. She has remembered to turn the label toward the wall even though she loves seeing it. It makes her smile while she uses the toilet. God, she misses him. It's not like he wants to be gone. He's the one at work to pay for their needs: food, shelter, babysitters.

Annie had always planned on being herself, but that got thrown out the window the moment she opened her door to an Asian girl dressed in jeans, an itchy-looking tight sweater, and little gold hoop earrings, most likely from Claire's. She remembered a girl from the park the other day, a young babysitter with a raspy, I-had-such-a-killer-night voice, telling her charge: "Come on, homie, let's cruise this-a-way." Annie wanted a babysitter like that, but this girl was nothing like her.

The girl took a step into her home as if entering a hot tub full of hippies. Annie immediately apologized for the mess and used exaggerated hand gestures to illustrate her hectic morning, tagging on an *agghh* for good measure. Girls like Jenny with their clean nails and outfits from Express made her feel loud, grubby, and gigantic. Jenny's eyes kept darting around. Her smile twitched at half-mast. Annie wondered: Do I hug her? Shake her hand? Inquire about her hobbies?

From the mother's chat group she knew the questions she was supposed to ask: "Do you know CPR?" "Have you had chicken pox?" "Do you cook or clean?" But this seemed so nerdy, personal, and bitchy—in that order. Plus, Jenny was recommended by Tabor Boyard, whom Annie only virtually knows through posts on SFMC, yet through Tabor's various postings and inquiries about personal shoppers, colorists, nut-free preschools, and home organizers, Annie has gleaned enough information to feel that she knows her intimately.

She knows that Tabor has a three-story home in Ashbury Heights (a necessary detail for the curtain consultant inquiry), a 1.5-year-old girl (preschool consultant inquiry), and brown roots (colorist reccs?). She also has a dog walker, a yoga teacher, and a personal organizer, whom she highly recommends: "She's only eighty dollars an hour and now my spices are all in a row. She also organized my bathroom in such a way that I never dreamed possible. She put all of my makeup brushes in a labeled container."

Annie wanted to write back that she would have done that for a shot of Patrón.

The woman has learned how to outsource her entire life, and while Annie has come to loathe her a tad (her heart rabbit-humps every time she sees a message from Tabe@hotmail.com), she has also come to trust the woman and value her opinions more than her own. And so, because of Tabor, Jenny was let off the hook—Annie didn't need to know if the girl had a criminal record. She'd only be there for three hours on Tuesdays and Fridays anyway while Annie was in the house. She didn't need to know about mumps or drug use. She just had to know how to keep her.

That first day Annie put Max down so he could demonstrate his version of crawling. She expected the new babysitter to laugh and then they'd have something to talk about, but Jenny didn't laugh and Annie didn't know if her horrified look was in reaction to the way he moved or to him picking a cracker off of the floor.

"Oh, no," Jenny said. "That's dirty, Max. Dirty."

Annie always let him eat from the floor, but this time she said, "Yucky," and swooped in like a booby bird. "Yucky! Dirty! Mommy will put it in the rubbish."

She put the cracker in her pocket, then later in her mouth. From that first day she knew that this girl would require a cleaner act.

"You know how it is," Annie says to Mele. "It's like when you meet goody-goody mothers. You pretend to be goody-goody, too, and then you have to keep up the act, inserting your true self gently and slowly."

"Yes, but eventually, you have to put it out there," Mele says. "See what happens. I know what you mean though."

"Oh God!" Annie sees the rolling papers she left on the counter of the office nook last night. She had gotten an eighth of Sour Diesel from a father at Max's Little Bears Music class, and the stuff made her terribly forgetful and gave her delusions she mistook for creativity.

"Can you imagine if she saw these?" She holds them up, then puts them in her pocket, contemplating a brief backyard hit, then remembering she has to drive Jenny to Tabor's later this afternoon. She can drink and drive pretty well, but smoke and drive? Forget it.

"So what if she saw those?" Mele says. "I'd be thrilled if I were a babysitter."

"She wouldn't be. That's what I'm trying to get across."

"You never know," Mele says. "Remember we thought Barrett would be high-maintenance and I thought you were going to be psychotic?"

Mele scoops Ellie out of Max's high chair and kisses her on the head. She walks toward the front door.

"It's unfair," Mele says. "In movies there's always the eccentric crazy artist and his repressed secretary, nanny, or assistant—they learn from each other—she's afraid, yet reverent, blah, blah, blah. But if the mom's weird she just gets shunned or reported to Child Services. You shouldn't have to put on such a show. She's the babysitter, not a mom. Not Tabor. You don't have to clean for her."

"I know," Annie says, following them out. "But she worships Tabor. I'm Tabor's opposite."

Annie thinks of things like fruit Jell-O molds and children's cereal. Nothing about her feels real anymore. She is monoglycerides. She is cellulose gum.

Shortly after Mele leaves Annie hears the familiar knock. At least they're settled into a routine now and the awkwardness of being an employer has lessened a bit.

"Come in," she yells and wipes the snot under Max's nose, then wipes her hands on the dishcloth hanging from the oven. There. Her house and life are waxy like the bald head of Mr. Clean.

Jenny walks into the kitchen holding her keys and phone, and a little faux Coach purse, which is evidently too small to hold her keys and phone.

"Hi, Max!" she says.

"Can you say 'Hi'?" Annie says, and when he looks up and grins, pumping his arms as if trying to take flight, Annie feels stage-mother proud. They watch him flap, then look at one another and grin. Fuck, it's still awkward, Annie thinks, then remembers a task she saved just so she'd have something to do during the babysitter-getting-settled time.

"How are you?" Annie asks. She opens the fridge and takes out the snacks, which have been premade to make things convenient.

"I'm good," Jenny says. "Busy."

"This is just some apple and cottage cheese," she says, holding up the purple container. "I got you some things, too." She gestures to the energy bar, yogurt, fruit, soda. "Everything you need should be right here. There's some strawberry tart here, too, that I made this morning."

"Oh, thanks!" Jenny says. "You didn't need to get me anything."

Oh, but she did.

"Should you provide food for the nanny?" a mom asked the chat group, and one of Tabor's replies said, "an extra ten or fifteen bucks isn't going to make a difference to us, but it affects the way they work for you dramatically."

There were other responses, too, ranging from angry: "Have you ever been given food on a job? I don't think so. Let them fend for themselves" to empathetic: "We make our nanny rice because she's Chinese," but it was Tabor's response that got her. She used the word, *us,* assuming that all the women in the group were like her, that an extra fifteen bucks a day, on top of babysitting money, was nothing to all of them and that every woman in San Francisco had the luxury of being so kind.

And so: baked goods and energy bars with names like Max Out and Cheetah. This is what Annie can provide, and she hopes it's enough.

"They're here if you need them," she says as kindly as possible and then excuses herself to her office.

"Work hard!" Jenny says.

"I will!" Annie says.

Annie slouches in front of the computer. She holds a chunk of her hair under her nose and looks at her design of a new onesie with a baby on it, its thought bubble needing a thought. In the bubble she types: "Who's My Daddy?"

Is that funny? Is the reference to "Who's Your Daddy?" too nineties? Maybe she should just leave the thought bubble blank—parents can fill it in for themselves, letting the world know who they are. They do that anyway—make statements via their children's clothing. "I was once cool!" they insist with Ramones or Che Guevara onesies, even though back in the day they were probably about as punk rock as a science fair diorama.

She clicks onto another window. All she wants to do is watch You-Tube videos and read people's stupid status updates. Georgia is wishing it were Friday! Barrett took a photo with Instagram! Maybe the blank thought bubble could work as a kind of baby status update. "Aiden just pooped in his cloth diaper!" parents could write in, or "Jaiden just got circumcised! Ho Snip!"

She stares, hands poised on the keyboard. She goes back to smelling her hair again. Work just isn't working, and she's convinced it's because Jenny needed to come on Fridays. She feels her most optimistic on Fridays, standing on the precipice of the weekend, those glorious lazy hours. That's the upside to having a husband who works so much—on weekends she can drop Max onto his lap and say, "Your turn," and then mothering becomes something thrilling and distant—a spectator sport, and she's the owner of the team.

This is the fourth week in a row where this Tabor lady obliterated her Friday morning plan to work a little and then enroll in the Bar Method, supposedly some difficult workout class that she's in desperate need of, seeing that she has enough skin on her stomach to make drums for an African tribe and her breasts look the same as Barney Frank's. She bets Tabor has one of those crazy MILF bodies every mother seems to have these days. Annie has sweatpants that say MILF on the butt, and it's clearly a false advertisement. She's not even a Mother I'd Like to Cuddle With. Brian treats her like a Mother I'd Like to Scratch My Ass in Front Of (a MILSMAFO?), and why should she have to primp when he doesn't bother to? His body is pale and plush, his strong face beginning to sink inward like the middle of a bell pepper. His penis is reminding her more and more of the muppet Gonzo, and when he bends over naked to put on his boxers, it's as though a bouquet of ferns were sprouting from his ass. And yet, every day she texts him: *Home tonight!?* His absence is most felt when she's in bed and there's something funny on television, her laughter echoing in the room, and she knows if he were there he'd be laughing, too. She pictures him in his hotel room just as alone.

She pulls up the graphics of her mothers. All of them are fabulous, long-legged and angular, phones in hand, oversize sunglasses on head. One hand pushing a Bugaboo, the other hand holding a huge handbag or a martini glass filled with an icy pink or blue liquid, depending on the sex of the baby, who is always smiling. She gazes at her creations. If brought to life, these girls would travel in herds and use the word *momtourage*. They wouldn't have husbands like Georgia's, who yelled at her in public about the two-sheet rule (using no more than two squares of toilet paper per pee).

They wouldn't be single like Mele, and if they were it would be "fabulous," and they'd write books about being cool and hip, single, hot moms. These women weren't like Barrett, the ex-cheerleader who looks the part but whose mind keeps her from full immersion. Barrett is too funny, too judgmental, too independent and short. These moms perhaps resemble Henry's wife, though his wife has to have some good qualities since she is married to Henry—that's automatic points, like writing your name on the SATs.

She looks at the graphic of the mom for her newest apron. What would you do for fun? she wonders. Talk to me. She imagines their voices, all based on people she's met and things she and Mele have overheard on playgrounds:

"I have dinner parties," the graphic says. "I have them in my newly designed garden, which features manicured European-style plantings and Stockholm guild-stamped Swedish rococo chairs with blue velvet seats. Because of the economy, at last week's dinner party my husband thought it would be really funny and yet responsible to get cheap beer and everyone drank it and said, 'God, remember we used to drink this?' It was especially humorous because our friends have respectable jobs: one's a CEO, one's a state senator, one is the granddaughter of the man who invented mini–condiments packets."

The next graphic is of a young, socialite kind of mom, who in real life would follow practically every assertion with "That's my motto." Even though she doesn't cook she buys these aprons as gifts for friends. The friends laugh, as if they're prank gifts, like edible underwear. *Aprons? How kitsch! How retro! I could wear it to the library gala—isn't the theme* Mad Men? *Oh, that would be ha-larious.* How do you have fun? Annie asks.

Well, fashion is my passion and my kids can't get in the way of that," she says. *"I was just praised in 7x7 for my fearless combining of a vintage Dior silk organza jacket and a bubble skirt from Target. I'm known for my whimsical approach, for pairing couture with fuchsia tights and microminis. The thing is the media can't pin me down, and so they keep tracking my fashion moves. One day I'm all Hawaii surfer–plantation owner, the next*

I'm all ice princess in ivory, cream, and ecru. Most of my closet is vintage or custom-made, but I also shop at Helpers Home Bazaar at Ghirardelli Square, which benefits retards.

Annie remembers reading this in an actual interview. This actually came from someone's mouth. "Why do I spend so much time creating and disliking you bitches?" Annie says. *Because we're real,* they answer. And it's what the company wants. Why would they want some graphic for cocktail napkins of a mom using a breast pump or crying from postpartum?

She hears Jenny's voice in the kitchen. An hour has passed and she hasn't done a thing.

"I don't have much fun these days," she imagines saying to Jenny. "When I was your age I was interested in gin, skinny boys with big ears (think ghetto Abe Lincolns), and going sledding after eating a Taco Bell gordita with shrooms in it."

Though she won't say this, of course, she decides to give herself a challenge:

Say something real today. Something revealing. Something true.

Sadly, this may be Annie's favorite part of the day: driving Jenny to Tabor Boyard's. Each time she hopes for a glimpse of her. The actual driving part, however, isn't as thrilling. Jenny always sits in back like a scared tourist.

The loud and obnoxious DJ whom Annie loves is talking about being on the couch with his hand down his pants. "I'm not masturbating," he says. "It's just how guys rest. We're just checking in with ourselves, you know?"

She pretends to be disgusted and presses seek, landing on a bubble gum pop station. Jenny begins to sing along with the song—a love ballad with lots of oohing and melismata. The singer manages to sing *you* at a variety of pitches, building and adorning it as if the word were a wedding cake.

"Vocal diarrhea," Annie mumbles, and yet she wants Jenny to hear what she has said. Forget CPR, forget TrustLine certification. If you like her humor then you've passed.

"What?" Jenny says.

"Her vocals are like Christina's," Annie says, backing out of the joke. "Aguilera." She mispronounces the last name so that it sort of rhymes with *diarrhea*.

"I love her," Jenny says, then starts to make Max's Piglet doll dance to the song. Max neighs.

"I love Piglet," Jenny says to Max. "Do you love Piglet, Max? Do you love Pooh? I love Pooh."

Oh, come on! Annie stifles a laugh. How she wishes Brian were in the seat next to her so they could stifle laughs together.

She turns off Seventh, climbing up the back way to Ashbury Heights.

"Any chance you can come this Friday?" Annie asks.

"Shoot," Jenny says. "I'm supposed to be at Tabor's for sure, but I was thinking—it might be okay if Max came there? I could ask if it's okay or even if she wanted to do a nanny share on Fridays."

"That would work," Annie says, in a way that hides the fact that she's thought of this countless times. A nanny share with Tabe.

"Purse—that's Tabor's little girl—she's the prettiest, sweetest thing."

"Purse?"

"It's short for Priscilla. She's a really calm, friendly baby."

Max makes a braying sound.

"Max would love it," Annie says. Maybe she and Tabor would hit it off, too. You never know.

"It's super easy over there," Jenny says. "They have tons of toys. Their whole downstairs is pretty much her playroom."

"How nice," Annie says, embarrassed by her home. She imagines Tabor's so rich and so together that the floor space between the fridge and the wall is spotless. "Max, you could play with a new friend!"

"Does he interact with other babies yet?" Jenny asks.

Annie thinks of him with the Panhandle babies and kids. "He notices them more now, but doesn't really interact."

"Just parallel play?"

"Yeah," Annie says, not knowing what that's supposed to mean, but then she gets it, and doesn't understand why "doesn't really interact" had to be translated into what she calls "baby bullshit language"— *tummy time, CIO, separation anxiety,* and so on. "Toddler bullshit language" is even more loathsome: "We need to calm our bodies, Isabella (or Gabriella, Ava, Bella, Ella)." "Use your words, Dash (or Gabe, Brody, Parker)." It's like yoga language: "Honor your intentions, bring awareness back to your breath, squeeze out the toxins."

"He loves his parallel play," she says, knowing that this isn't the time to reveal anything about herself whatsoever. Now is the time to impress, to have Jenny go to Tabor's and tell her what a classy, smart, together mom Annie is. For fun she does yoga! For fun she scrapbooks! She needs to say something like that and remembers that god-awful mani-pedi moms' party she went to the other night, in an attempt to embrace her husband's absence and enjoy herself.

It was hosted by SFMC, and she sat in between a brunette who talked like a drag queen and an obviously new mom who had her hair pulled back into one of those severe ponytails.

They were chattering back and forth about pumping and dumping. The woman with the bitchy ponytail was explaining her circumstances: "If we have to go out I'll nurse first, then when we get home I'll pump out the spoiled milk. I wait a few hours so that most of the alcohol can get metabolized? One time, though, oh my God. Drank way too much, and when I pumped, I could actually smell the alcohol in the milk and so I'm like, 'I'm not giving Brayson that!' and so I pumped and dumped every two hours for the next twelve hours and supplemented with formula so I wouldn't give him an infant hangover? But because I pumped so much—total rookie maneuver—my body signaled my glands or whatever to make more milk and I got totally engorged. I looked like I had a botched surgery! That was *not* fun at all. I don't even drink wine anymore—it's dehydrating and there are all these pesticides on grapes? I've been sticking with beer because I know the yeast in beer stimulates milk production? Have you tried Otter Creek organic ale? It's pretty good—it's local."

Fuck me, Annie thought. Or: fuck me?

The woman on the other side of Annie was quasi-listening, dismissing everything she said with quick shakes of her head. Annie could just see the words on her tongue waiting to be released like gas bubbles.

"Forget it," this other, been-there-done-that woman said. "I have three kids."

Ah, the three-kid exemption. When chicks pulled out this card you were just expected to bow down.

"After my first C-section I was on around-the-clock narcotics, still breast-fed, and Caitlin was fine. A bit unresponsive, but we both got sleep. You don't need to dump, trust me. All my kids have turned out fine. And you want to know the truth? Alcohol breast milk is better than formula any day. The mothers who use formula are the ones who need to worry about the poison they feed their babies. I mean why wouldn't you breast-feed?" She grabbed her left breast. "What else are they for? It's like having eyes and not using them to see."

Annie turns onto Tabor's narrow street. "I've been meaning to tell you," she says. "I had the best time the other night. My girlfriends and I had a mani-pedi party. We reserved the salon and got the full treatment!"

"Fun!" Jenny says. "That's so awesome. I've always wanted to do that."

"It was so fun," Annie says.

"Fun," Jenny says.

"Super fun. So . . ."

Annie thinks of the Korean woman who worked on her as though she were a horse. The woman was so fast and rough. It was like she wanted to hurt Annie, and she kept talking to the manicurist next to her and Annie knew they were talking about her sweaty hands.

Annie stops in front of Tabor Boyard's home, which must have views all the way to the Marin Headlands. Jenny opens the door and says good-bye to Max.

"Don't forget these!" Annie says, passing Jenny the tin of dulce de leche brownies through the passenger window. "You know how I have fun!" Her June Cleaver tone grates her ears, but Jenny's eyes light up.

"Oooh, thanks," Jenny says. "I'll share with Tabor."

"Yes! Please do!" If she couldn't go to exercise class then Annie would give up sweets and make Tabor fat.

"I'll let you know about Friday," Jenny says.

Annie keeps her face as still as possible, not wanting to reveal her hope or her annoyance from having to wait in the wings. Jenny walks into the house, and Annie slowly pulls forward. This is the part she likes. She lowers her sunglasses so she can look out the corner of her eye at Tabor's home. It's brown with a creamy yellowish trim. She bets the paint is called Thoroughbred Brown and Golf Shirt Yellow. Every time she leaves she scans for another detail, for something she's missed. She takes a last look back, spying the glimmer of a garden fountain. She says something to Max while looking lest she appear to be openly gawking, having the owner of the home mistake her curiosity for jealousy or worse, admiration.

*   *   *

Friday: no call from Jenny.

The following Tuesday, Mele comes by with Ellie. Annie is making Baileys brownies and pours some Baileys into her coffee. "Want some?" she asks.

"What time is it?"

"Noon."

"Okay."

She pours some into Mele's coffee, checks the chocolate in the double boiler, then sits down.

"Brian still gone?" Mele asks.

"Yup," Annie says. Still staying in Palo Alto. She calls him at night, always with the intention of speaking calmly—it's not like it's his choice to be gone—but it always goes south. She assumes the position of haggard housewife, raising their child alone, sleeping alone, and she always hangs up angry with both him and Fletcher Webber IV.

She pours in more Baileys, though not too much since Jenny will be coming soon. She looks at the clock.

"Where is she?" She gets up to give the pot of chocolate a little stir. "And she could have called on Friday and at least let me know. I don't see why Max just can't go over there. It's like I'm not mom enough or something. I get no respect."

The kids come back into the kitchen, Ellie walking, Max straddle-hopping.

"Do something about it!" Mele says, bringing her fist down on the counter. "Do something!"

The women laugh for no reason at all. They laugh because it's Tuesday afternoon and they're drinking Baileys and making brownies. Annie decides to ease up a bit and enjoy her friend's company. She shows Mele some of her favorite dessert recipes, and they have their typical scattered banter fueled by

Observations:

"I hate it when my boobs sweat. You know, the underneath part?"
"I hate that!"

Questions:

"Were you horny when you were pregnant? I masturbated constantly."
"I felt like an ape if I did that."
"I almost humped my bedpost. Oh, do you still want to do that kids' craft thing? They've got paints and shit."

Criticisms:

"He should so be potty-trained by now."
"It's like she's in a diaper coma."

And Notes on the Past:

"Did you ever get the crab call?"

"The what?"
"The crab call. You know—'I have crabs and I'm calling you and the other people I've slept with to tell you about it so you can shave your hair off and take crab pills.'"
"I can't believe someone called to tell you. I wouldn't call."
"He was all business about it. Offered to make me an appointment."
"Whoa. That's the kind of guy who'll take care of a baby. He'll do night feedings."
"I know."

"So did you have crabs? Are they actual crabs? Like with pincers?"

"Didn't have them. That's why I wouldn't call. I mean he endured unnecessary embarrassment. He will forever be the guy with crabs."

"Forever Crabby."

"It was my fault. I was such a slut back then. I always slept with people right away. It was my thing."

"I've only slept with three people other than Bobby."

"Really? You seem slutty. Like you'd be recognized by the back of your head."

"Oh, please."

The exchanges usually end in a gale of laughter. One such gale is particularly explosive, so powerful in fact that they don't hear the front door open and the pitter-patter of little feet. It takes Annie a moment to notice a little girl in her kitchen, wearing a brown onesie with a kangaroo on it and a pink tutu-like skirt with an embroidered pouch.

"Oh my God!" Annie yells. The little girl stops abruptly in front of Max and raises her fist, then sucks it with a smile. Jenny comes in after her, and the women are rendered silent.

"Jenny!" Annie says.

"Jenny!" Mele says.

Jenny has on her usual expression—that uncomfortable compulsory grin and nervous eyes. Annie feels like a predator. Jenny always looks afraid.

"Hi," Jenny says. "Sorry. Tabor got stuck and I thought it would be okay if I brought Purse over here." She guides Purse by the shoulders toward Annie. "I hope it's all right."

"Of course," Annie says, unable to stop looking at the little girl. Max looks like a thug next to her. He ogles her, smiling and shaking his head as if he can't quite believe she's real. He looks from Jenny to Purse and bangs his fists on the shape keys of a toy. "I'm a triangle!

I'm a circle!" the shape keys sing, and now he looks like a thug with special needs. Where did that term come from in the first place? Everyone in the world has special needs. Purse gently wiggles her hips to the sounds of the toy, looking back at Jenny either for approval or just to acknowledge the entire audience.

"So cute," Mele says.

"Cute," Annie says.

Jenny has her hands on the little girl's head.

"We didn't hear you come in," Annie says.

"I called out," Jenny says. "But it was loud." She looks down, and Annie thinks back to what they were talking about. It's irritating, really. Why bother cleaning up your act if you're going to be caught talking about venereal filth?

"So what's Tabor so busy with?" Annie asks.

Jenny rolls her eyes, a gesture to establish her and Tabor's intimacy and perhaps, their lack of. "She has this fund-raiser for her old sorority. And her son's nanny is on vacation . . ."

Sorority, Annie thinks. Why, of course. In college those girls had backed away from her as if she were toxic, except for a girl named Heather, who was always looking for speed, and Annie would oblige, totally overcharging her for quarters.

"I'm super busy, too," Annie says, thinking of her graphics, her moms, her momtourage. "Just like Tabor!" Annie says. "I've been so busy, too. Hey, we're doing the share already! Purse is here today. Max, you can play at Purse's on Friday! She has a huge playroom! She has everything!"

Jenny laughs uncomfortably, looking at Mele for solace. "Watch out," Mele says and looks down at Jenny's pink boots, which look like they're made out of yak.

Ellie twirls some pink yak fur around her pinkie.

"Sorry, sweetie, I almost stepped on you!" Jenny says.

Ellie holds up a toy, but brings it to her chest when Jenny tries to take her up on her offer. "What do you have?" Jenny asks.

Ellie holds it up again, handing it to Jenny, who still hasn't even said hello to Max, really. Purse giggles at Ellie moving the toy around. The girl is so cute it's freakish, disgusting even. She looks up at Annie, her eyes deep, dark, and beautifully coy. This girl will sail through life like a schooner.

"So that would be fine, right?" Annie asks. "If Max could go to Purse's on Friday?"

"Um," Jenny says, pretending to be distracted by Ellie. "Sure, I'll check to see if I'm even going to be there."

"If you're not then you can just come here. Either way—we get to see Jenny on Friday!"

Annie's face is hot with determination and Baileys. She can tell that she's even making Mele uncomfortable. Jenny doesn't respond. Are Ellie and her little toy really all that fascinating? That's when Annie sees what it is.

"Max, your favorite toy!"

Jenny, welcoming the redirection, holds up the top-like figurine. Max baas in delight and straddle-hops over to Jenny.

"It's the butt-plug toy," Annie says, diligently keeping watch over Jenny's expression. She doesn't flinch.

"Oh my God," Mele says. "That's what it looks like."

"Doesn't it?"

A smile seems plastered onto Jenny's face. She's ignoring the butt plug and pretending to be fascinated with a Glad lid that Purse is using as a tambourine.

"I buy all these toys and this thing is what he loves," Annie says. "I don't even know where it came from."

Jenny is walking Purse out of the kitchen. "Come on, Max," she says. "Let's let your mom get back to her things . . ."

Purse follows Jenny while glancing back over her shoulder. Max hops after her.

"That was chaotic," Annie says when they've left.

"You seem irritated," Mele says.

"I don't understand how she feels so free to bring that child here, but she has to check to see if Max can go there. It's totally classist."

"Um, it's not like you're living in the Tenderloin or something."

"Yes, but clearly, I'm not *Tabor Boyard*. I don't go to the *Bar Method*. I wasn't in a *sorority*."

"Yes, you only went to *Barnard*. You just bake desserts on the *Wolf range*. And drink coffee from a *machine built into your wall*."

Annie remembers the brownies and takes them out of the oven to cool. The smell of them tamps her hostility and turns it into hunger. She could eat the entire pan, but remembers that some are for Jenny.

"Do you think she heard us?" Annie asks.

"Yes," Mele says, "but you shouldn't really care."

On Thursday, Annie waits for a call that never comes. On Friday she waits for a call that never comes, and on Tuesday she waits for a baby-sitter who never comes.

Annie calls Jenny; she texts, she emails, and when there's still no response she sends an email to Tabor, inquiring about the state of Jenny, the health of Jenny—perhaps something happened to her! But Tabor doesn't respond either.

Finally, the next Thursday, Jenny emails that she can no longer sit for Max because of her busy schedule. Annie is brought back to seventh grade, being told via note that she's being dumped, and just as she did in seventh grade she questions herself: What did she do wrong? Was she not generous enough, pretty enough? Did she not have cool things? Did she not provide enough benefits?

She calls Mele. "Jenny quit. I shouldn't have pushed Haight Street on her. I told her to go there one day to shop. I shouldn't have asked if Thursday was still the party night."

She remembers that Jenny had just ignored her and grinned at Max so closely you'd have thought she was using his eyes to check for lipstick on her teeth.

"I swore, too," Annie says. "Once or twice, I think."

"I think you had her at *butt plug*," Mele says. "Or *crab call*."

"We shouldn't have done that! What kind of people are we!"

"Um, normal?"

"But you're not normal," she wants to tell Mele. "You're single and obsessed with a man who doesn't love you." Annie wipes the skin below her eyes, confused by her tears. She looks at Max in his high chair eating a banana. He liked to take huge bites of his food, then hoard it for hours. Music plays on her computer in the office, and his head bobs so that he looks like a fifteen-year-old boy, headphones on, walking down Market while sucking on a billiard ball. She left you, she thinks. How can she leave you? How could she not cherish you? Her son loves Method Man and Clifford the Big Red Dog. He loves wearing her underwear around his neck like necklaces. Panty leis!

"I'm not a good mother," she cries. Mele remains silent. "I need to be one of the moms on my aprons. I need to love mani-pedi parties, pop champagne, and yell, 'Whoo-hoo. Girls' night out!' or whatever."

"Forget all that," Mele says. "Put yourself on the apron."

Annie is about to say that she's just lonely and she's been drinking too much of the alcohol meant for her cooking. She went to Barnard. She has an MFA in graphic design from California Institute of the Arts, and yet what does she do with all of that now? She bakes brownies. She makes designs that everyone seems to be doing on Etsy. She knows everything adds up, but the sum is so vague right now and unsatisfactory.

"I don't know why I'm so upset," she says. "I'm fine. I'm fine."

I want to fit in with people that weren't nice to me when I was young, she thinks. I'm lonely, she thinks. I miss Brian. She had wanted to hire someone with whom to raise her child.

When they hang up she goes to look in on Max—there's nothing better than watching your child sleep. Here we are at the end of the day, she thinks. Here you are safe. And Daddy is out in the trenches working for us. Sometimes, life is simple and amazing and the sum of it all is right. But then the moment passes and you're left wanting. Annie kisses her son on the forehead and then she goes to the kitchen to satisfy something she cannot name.

The next day Annie parks in front of Tabor Boyard's home, turning her tires in to the curb. It's Friday. Jenny will be here soon.

"Jenny forgot some things at our house," she says to Max. "We have to return them. Maybe we'll see Purse. Did you like Purse?"

She can't wait until he's at an age where he can answer her questions without knowing her motivations. Jenny is walking up the hill from the bus stop. When she sees Annie she does a kind of full-bodied hiccup, but manages to keep moving with a happily surprised expression on her face. She comes to the passenger side of the car and Annie puts the window down.

"Hi," Jenny says. "Hi, Max! What are you guys doing here?"

Annie knows that if she doesn't mention it, Jenny will pretend that she never quit, that she never worked for Annie in the first place. She can't stand shy people. This is what they always do in the face of tension and conflict—pretend nothing has occurred.

"I wanted to touch base," Annie says. "Since it took you a while to email and you don't return calls."

"Oh," Jenny says and nods, an infuriating grin on her face.

"So you've been really busy?"

"Yeah. Really busy, so . . ." She looks to both sides of her, then back at the house.

"It must be hard to juggle everything," Annie says. "School. Work. Max. Purse."

"Yeah," she says. "I couldn't juggle everything."

Teachers must feel good when students ape their sentiments, but Annie knows Jenny's just saying what she thinks will make Annie leave her alone.

"You didn't like me," Annie says. "Am I right?"

"I like you." Her face pales. She looks like she's going to barf.

"My language," Annie says. "You don't like the way I speak or act, right?" Annie's voice is calm, not at all angry or defensive. She really does want to understand. "Do you think I'm a bad mother?" she asks.

"No!" Jenny says. "No."

"Why couldn't Max come here on Fridays? Why could you bring the girl to our house, but Max can't go to hers?"

Jenny uses a smile to deflect everything Annie just said.

"Well?" Annie asks.

"It just isn't a good fit," Jenny says. "Purse is walking and interacting and she's starting elimination communication and Max isn't doing that so—"

"Are you serious?" Annie asks. Why can't people just say 'potty training'?" She can't imagine teaching Max to say, "Elimination." He will say, "Poop." He will say, "Mommy, I crapped my pants."

"Tabor's doing this intensive E.C. training thing and so Purse isn't—"

"So maybe Max can join after she's fully E.C. fluent or whatever?"

Max baas from the back, and Annie wishes she had bothered to clean her car. Random papers and leaflets are on the floor on the passenger side. The clutter, the mess seems endless. At that moment she believes that a stray Pirate's Booty could make her cry.

"Moms are like me, too, you know. We're not all like Tabor."

"Okay," Jenny says.

Annie shakes her head. She is never going to get an answer. She is never going to get in or through, and of course she was prepared for this.

"I'm sorry it didn't work out," Annie says. She looks over at the cellophane-wrapped brownie on the passenger side, not sure what she should do with it or what she was thinking. "This is for Tabor." She holds up the treat.

"Wow!" Jenny says. "She'll love it. She loved your last batch."

"It's quite big," Annie says. "And extremely rich. You really only want to eat half."

"Okay," Jenny says. "Maybe we'll split it. Bye, Max!" She makes a face to indicate sadness.

Max makes a noise that reminds Annie of a cartoon character expressing disbelief. *Huh???*

"Say bye," Annie says in a sweet, upbeat tone. "We won't see her again."

It's only when she explains to Mele what she has done that the possible consequences materialize before her eyes. She thinks: lawsuit. She thinks of Brian, how he'd have to work for his own family pro bono. His firm—its rich (and slightly smarmy) history—they've defended the Black Panthers, Hells Angels, Snoop Dogg, and the Symbionese Liberation Army, and now they'd be defending Annie Lane from West Portal, apron designer, mother of a nonwalker. All Brian's work would be for nothing. Tabor Boyard will sue them so bad that all they'll be able to afford is that one-ply toilet paper and mommies like the ones on her aprons will be like "Oh my God, is she okay? I mean should we organize a silent auction?"

"Annie," Mele says. "I asked you a question." They are sitting around her kitchen island. "How many did you give her?"

"Just one," Annie says. "A big one."

"Who do you think will eat it? Do you think she gave it to Tabor or kept it for herself?"

Max sits at her feet, moving the butt-plug-like toy along the floor like a race car. She wishes Mele, of all people, didn't sound so frantic. Mele was supposed to keep her cool, meaning that this whole thing was either really bad or Mele was just sniffing out a good story she wanted to pillage.

"I told her to 'take half,' or to only eat half. That's code for 'It's a pot brownie.'"

"She doesn't know the code!" Mele says. "Jesus, Annie! She's the girl in the computer lab on a Thursday night. She's not doing a keg stand or a bong hit or tripping out watching Mickey Mouse getting terrorized by brooms!"

"It was a weak batch," Annie says. She feels like she's getting questioned by cops. She tries to remain still, and has kept on a pretty good poker face, but her hands are clasped tightly, her shoulders tensed up near her ears. "She's probably never even heard of a pot brownie before anyway."

"Great. She'll be tripping balls."

"But what I'm saying is that she won't know it's from the brownie. She won't put it together. Like when dogs get tranquilized—they don't think, Yup, I'm being tranquilized. Right?"

"Maybe," Mele says. "But what if she gives it all to Tabor? Or worse, a child!"

"She wouldn't do that. The kids are in an egg-free, dairy-free, inorganic-dessert-free zone. That's what Jenny told me. And if she gives it all to Tabor, then great. That was part of the . . . plan, not like I had a plan, but . . ."

"You don't even know the woman," Mele says. "What were you thinking?"

Annie watches Max fly the butt plug. "I don't know." Max brings the toy to his mouth, and she snatches it from his hands. "No," she says. "You could choke."

He begins to cry, and she picks him up, moving her hand in circles on his back.

"Sorry," she says. "Sorry I scared you." As a mom she feels there's just so much to be sorry about every day.

"Don't judge me," Annie says, but Mele says something that makes her feel better.

"Why not?" Mele says. "It's what moms do. And it's okay."

"Okay," Annie says and smiles at her friend, who is still here, after all.

At the park, Mele and Annie gather their things, preparing for departure. Mele rounds up their trash: an empty bottle of hand sanitizer, orange peels, a plastic baggie she stuffs into the pocket of her tight jeans with a strategic mid-thigh tear. She walks to the overflowing bin and lets go. The hand sanitizer makes her glum—this invention that no one really needs.

Like Annie, Mele will return to an empty home, and Mele wonders if she has it better in a way. She doesn't expect someone to be there—she isn't missing anyone. Yet, hearing it that way in her head just makes her miss and expect someone even more. She wants Ellie to be enough, but perhaps that isn't the healthiest desire. Little Ellie will become medium Ellie and then big Ellie, and she won't want to be the only thing that sustains her mother. Mele will need to find other ways to have fun.

She goes back to the table to get her bribe: PEZ. Annie has Max on one hip, her diaper bag on the other. Mele loosens her friend's hair tucked under the strap.

"I can give you my recipe for the brownies if you want," Annie says. "I have a good cookie recipe, too."

"I'm not sure if that would fly," Mele says.

"It might. You know moms in San Francisco do it. No judgment, right?"

"Okay, maybe," Mele says.

She likes the idea of Sloppy Joes with "Shrooms," in quotes, of course, paired with an elegant, inflated, Tabor Boyard salad. Also, Baileys Brownies, and why not? The recipe for Annie's "Just Eat Half" Brownies.

"Ellie, let's head out," Mele says, waving the PEZ. Ellie spins on the tire swing, looking up at the sky and saying, "Boppity, boppity." When she sees the candy she slows to a stop, then staggers to her push bike like a drunk.

"I wonder why Henry didn't show up today?" Mele tries to say this in the same way as she'd say, "I wonder if it will rain tonight?"

"He took his kids camping," Annie says.

"Oh," Mele says, a streak of heat moving across her chest. Maybe he and Annie have the same kind of friendship as he and Mele do. Maybe theirs isn't at all unique. Their dinner last night meant nothing. A hamburger is just a hamburger.

"Why are you asking about Henry?" Annie says.

Ellie gets on the bike and puts out her hand.

"Just asking," Mele says, clicking out the candy. "Why?"

"No reason," Annie says. "No judgment." She raises her eyebrows.

"Because I'm thinking about him," Mele says, being honest with her friend.

How do you unwind?

My friend Annie unwinds with pot, though she isn't comfortable telling anyone this. She has trouble talking with other mothers. She rolls her eyes at the acceptable truths and complaints—"We're tired! We're sick of the kids! We hate changing poopy diapers! We can never shower!"—and the acceptable definitions.

At the last SFMC meeting, this "unwinding" question came up with a group of moms. I looked at Annie, wondering what she'd say. Usually she just smiles and looks down, but she said to the group as if they were cross-examiners: "Mani-pedis. I get mani-pedis."

Another woman said that to unwind she exfoliates. Yes, that's right. Exfoliates. She takes long showers and tells the kids that Mommy is not to be interrupted. She clarified to us that she doesn't use exfoliants from drugstores but rather, sophisticated scents with ingredients like brown cane sugar, Malaysian citrus, fennel, seaweed, and basil. "My husband says I smell like a pizza," this woman said.

Annie and I thought she was making a joke, but then she added: "He has a poor nose for things—he's from Minnesota."

"Wow," Annie said. "I should try it."

This prompted the woman to go on. "You should! My latest exfoliant is a blend of black currant and Bulgarian roses. I also light scented candles—it's sort of like pairing food and wine. The flavors all complement each other, but it has to be the perfect combination. I get lead-free wicks. *Do not* buy the scented candles from drugstores. They're all cheap imitations and smell like, like, you know—a public restroom." She sniffed the inside of her wrist. "Here. Smell. Delicious, right?"

Like a pizza.

Annie and I looked at each other and we seemed to be communicating the same thing: this conversation is happening. This is what we're up against.

All Annie wanted was to be able to eat a brownie, then change her Facebook status to "I'm so high I can see the curvature of the world!" and get back comments that say "LOL!" "OMG!" "Got any more?" and "Me, too."

Annie wanted her child to be able to go to any mother's house. Annie wanted to be counted. I *am* going to include Annie's brownies. They can be a bonus recipe. Because she exists here among us, and she's a great mother and a fantastic, loyal, and exciting friend.

If you decide to make these, that's your own deal. Don't sue, judge, or complain if you end up curled into a ball watching *Ocean's Eleven*. It's better than a mani-pedi party, that's for damn sure.

METHOD

Bring water to a boil, then put in a stick of butter and a load of marijuana (separate the seeds first—Annie plants hers in a nearby park). Let it cook for a half hour, then quickly strain out the plant matter. In your normal brownie recipe, replace the butter or oil with the new butter. Annie calls it "cannabutter." Your kitchen may smell incriminating, but boy is it a treat. Now who's the sneaky chef?

I decided not to post the supportive responses since that would violate people's privacy. I just wanted to tell the positive mothers thank you for your overwhelming responses. Beth, maybe you'll understand if your child is attacked and the perpetrator's parents can't communicate. Fingers crossed.

—Renee Grune

Renee, your comments are completely inappropriate. For you to make a personal attack on an individual who was offering sound and logical advice in a nonthreatening environment is an extremely immature response. Did it somehow slip your mind that you posted to this forum for advice, regardless of its content? Your actions over the last day can easily be described as bullying. The biggest threat to your son right now is not a child at the playground. It is you. You need extensive therapy.

—Lee Laughlin

Chill out, Renee. A little shove never hurt anyone. We used to get clotheslined in Red Rover and totally walloped in Dodgeball. Look at us now! I'm kissing my muscles. Give me your address. I'll send you some brownies.

—A.L., West Portal

You need to make sure the wood toys use the most eco-friendly type of wood, like sustainably produced hardwoods. Avoid wood from threatened domestic redwood and overseas rain forests! Check the edges of toys and puzzle pieces for layers of pressed woods, like plywood and particleboard—ugh! They contain glues that emit toxic fumes. And watch out for paint finishes! Some use lead and solvents that severely damage your child's developing brains. I beg you—find finishes that use linseed, flax, walnut oil, or beeswax.

—SFMC answer to "Where is the best place to buy wooden toys?"

How have your friendships from SFMC changed your life? What do you value about them? Have these friendships made you a better mother?

I signed up with SFMC and went through a few mismatches before landing on my current one. My first try lasted a day. Ellie could only sit at the time. Her play involved mouthing things and bouncing on her diapered butt while clapping.

The meeting spot for my first playgroup outing was Golden Gate Park playground, but there was just one other mom there when Ellie and I arrived. The woman and I waited in the sandpit for the others, breezing through the standard topics: child's exact age, sleeping and feeding schedules, what we were strolling, where we lived. Conversation was a bit tough. She was a mommy natural—the kind of mom that wears those hideous baby slings made from what appear to be curtains, sings "Baa, Baa, Black Sheep" with utter abandon, dresses her babies in clothes that are itchy, butch, and biodegradable, and wears hats that look like they're made out of worry dolls. I don't think she liked me very much—maybe she smelled the ethanol on me or saw Ellie's disposable diaper. I couldn't tell if her baby was a boy or a girl, something intentional, I assumed, since it was one of those organic, free-range babies dressed to look like a migrant worker. Mommy Natural was beginning to drive me nuts. She repeated every action the babies made. Hers picked up a shovel.

"You've picked up a shovel," she cooed.

Ellie picked up a plastic pail. "You've got a pail."

Hers looked around for more toys—"You're looking for a new toy. You like her bucket. Ooop, Bodhi, no no. She's playing with the bucket. Can you share? Are we learning to share?"

"I'm still learning that," I said, trying to be funny. I had to put it out there, but she just looked at me in that condescending, Green Party kind of way.

"I mean, we all are," I rewrote, trying again. "As a civilization."

"That's true," she said.

Christ. Fortunately, Ellie pooped, and I thought, I should, like, leave, and I did.

I didn't realize then that the SFMC experience could get much worse, that I'd go back for a group reassignment only to be placed with women who ate mommy naturals for lunch, then worked them off with their trainers. They were the true SFMC moms: Bugaboo strollers, Mia Bossi diaper bags, good bodies, expensive sunglasses, cute snack organizers (not Tupperware), vinyl throw mats with polka dots, and babies who only wore clothes with nonbaby motifs—brown stripes, bamboo, goldfish, and lemons.

This is the kind of mom whose kid will wave around a wand and the next thing you know she's hired a maestro for conducting lessons. The kind of mom who will sit primly at her computer and ebicker with other moms about raw versus soy milk.

My first playgroup meeting with them was at Betts's home. When I arrived I wondered if I had made a mistake with the address and was entering a decorator's showcase.

Betts opened the door wearing a silk blouse and white flared pants. She looked like she was going to the Golden Globes, and she wasn't holding a baby. She looked like she had never held a baby, just a Pomeranian in a Burberry raincoat, and I wondered if babies were discouraged at playdates. Should I have left Ellie at home?

I bounced Ellie in my arms and said, "Can you say 'Hello'?" something I find to be stupid, but asking your speechless babies to say hello was the new hello. Plus, Ellie felt like a ticket, the only way I'd ever get into a joint like this. "Where's your little one?" I asked.

"Oh, she's with the nanny getting changed," Betts said. "Poopy dia-per." She made a face like a cat coughing up hair, which I automatically imitated because I have this habit of assuming the voices and facial expressions of those around me not so much to be liked but just to blend and get things over with (I was a kiss-promiscuous teenager for the very same reason).

To blend even further I almost lied and told Betts that my nanny, Svetlana, couldn't make it because she was folding my laundry and massaging my Pomeranian, but I was wearing a black hooded sweat-shirt with spit-up on the right pocket, and jeans that were cut at the ends versus properly hemmed. I had intentionally dressed down think-ing I was about to meet a bunch of frumpy moms who scrapbooked and bargain-hunted. It was glaringly obvious that I didn't have a Svet-lana, but I took some comfort in the fact that it was a Lululemon sweatshirt and Paige jeans. They'd know I tried and that I was at least middle-classish.

Betts led me to the living room and introduced me to Lana, Amber, and Courtney. My playgroup. Four moms who, I quickly learned, all lived in Pacific Heights or Presidio mansions and enjoyed sitting and looking at their babies while talking about feuds, fund-raisers, and pre-schools. Week after week I'd sit and watch the babies play with wooden animals and wooden grocery items. Only wooden toys were allowed in Betts's household, not because of safety concerns but because plastic figurines didn't blend with the home's décor, whose theme seemed to be "I am very wealthy and hell to the no will I allow cheap crap from China up in here."

All of Bella's baby furniture and toys looked like small versions of what Bella would own if she grew up to be a woman who summered in a vineyard and hung paintings in her kitchen with titles like *An Elegant Flower in a Modest Garden.*

One of the moms, Lana, had a habit of speaking for her baby. For example, she would say, "I love that chair. Where did you get it?" then switch over to her cartoon voice, pretending her baby, Gabriella, was speaking and not her.

"I want one, too!" she'd say, leaning down from the sofa to move Gabriella's hands around. I'd look at Gabriella, then at Lana. It was like watching a ventriloquist. I hate ventriloquists.

Amber was different from the others. She belonged to a fitness moms' group called the Hot Moms Club and was always pushing us to call ourselves that, too. She brought it up jokingly and frequently, like when you're trying to establish your own nickname. She'd sneak in sermons on hotness.

"Put yourself on the to-do list," she'd say, or "Learn how to rock your best assets."

I sometimes caught Betts looking at her in this patient, oh-dear-you-must-be-new-money way. I liked Amber and even considered asking her to join our current group, but I haven't run into her since. We belong to different playgrounds, I guess.

I liked that she wore tight jeans with her muffin-top stomach pouring over the rim and how she'd sometimes grab the flesh and say, "Rock it. Own it. Love it." I liked how sometimes she'd stare at her son, as if to say, "What's your frickin' deal?" whenever he was making his lit-up imp face while pointing at something and grunting.

Courtney was just plain mean. She had a raspy voice and sun-beaten skin, wasn't that pretty, but had blond hair so was hot by default and knew it, but not the default part. She was always dressed in outfits that you'd see described in magazines as "festival ready." She'd eye me like I was infiltrating some kind of top-secret poodle club. They'd be talking about someone's divorce and she'd suddenly ask, "Have we seen your house yet? I mean, your apartment?" Her gaze would move from my Target shoes up my body to my face and hair, which is usually in a messy bun. She'd give me these full-on catty scans. It was like being strip-searched. I would always answer, "You guys are welcome to come over anytime," knowing the bee-atch was playing psychological chicken.

Then there was Betts, the queen. She seemed to live on sardines and hot water and would complain endlessly about her waistline, which was the size of a power cord, if that.

Her home was supposedly inspired by a castle in France. Three stories, marble floors, carpeting a baby could drown in, drapes so heavy they'd crush a monkey, chandeliers that could flatten Betts to such an extent you could probably fax her to St. Bart. She lived up so well to her stereotype, but I respected her because she never professed to be anything else. Once I met her at a playground and she was holding Bella and laughing. I started to take pictures of them, and Betts said, "Oh wait. I'm smiling too hard. The bottoms of my cheeks get all wrinkly," and then she mumbled, "Fun can be ugly."

I laughed, which made Betts smile confusedly. She eventually caught on that I was laughing at her comment. She lit up, thrilled that she had said something amusing, something she probably didn't do very often.

"Well, it's true!" she said, then continued to remark on her comment, as the unfunny often do, reducing something wild and unstructured into a cloying sauce.

Mainly my days were filled in that living room, smiling at the babies. I thought this was all that existed. I was two months in and lost all hope that I'd ever be myself again. I'd feign interest, make happy and surprised faces when someone picked up a block. Then I'd give up and stare at the Golden Gate Bridge in the distance—I was never into other people's babies, especially those four. Bella was a tank. Gabriella looked like she was on Klonopin, and Lexi eerily resembled John Madden. I liked Oliver, even though he'd creep me out sometimes. He had a disconcerting expression like he'd just had sex and was telling his friends about it. His laugh was also a bit diabolical. Like he'd just screwed over a drug dealer named Fang. I think he resented his botched circumcision. Ouch. Sometimes I'd pat him on the head. I don't dislike you, I'd think.

I was resigned to this group, until one day I did something and couldn't go back.

It was another day at Betts's house, and this time we were brainstorming how to help single moms who had been laid off—me, basically! We were told to bring bags of clothes and things we didn't want. Betts wanted to send something along with the clothes.

She had provided her usual political fund-raiser-like snacks—cheese and fruits, crackers, dull mini-sandwiches, and pastries from Tartine. I almost suggested forgoing the snacks. The spread could feed the laid-off mothers for a week, but I nibbled on a piece of cheese (of all things).

Oliver threw a block, and it whizzed past Courtney's head. She covered her ears as though it was a passing F-16.

"Sorry," Amber said. "He's going through this block-hating phase. Hey, that's an idea. Duh. We could send the mothers toys that our babies aren't really into anymore. Oliver is so over the Harmony Ball rattle."

"But I love my Ballino clutching toy!" Lana said, using her stupid cartoon voice that made me want to push her off a cliff every time I heard it. POW! SPLAT!

"Oh, God, Bella loves the Ballino," Betts said. "Loves it. It's a godsend."

"Your nanny's a godsend," I wanted to remind her.

"And I love that it's made from that good wood," Courtney said.

"I know. I love that wood." Lana bounced her palms on her thighs. I couldn't imagine a baby topic propelling me to use hand gestures. I felt many notches below my peers on the vocal and fervor register, and it made me wonder if there was something in me that was missing. Was I a bad mother for my lack of facial expressions and hand gesticulations? Should I start drinking before talking with other mothers? Because wine makes me a little more passionate.

"What toys is Ellie into?" Betts asked.

I looked at Ellie, who had crawled toward a pink rocker. Cords, I thought. Cords, my phone, and panty liners. Oh, and she loves plastic bags.

"The Ballino clutching toy," I said and moved my hands. "Loves it. Can't live without it. Screams when I take it away. She doesn't scream, really. More like a high-pitched moan." I talk too much when I'm nervous, and my lies get absurdly detailed. I had no idea what a Ballino clutching toy was, though I assumed it was wooden and expensive. I bet I could show them a two-hundred-dollar wooden dildo and call it a Baby Genius Wand and they'd buy it.

"But do the mothers really need more junk?" Betts asked. "What about going to Whole Foods and putting together a package of organic baby foods and those bear things? Bella loves those bears, and they don't have sugar."

"They have organic cane," I said. "That's just a fancy way of saying sugar. It's sugar in disguise."

The room was silent. A baby coughed. It was like I had offered a bunch of anorexics a hoagie. To soften my remark I looked at the babies and sang in a Barneyish voice, "Sugar in disguise! Sugar in disguise!"

Lexi screamed and pulled her own hair. Courtney rolled her eyes.

"Really, Lexi Jones. Get ahold of yourself. Does Dr. Jones need to have a talk with you?"

Courtney's husband was a doctor, Dr. Jones. She liked reminding everyone of this, and I kind of admired the way she worked his profession into every conversation I ever had with her. She was an expert weaver.

"It's hard to figure out the best way to help besides just throwing cash at people," Betts said. "Zack and I already do a lot of that. I wouldn't want to hurt anyone's pride."

"Same with us," Lana said. "A lot. We give a lot."

I would love people to throw cash at me. I wouldn't feel degraded at all.

"Maybe," Lana said, "we could give them jobs! We could always use help around the house. Maria didn't have any experience when we hired her, but it just came to her naturally."

"Or what about nannying?" Courtney said. "With Doug in the ER round the clock I've been looking for someone to fill the four-to-eight slot, but I'm not sure I'd feel comfortable hiring someone without references, and who knows how to contact their references? Or maybe they've never even nannied in the first place."

"Maybe it will come naturally," I said, and because I was feeling sassy and pissed off I gave the women that scandalized hypersmile they were always using and said, "Maybe we should send them certificates for spa treatments! You know, like what Gavin Newsom did for the city's public school teachers a while back? They could use some pampering."

They all exclaimed, thinking this a brilliant idea, like I was really onto something. Mele Bart had found the perfect thing that would save the unemployed: seaweed wraps and foot rubs. My sarcasm, when not understood, makes me feel incredibly isolated.

"I could ask my facialist for a donation," Lana said. "She's so amazing and brilliant. Like she uses all this science so it's like actual—"

"Medicine," Courtney said.

"Exactly," Lana said. "She says that excess sugars bind to the skin's collagen. That's what makes wrinkles, so she gives me this serum that stops the sugar molecules before they can reach my skin." She touched her face.

I wanted to touch her face, too, then squeeze it as though it were one of those stress balls, but I reminded myself that I was older now. A mother now. All grown up. I did Pilates. I sometimes bought educational toys. I had four strollers, one for walking, one for running, one for walking short distances, and one for a fake baby. I was more like these women than like the ones they were trying to help, and women like Betts did much more for people than I ever could or, quite possibly, would.

Still. Having first world problems doesn't mean you're not allowed to feel desolate and bitter. It can't keep you from wanting.

"As for your things," Betts said. "My foundation will organize the items. We're trying to do a big delivery next week."

Foundation. Courtney, Amber, and Lana fluttered at the word. I had heard them all talk about their charity work—the Modern Ball, Denim & Diamonds, Paint the Town Red, the Junior League Fashion Show, and I knew their husbands played in polo, golf, and tennis matches to help kidneys, hearts, and livers. But their names weren't synonymous with charity. There weren't events with their last names in the title like Betts's; she ran the Galley's Guide Me Gala, an annual auction that secured guidance and sponsors for inner-city kids.

Lana, Amber, and Courtney didn't have foundations, and this was their ultimate goal: creating a kick-ass charity, or finding one and working their way to the top, making it into the event of the year, brainstorming how to top the others: celebrities, famous chefs, DJs, themed lounges, fab decorations, pole dancers, and auction items that would really stick it to poverty. End homelessness by sailing in New Zealand or by relaxing for a week in Zanzibar, where you're woken by the smell of coconut bread baked in a woodstove by your personal chef. This is for you, you poor and sick people. We will go to Zanzibar for you.

"Should I take the bags somewhere?" I asked, needing to give myself a time-out.

"That would be great," Betts said, staring at the spot on the carpet where Gabriella had spit up. "You can take them to the kitchen. It's through that hallway. Go past the foyer, then take a left down the corridor through the atrium, then on your right you'll see a sitting room, take another right and you'll see the dining room, and just go straight from there. You can't miss it."

I looked down the hall to the black marble foyer, then gathered the bags, feeling like a hobbit embarking on a long journey. I ventured forth. The shopping bags were heavy. They were from Coach, Neiman Marcus, Giggle, Saks, and J. Crew. I felt like a lucky hobo.

As I said, I offered to carry the bags not so much to be helpful but because I needed to be alone. Also, I was dying to know what was in them. My bag was filled with the things I felt I could part with. It took me so long to fill it, so much back and forth. I rescued at least three things just moments before I entered Betts's home. I saved my platform shoes with cork wedges just in case someone declared them in style again. I rescued E's stuffed monkey and a pan she could use for pretend cooking. I had no right to judge these women and understood that part of it was jealousy, but there was something else, too, rooted in a disappointment in friendships, my expectations and hopes for them. *What do I value about the friendships I've made in the SFMC community?* At that time, I didn't value a thing. Friendship was like a cold. I was just hunkering down, trying to get through it, hoping for future health.

When I finally got to the kitchen, I put everything down, looking around for nanny cams. The kitchen was dark and elegant, lots of copper and burnished brass. I peeked into a bag, making a face like I was searching for something so if someone came in I could say, "Where is that thing I put in there? I can't seem to . . . Oh, never mind." I was an actress in high school, or at least thought of myself as one, and the skill has come in very handy in my life, especially now as a mother.

In bag number 1 I spied smoked trout, sunless tanning cream, and clothes that were no longer in style—peasant skirts and velour sweat suits. I imagined someone saying, "I'm not wearing this busted-ass skirt. I'm not eating this smoked shit. Fish in a box? That's nasty."

But then I saw something that caught my eye: a black belt, something I've been looking to buy, a nice black belt that isn't from Forever 21. I extracted it from the bag as if playing Operation. It wasn't too thin or too wide. No loosened threads or chafed leather. It had a sturdy silver buckle that could be used as a weapon if needed. I ran my hands down the rouge lining, then spotted the label: Hermès.

I put it around my waist. Hermès—that soft, lofty word had, against my better judgment, made it not just a belt but a perfect belt, a belt that could dress up jeans or transform a dress; a belt that could take me into my golden years. I was trying to get a glimpse of it in the reflection of the oven when a woman came into the kitchen with a bucket of cleaning products. I was too embarrassed to take it off, so I pulled my sweatshirt down over it.

"I can't seem to find my . . . Oh, never mind," I said.

The woman ignored me.

"I'm just dropping this stuff off," I said.

"Yes, ma'am," she said.

I wanted to tell her that I was different from the women out there, that she didn't have to call me ma'am. I used to have Mexican friends. Granted one went to Harvard and the others worked for my grandmother, but still. I'm biclass—I can swing both ways.

Then Courtney walked into the kitchen.

"Oh, hi, bon journo, Cecil. Como sta?" She turned to me and asked: "You having second thoughts?"

"What?"

She gestured to the bags. "Giver's remorse."

"Oh, no, I was just making sure I didn't forget to put this emergency kit in there. It has Band-Aids in it . . ." I tried to trail off. "Little sewing needle."

Courtney started to go through the Saks bag, the one where I got the belt. She was pulling out clothes, leaving them on the floor. "I meant to take some of this stuff to a consignment shop." She held up a pair of high heels. "These," she said and continued to rifle around. "I thought I had this belt in here, too."

I knew this was the time to take it off. I could act my way out of awkwardness. If Courtney were my friend, it wouldn't have been awkward at all, but I pulled my sweatshirt down further.

"What the hell?" Courtney said. "Where is it?"

"Weird," I said.

The window had closed. There's a point when too much time has gone by to ask someone what his or her name is if you've forgotten it. This was the same situation—too much time had gone by for me to take off the belt. I couldn't have said, "You mean this?" pointing to my waist. I had passed that point and I was trapped. For a moment, I felt panicked and a bit sick, but then I began to feel better. It was like shoplifting, something I used to do sometimes with my friends in college. At grocery stores we'd buy our groceries, but would steal something, too. I don't know why we'd do this. It made a mundane errand fun, I guess, and we were showing off for each other, and naïvely thinking we were doing something to the system, the big chain stores. With Courtney I had that same feeling of exhilaration and badassedness. *I'm going to steal your goddamn belt.*

Courtney made a sound of frustration, then walked toward the hall with her rescued heels.

"Maybe it fell out in my house somewhere," she mumbled before disappearing into the maze. I was relieved to be alone again—the lie around my waist was becoming loud, like a telltale heart.

I walked out of the kitchen and back down the hall, looking at the details, the art, the cleanliness, all these things I may never have. I felt like a sloppy child, or like my old self, the college girl, needy and hungry for the extraordinary, for something that would set me apart from people who wouldn't have me anyway. My shoplifting high was gone. Being bad is just a reaction to feeling marooned.

When I got back the women were looking at me as though I had done something wrong. I almost confessed, but then Lana smiled apologetically and I realized they were talking about me.

Courtney quickly gave something to Betts. A check.

"This is just for the charity," Betts said. "But don't feel obliged." She looked at Ellie, who was smiling, all gums. "It's fine," Betts said. "We have a lot here."

Was it really that obvious? Did I look poor? Did it come off of me like a scent? Or maybe it was just that I didn't know them before this, and they know everyone in the city you're supposed to know.

I could have written a check—not like the ones they were probably writing, but I could have done something. It was more humiliating to not be included at all.

"I don't have my checkbook," I said, and I didn't. "But . . . next time."

"Okay," Betts said lightly. "Next time."

I picked Ellie up, and waved her little hand for her. "Off to nap. Bye, everyone," I said in my voice, in Ellie's voice. We were a united front. Then I walked out of the house with a beautiful baby and a beautiful belt.

What am I going to teach you? I buckled my girl into the car seat. How are we going to move with confidence? How are we going to fit?

I closed her door, looked back at the house, then took the belt off, leaving it on the sidewalk. It had fallen from Lana's bag, mystery solved. I felt its absence, but it was just a belt, and this was just a big home, and those ladies in there were all just mothers who probably felt just as alone at times. I left them all behind and never went back.

Do I value the SFMC friendships I have now? Wholeheartedly. Friendships are meant to strengthen you, not deplete you. Now that I'm a parent friendships will most likely be ever-changing as my child grows. Children lead us to our company. For now, there is Georgia, Barrett, Annie, and Henry, my company, and I don't know what I'd do without them.

Any suggestions to make SFMC playgroups better?

I got a little teary there for a moment. Okay, moving on. Yes, the whole registration process could be much simpler. I remember signing up online, what an arduous process that was. I was pregnant and sweating profusely after having tried, and failed, to come up with a suitable username. After each attempt I was informed that my username either was taken or was missing a key element—a capital letter, a number, more letters, a space. I even tried FuCkU69!H()_, and got: "This username has been taken." Is the SFMC chat group, which is really just a forum for mothers to harangue, boast, rant, judge, ridicule, malign, and passively aggressively battle, really that top-secret?

Also, for playgroups I've learned that you pair people up by zip codes, a.k.a. tax brackets. When I signed up I was still living in a Pac Heights studio. That's why I got placed with Betts and the funky bunch in the first place.

Perhaps pair people up in a way that moves them out of their bubbles. You never know where friendships could strike.

My friends are the perfect example. They've been so supportive this past week, the wedding just a week away. Even though Annie thinks it will just rub salt and the whole spice rack into the wound, she has offered to come over to help me get ready.

"I'm really good with makeup," she said the other day. She squinted at me, planning her strategy, then cupped my face and smiled, which completely warmed my heart.

I still haven't asked Henry if he wants to go—the delay due to the fact that I haven't seen him since he left for camping, and because it hasn't really been on my mind. I've been working on this book and looking over my old writing from grad school. I've been hanging out with the girls—I even went to the Embarcadero Farmers' Market with just Georgia, friendship striking on a warm day by the bay. We watched our kids play on the pier and ate the most delicious almond cherry scones.

They know if they stamp Cinderella or a talking sponge on a box of cookie cereal we'll be too tired to argue. Why can't they put Elmo on kale bags! Only the crap gets the fun.

—Moms at the Discovery Museum watching their kids eating princess fruit chews, which have no fruit in them whatsoever

EAT CAKE

t's a sunny day in San Francisco, which means everyone is out in full force with their Frisbees and pit bulls. It's like being at a music festival. The Panhandle playground is packed with kids, buzzing with excitement and intermittent cries from some unfortunate child. Parents perk up at the cries, then settle back when they realize it isn't their child. Some don't even look up, the sounds of their children's cries firmly imprinted.

Mele reads a magazine on the bench while Barrett finishes her phone call. She spies Ellie climbing up the play structure stairs and accidentally knocking down a black child. She'd rather not get up to help—if it were a white child she wouldn't—but she doesn't want anyone thinking Ellie's a racist. It's been on her mind lately, as Ellie will say things every now and then that give Mele pause about the best way to answer. Ellie asked her Indian friend, Amita, in daycare, "Why is your skin like that?" Amita didn't know what to say. She shrugged. "No one told me why."

No one seems to have noticed the accident, and the knocked-down child is already standing, contentedly continuing on. It would have been racist to have gotten up, she thinks.

143

Barrett ends her call and shakes her head. She runs her family like a company. Mele wants to talk to her about the wedding. She values Barrett's opinion, sort of like Annie deferring to Tabor Boyard.

"Do you think?" Mele asks, then stops when Ellie catapults off the purple slide and screams, "Dora! Dora! Mommy! Mama!"

She scans the playground for a Dora doll, T-shirt, shoes, backpack, book, cereal box, corn syrup pops, whatever the little minx has affixed herself to.

"Dora!" Ellie says again, and Barrett sighs. "Look to the right. The gate."

Mele looks toward the gate, where the blond in-vitro twins are being strolled into the playground by their nanny. Their short, Mexican nanny with black bobbed hair and blunt bangs: Dora.

"Oh," Mele says.

"Dora!" Ellie says, pulling on Mele's white T-shirt.

"No, sweetie," Méle whispers. It's happening again. "That's not Dora. We don't know her name. It could be Louise or Mary."

"Or Dora," Barrett says.

"It really does look like her," Mele says. If Dora was fifty-five and taking care of two blond girls who kept shouting, "Look what I can do! Look what I can do!" A Dora who had stopped her adventures and explorations and spent her time parked on a playground bench, grinding up flax to sprinkle on tofu haute dogs and other foods said with finger quotes.

Ellie continues to stare, not entirely convinced that this isn't Dora at her second job. She walks toward the twins and stands in front of them, checking things out.

"What do I do?" Mele says. "The other day she yelled, 'Albert's dad!' when she saw our Asian neighbor in the hall, and she's starting to say it whenever she sees Asian men. So I say, 'No, sweetie, that's not Albert's dad. He just looks like . . . And I had to stop myself. I couldn't say he looked like Albert's dad. That's totally racist, right?"

"Right," Barrett says. "Racist. Oh, you don't even know." She shakes her head, and looks like she's holding back from saying something.

"What?" Mele says with a hungry look.

"I don't want to be that person who follows 'I saw a shark' with 'Yeah, well, I've been bitten by one.'"

"But I like shark-bite stories!" Mele doesn't mind being one-upped or talked down to by Barrett. She has always looked to her for advice, from choosing the right stroller and the right diapers to knowing the best times of the day to go to Costco and Trader Joe's, and now Barrett could help her to teach Ellie that not all Mexicans are Dora and not all Asians are Albert's dad, subtly blending in life lessons, hiding them like sweet potatoes in pancakes.

"Some things went down this weekend," Barrett says.

"What happened?" Mele asks and prepares to be priest and translator. "Can I use it?"

"Sure," Barrett says. "Make it into a cake."

BARRETT'S
FABULOUS LIFE

arrett is watching the Fabulous Life of someone or another, some teen singer who claims she wants to be a mom before she gets too old to enjoy it.

"I want to be able to play with my kids," the pop star is saying. "I want to go shopping with them. I want two boys and two girls." The singer giggles, as if she has said something funny.

Barrett's son, Jake, flips the channel—he always flips it right when she's starting to get into the groove of a show.

"Just pick something," she says, eager to relax while she has one kid down, but Jake's cell phone rings and he tosses the remote to the other side of the couch. His ring tone is a jazzy riff that makes her panicky. It's so strange—Jake's phone is ringing and yet both she and Gary, the only people who call him, are in the room. This has been happening all week, but still, she can't get used to the sound, to the way Jake will jump a little, feeling his pants pocket, then looking at the

147

screen, casually, as if it were something common. It's been happening ever since his commercial aired a few weeks ago.

She supposes it's a good thing—she has always wanted him to have more friends, yet at the same time he was perfectly fine without them. Active, funny, charming. She never really noticed his lack of friends except those times when a crew of boisterous boys would pass them on Chestnut; she'd feign the need to duck into a shop, pulling him in after her, but when she did this she felt guilty because it forced her to admit he needed protection, or that there was something wrong with him in comparison to those other boys. But ever since his cell has been ringing "off the hook" and he was starting to say things like "I'm going over to Hat's house" (Hat? Hat!), she wishes he were the old, friendless Jake, because that Jake seemed to work harder.

"What's up?" he says into his phone. "Nothing much. Yeah, I know who you are."

Barrett scans her son slumped on the sofa, then tries to get Gary's attention, but he has gotten hold of the remote and is watching, open-mouthed, a show about battleships. She bets he doesn't even notice the changes in their son. He's as observant as a carton of eggs. When he finally looks over at her, she gestures to Jake, but Gary looks behind Jake to the back door.

"What?" he says.

"Never mind!" she yells, furious his mind isn't tuned to the same station.

"Um, I guess so," Jake says. His legs are spread so wide on the couch! He never used to take up that much room. He puts his hand over the crotch of his jeans and pinches at himself like he's trying to pluck a grape.

She sighs loudly, and both boys look at her and give her peevish little smiles. They're trying to *lull* her, because she has complicated moods and desires and they both know that talking to her only makes it worse.

If they only knew that these crooked little grins made it doubly worse.

Jake ends his call. She makes herself wait five seconds before speaking. That's another thing about her husband and son. They can talk on the phone and when they hang up they'll just sit there like nothing happened. You're supposed to talk about what you talked about on the phone! It's like they're from the Paleolithic period.

"Who was that?" she asks. Cool tone. Nonviolent posture. Eyes on the television, the ships marching across stormy seas.

"This girl from homeroom," Jake says.

"What did she want?" Barrett asks.

"Dad, change it back to what I was watching, please."

Poor Dad, Barrett thinks. He's so transfixed you'd think he was watching porn or football. He never gets to choose, but when you have no opinion or knowledge of program schedules, you have no authority, so that's his problem. Gary changes it back to the singer's fabulous life. She displays the contents of her refrigerator. "I'm obsessed with Coke Zero," she says.

"You guess so about what?" Barrett says.

"What?"

"You said, 'I guess so,' on the phone. You guess so about what?"

"Jeez. Listen much?"

"Well?"

"She was asking if she could come to my birthday party."

"To Waterworld with you and Tyler?"

"No, remember I said I wanted to have something at the house now, like at night."

"That's fine," Barrett says, even though she had her mind set on the water park. She loves water slides and amusement park food, and enjoys seeing her son with Tyler, a boy with hair as red as a rooster's wattle, because he, too, is cool yet solitary, the kind of kid who'll grow up to be a drummer.

"What, exactly, is this party going to be like?" Barrett asks. "I need to know what to buy, what to expect. Should I invite the parents?"

"No!" Jake yells. "Just, like, I want to ask a lot of people. And we'll just hang out. I've never really had a big birthday."

"Your second one was huge!" She remembers the balloon man they hired. He twisted the balloons into a jet pack Jake could wear. She couldn't fathom it on him now. It would be so small—like a growth.

"That doesn't count," Jake says.

The pop star walks into her bedroom and points at various things from her childhood, which was what, a month ago? From watching this show Barrett has learned that no one reads and everyone loves the movie *Scarface*.

"How many kids are you thinking?"

"I don't know. Fifty?"

"Fifty! Do you know fifty kids?"

"Yes," Jake says, and Barrett senses that this is strange for him to admit.

She wants to ask where these kids were before the commercial aired, but feels this would be cruel. Jake is aware of the connection. It's the reaction to sudden fame that serves as the true test of character, and so far he's doing very well.

She doesn't really get the appeal of the whole thing. About six months ago a cereal company called for video submissions from kids ages ten through thirteen doing whatever they do on an average day. Jake sent in clips of himself skateboarding at Golden Gate Park, riding his bike in the Presidio, and playing in the water at Crissy Field. For some reason it won. They probably liked the whole San Francisco thing: the Haight, the bridge, a kid in the city eating Jumbo O's on the Muni. Now Jake and Stubs, their feral corgi, can be seen running out of the ocean. Jake can be seen walking down Union, reaching into a box of Jumbo O's, tossing some in the air, then catching them in his mouth as his friends laugh and pat his back. She doesn't like this supposed "reality" ad. Who are these friends? And who is that fake mom pouring the cereal for him? Like a twelve-year-old can't do that for himself.

"I want one of those cool parties," Jake says.

"No way, mister!" Barrett yells.

"Honey," Gary says. "Why are you yelling?"

"Because! We're not going to be one of those families who do those sweet parties!" Gary's expression is blank and dumb. "It's this trend," she explains. "There was this show years back about kids who throw extravagant birthday parties. They'll come in on the back of an elephant, they'll wear designer clothes, they'll belly-dance in front of their peers, and then at the end they get a car, and not like a Corolla. They get a Mercedes or a BMW. One girl got a sports car and an SUV. Two cars! It's just insane. The parents should be neutered."

"I wouldn't do that," Jake says.

"We will feed you, educate you, love you," she says, "but it's not our job to hire Kanye West to come to your birthday party, nor am I required to buy you an SUV."

"I wouldn't want Kanye anyway. And I don't want anything all crazy. Maybe we can get some KFC and we'll just hang out downstairs and listen to music and stuff. Maybe dance. Twenty people tops."

Dance! Barrett's heart melts, along with her hesitancy and skepticism. She trusts Jake, after all, and she wants him to have fun on his birthday, to dance with friends. Perhaps Jumbo O's has created a tiny portal into which kids can glide. His charisma, his style and agility, his humor have always been present, but now they can erupt for all to see.

"We should get KFC," Gary says. "I haven't had that for so long."

Barrett glares at her husband, who is taking off his socks and throwing them toward the hallway. Then he stands, holds up his leg behind him, and farts. Both Barrett and Jake laugh.

* * *

Today's the day of Jake's party, but Gary has to go to a funeral and he has taken Tara with him since the family requested children be there. His colleague's baby has died. The family was expecting it, but still. How do you wake up? How do you go on? Barrett can't think about it. She really can't—can't wrap her head around the child's death, can't come near to imagining what they must be feeling. You can't possibly know other people's pain no matter how hard you try to cram your feet into their shoes. You end up grieving for your own self and their loss becomes an object lesson. This makes her sad.

She looks out of her living room window, waiting for the kids to come. They live on a narrow street and, she's happy that no one's parked on the Mount Davidson side of the road. Maybe parents will park and come in, stay for a glass of wine, perhaps some bruschetta, salad, or salmon. She prepared for the possibility of guests. She has some dessert, too—lava cakes from Trader Joe's that she put in white ramekins to make it look like she made them herself. Then she remembers the birthday cake and feels stupid.

A car pulls up. She spies a boy in the passenger side, a younger girl in back, and a handsome father behind the wheel. Please come in, she thinks. She loves handsome fathers—it isn't that she flirts with them or anything, but they tend to give moments of her day (the playground, for instance, with Tara, or soccer games with Jake) a pleasant charge. She's way more into her kids when an attractive man is watching, and the feigned enthusiasm always turns into genuine enthusiasm, and so cute dads are good parenting aids, though in this town most of the dads are practically geriatric, or superuptight bores who probably bought their tools at Restoration Hardware. The guy out there, however, looks like he could change a tire. Unfortunately the boy gets out of the car without him.

"Jake," she calls. "A buddy is here."

"Don't call him a buddy!" he says, running to the door, his jeans making a swishing racket.

"Those are the biggest jeans I've ever seen!" she says. "And they're so stiff, and all bunched up by your shoes. Good God, when did you get those shoes! They're so white they're practically blinding me."

"I went shopping with Dad."

"Obviously."

"He got the same jeans."

"Oh, I believe it."

His buddy walks in, and Barrett stops herself from hugging him and asking about his hobbies. "Hello!" she says.

"Hi," he says.

"Come on!" Jake says and runs toward the stairs.

She's once again left alone and wishes Tara were here so she'd at least look like she had something to do. She straightens the living room, puts the *New Yorker* she found in the park on top of the *Us Weekly*.

She hears a car outside and runs to the window, spying a minivan with a MY CHILD IS AN HONORS STUDENT sticker and a license plate that says, MOM4BOYS. The minivan drives away, thank God. Whenever she sees those awful accoutrements she wants to stick to her car something equally offensive, like MY CHILD ISN'T OBESE or I AM FERTILE.

The door opens. In comes the new friend, a boy with sunken eyes, dark long lashes, and cheekbones like pomegranates. He has a concave trunk and clownish feet.

"Hello!" she says. "Are you the honors student?"

It takes him a moment, and then: "That's my brother," he says. "But his whole class got that sticker."

He's also wearing baggy jeans, along with a huge sweatshirt, which is covering up a gold chain necklace.

"Nice bling," she says, trying to be down.

He flushes as if she caught him masturbating. "It's okay," she says, then points him to the stairs.

Three girls, all with braids in their hair like they'd been in Jamaica or at Burning Man, are next to arrive. Barrett is on her knees on the couch, watching them walk up to the door; then she turns around and sits facing forward and flips through *The New Yorker,* but then thinks this looks too staged.

She gets up and opens the door.

"Hi, girls," she says.

"Hi," they all sing. They smile at her like she's dying, cursed with some old-lady affliction. One of them carries an expensive handbag, and Barrett wants to tell her that she shouldn't even care about labels until she's twenty-four.

"The boys are downstairs." She points to the stairwell.

"Thank you!" one says, and then they giggle like that TV pop star, tittering at jack nothing, just filling dead air with dead laughter. She feels like it's too late for these kids, the girls especially, like they've crossed a line and can't come back. She thinks about that dreadful *My Super Sweet 16* show, the last episode she saw, the birthday girl and her posse preparing for the party.

"We're pretty and popular and wear nice clothes and people sort of look up to us," girl one explained.

"So, like, this party could seriously affect our reputations," girl two said.

Then the camera cut to a nonfriend, a brunette whose eyes kept darting from side to side, and she said, "Kaya's, like, relic-collecting rich. Like, I heard she has Napoleon's bathtub."

It's too late for them to be fully human. Their fates are sealed. They'll be giggly and mean now, fake and dumb later, then as mothers they'll arm their kids with pukey cute gear and give them pompous British names. Fuck, she's in a bad mood.

Barrett was a popular girl, she supposes, but popularity was completely different when she was in school. She recalls her blond hair soaring while she danced (all fists and forearms) and drinking wine coolers. That's what made you popular back then. Big hair and Bartles & Jaymes. Now it's all about handbags and hashtags and phones, for crissakes! Kids these days are so messed up.

She tiptoes to the top of the stairs and hears a hoot of laughter and then a girl say, "Sick! What are you? Like six?"

She walks back to the couch and watches another car pull up, then reverse. A woman is behind the wheel and she's parking. A parent is going to come in! There aren't any brag-hag bumper stickers on her car either. Barrett walks to the mirror by the front door and widens her eyes and turns her head to the right. Then she walks into the kitchen so that when the mother knocks Barrett won't be right there. She's pretty sure the mother parking is Christine, one of those "cool" moms, who isn't cool at all but bills herself that way and is part of the little cool-mom clique that Barrett despises and desperately wants to be a part of, more to avoid being grouped with the dork moms than anything else.

After the knock Barrett waits a second, then opens the door with a spent yet friendly smile on her face so that she looks as though she's been very busy, yet is happy to be interrupted.

"Hi! Come in!" she says to Christine and her daughter.

"Hi, I'm Christine," Christine says, looking around her living room.

"I'm Barrett," she says, though they've met before and see each other practically every day. "I think we may have met before."

"This is my daughter. Luella say hello."

"Hello," she says, flashing a smile. Literally. It's a flash, then it's gone.

Luella? Barrett thinks. Why, of course. The girl has a handsome face, made prettier by the fact that Barrett has to stop and think if she's pretty or not. The large nose is the hang-up, but in a way it ameliorates the face because you think, Wow, even with the nose she's pretty. She also has round, heavy breasts that would surely make any teen pre-ejaculate if he got ahold of 'em.

"Pretty name," Barrett says.

"I just wanted to make sure there were parents here," Christine says.

"I told you there would be," Luella says.

"Well, you said that about the last party, and your friend ended up going to the hospital."

"What?" Barrett says.

Luella rolls her eyes. "She would have had to go to the hospital with or without parents there. She couldn't find her inhaler, and the contractor was there to drive her. It worked out fine."

Barrett gives Luella a secret wink. "Everyone's downstairs," she says.

"I'll text when it's over," Luella says, then sulks away.

"Would you like something to nibble on?" Barrett asks Christine, horrified at the words that just left her mouth, but Christine doesn't appear to have heard. She's watching her daughter with intensity. Barrett knows the look. There's nothing more pleasing than watching your children when they don't know you're watching them.

"Would you like a glass of wine?" Barrett asks.

Christine's face lights up. "Sure!" she says, spoken like a true mom.

Barrett brings out the wine, pouring it beforehand because it's Bogle, her weekday wine. She brings the bruschetta, too, and can tell that Christine's happy to see both. After they get settled on the couch, they sit in silence for a bit too long.

"I love your house," Christine says, but Barrett's sure she's lying.

Another silence is saved by the bell.

"They just keep coming," Barrett says, pretending to be weary. She walks to the door and opens it to a mother, Maggie, and her son, who doesn't seem at all embarrassed to be accompanied by her.

"Hi," Maggie says. "I just wanted to thank you for having the party. I'm Matt's mom, Maggie."

"Maggie?" Christine says from the other room.

"Christine?"

Maggie peeks through the door, and both women issue that customary little greet-scream. Barrett can't imagine men doing this. *Pat? Andy? Ahhhh!*

Both Barrett and Matt watch them hug while giving one another awkward glances. She feels like she's on a blind date and tries to think of things to say. "So, Matt, Maggie tells me you like math and Kings of Leon."

"Okay, Mom," he says. "See you later."

"They're downstairs," Barrett says to Matt, noticing that a black comb is lodged into his dark curls. He walks away, and she almost calls after him: "Wait, there's a comb stuck in your hair," hoping to save him from embarrassment, but she assumes he knows this and that it must be a fashion statement, though she isn't sure what's being stated: "I have so much hair I can stick a comb in it." Or: "I'm so busy, I'll get to my hair when I'm good and ready." Or, simply, "Look at me. There's a comb in my hair. A comb!"

She's left fake-smiling at these women who are facing one another and speaking in hushed, aghast tones. Barrett forms the tip of the triangle, not really sure what she's doing here. She feels psychotic, clearly not part of the conversation, but it's too late now. She has to commit. It's like being in a store, two shoppers flipping through the rack toward one another. Who is going to move? Who is going to take her hand off the clothes and *go around*? Not Barrett. She never moves. It's her thing.

"God, you look so good!" Maggie says. "Did you get divorced?" she asks in an exaggeratedly sardonic, drag queen sort of way.

"No, no. I've been doing Pilates. It's such a good workout—"

"I love Pilates," Barrett says, committing.

"You know who *did* get a divorce though? Sheila Schatz. Isn't that crazy? She looks fantastic though."

"Like how?"

"I don't know. She just looks thin and . . . she's just got that divorced body."

"So do you!"

"Really?"

"Yes! I haven't seen you forever. What have you been doing?"

"Same old. What have you been up to?"

"Oh, the yushe. Superbusy. Really busy."

Barrett takes a step back, then another, until her steps take her to the sofa. She goes around.

She takes her glass of wine from the table, gripping it ferociously, and takes a deep sip. More kids stream into the house and she waves them in like a parking attendant. "Downstairs," she says. "Have a blast." She feels duped that these two know each other. Now they're talking about a friend who is moving to San Rafael.

"I told her to go see *Little Children*," Maggie says. "Going to that community pool—it's just like the one in the movie. Totally creepy."

"Great movie," Barrett says. "And book."

Both women turn to face her, and Barrett feels like she's in high school once again. She'd do anything to fit in, to have these girls like her, but in high school, unlike in motherhood, she never had to work so hard. Usually the blond hair worked as an E-Z Pass.

"I didn't know it was a book," Maggie says. "Oh, my God, we're reading the worst book in my book club. I mean it's not bad, but it's so serious and I can't get into it."

"We're reading *Baby on the Brain*," Christine says. "It's about this high-powered marketing director and she gets pregnant, but still tries to juggle everything? And her friends are all single, so she still tries to go out and keep up with that lifestyle, but then her parents die and . . . Never mind." Christine flutters her hands. "I don't want to ruin anything."

Barrett finishes the sentence in her head. Then her parents die and the protagonist discovers what really matters. Or: Then her parents die and she realizes she needs to think of others instead of just herself. Or: She realizes her single friends are all whores who'll end up alone and children are the best. She loves little Arabellabellalulu after all. Mele would just puke.

"I should read that," Barrett says, using her admonished voice because that's how you speak if you want to appear engaged just as cool teenage girls speak with that nasal, closemouthed, bored-to-death drawl in order to properly merge with their kind.

"Would you like a glass?" She lifts her glass to Maggie.

"I'd love one. Are you kidding?"

Both women laugh—*ha, ha, ha, we drink, we gossip, we're cool, hip moms!*—and Barrett goes to the kitchen like a servant. The kitchen is around the corner, so she can still hear the women. "Red or white?" Barrett asks.

"White, please," Maggie says. "Jake just started at Sterne, right?"

"No, no. He's been there since fifth." He had to take a test and undergo an interview, and waiting for the results was like waiting for the lines to appear on a pregnancy test after your fifth in vitro. She doesn't like that she can't see their facial expressions.

"Oh," Maggie says. "I'm not sure what he looks like."

"He's in that webisode thing," Christine says.

"That's right!" Maggie says. "He's a star."

"Well," Barrett says, walking back with Maggie's wine. "I wouldn't say star—"

"Now, what do you do?" Christine asks. "You work, right?"

"I'm in real estate."

"Aren't we all?" Maggie says, and the two women laugh, but Barrett doesn't get it. They start to discuss properties they know of and who of their friends are "in a rut" because they want to move but can't because it's such a poor time to sell.

Barrett figures she could do a little networking. She has already scanned their fingers, ears, shoes, and hair, and is pretty sure of their friends' price range.

"For most people it's a bad time to sell," Barrett says, "but it really depends. Homes in the three-, four-, five-million-dollar range and up—homes in that bracket are still going strong."

"I should have Trey call you," Maggie says.

"Tray?" Barrett asks. "As in, 'Carry this on a'?"

"He's dying to move."

"Sure," Barrett says, "I'd love to talk with him."

She walks to the bookshelf and grabs a bunch of business cards out of the bowl that holds business cards, miniature plastic toys, dust, and change. "Give one to your friend, and here's some extra." She hopes to God this could generate some new business, yet the people they know must have their own agents, top agents, Previews agents, agents that make you feel bad for walking into an open house. But you never know. Sometimes those agents are too busy for them.

"Would you guys like something to eat?" Barrett asks.

"Oh," Christine says. She looks at her watch. "Then we wouldn't have to drive all the way to Nob Hill and come all the way back," she says. The two women eye-conference, and Barrett looks away.

"Sure!" Maggie says.

"Great. I'll just put some plates out in the kitchen and come help yourself. There's salad and fish. Hope you eat fish. And I'll get another bottle of wine downstairs. I'll peek in on the kids!"

She thought this would make them want to sneak down the steps with her, but they're already immersed in another conversation.

"You're kidding me."

"No!"

"Are you serious?"

"Yes!"

It's because they're used to seeing their children with other children. They're used to seeing them at parties, or admired by their peers. Barrett has been dying all night to see this, to creep downstairs and behold her son finally getting the attention he deserves. He's like Cinderella. There the whole time, but denied the opportunity to mingle.

At the top of the stairwell she hears the deep bass of the music. It's so loud that by the time she reaches the bottom of the stairs she covers her ears. How can they have conversations like this? Before she walks by the family room to the garage, she prepares herself. She will walk quickly and glance casually toward the party. Then she'll get four bottles of wine so that on the way back she can pretend to have trouble carrying them all, and will have to move slowly by the scene while appearing to be completely occupied.

She makes her move, taking a quick glance up, and then she stops and steps back toward the stairs to hide.

What was that?

She peeks back out, then pats herself down for her phone, a typical reaction when faced with danger. She reaches for her husband, for communication with him. Everything has to be shared with Gary or else she is alone. Her need is similar to wishing you had your camera when you see something incredible. Her husband is the camera, an instrument that helps her capture things she appreciates, fears, or doesn't understand.

They are dancing. The kids are dancing. And yet they aren't really dancing. She thinks of *It's a Wonderful Life,* the scene where the kids are dancing on the platform over the pool, all quick and hoppy, like they're high on malt powder. The music is lively—you can actually identify instruments—piano, saxophone. That's dancing. She listens to this music from the last step on the stairwell—*Booty, booty, booty, booty knocking everywhere*—and sees her son gyrating his buttocks so rapidly it's like watching a hummingbird hovering over a honeysuckle. Then he slides to the right with his arms spread apart as if presenting a magic trick. After this arrangement he lifts his leg, a move she'd call the Pissing Dog if she had to give it a name, and gyrates with jackhammer speed.

She is so stunned to see Jake in this fashion that it takes her a moment to register the other kids. Girls are backed up against the boys, their asses gesturing wildly and their faces making *fucking* expressions. She finds herself envying this for a second—*I haven't made that face forever!* But this doesn't last long as she remembers that these girls are twelve and thirteen and just imitating someone making faces that a director in Hollywood says are fucking faces. Actual fucking faces aren't nearly as appealing, she thinks, thinking of her own and of Gary's face when he's mid-o, a kind of stroke-like cry for help.

She's sure the boys are all bonafied, or whatever the expression is—bonered up? Fully boned? Their expressions are very serious and focused, as if this were some kind of final exam. It's then she grasps what everyone's wearing. Basketball jerseys and baggy jeans, gold chains and baseball caps cocked over their eyes. The girls are in tight jeans, some in little shorts and tube tops; Christine's daughter wears a purple basketball jersey that's knotted below her breasts. She has on low-riding jeans, and a purple thong coasts over her hips. Barrett thinks of the show Jake watches about rappers' houses, how some will end in the "family room" with a shot of "how we do," which involves playing video games on a monstrous TV while scantily clad women dance around them, and by dancing she means humping nothing but dust motes, much like the scene before her. She doesn't want to embarrass her son, so she just gapes. She's gripped by fear that those women, those mothers, will come down and see what's going on. Or maybe they already know? Maybe this is "how they do," too? No. Not possible.

She peeks out and raises her arm, hoping the gold glint of her jew-elry will catch Jake's eye. She feels like she's stranded and trying to get the attention of a rescue plane. He finally notices her.

"Come here," she mouths, using her pissed and publicly humiliated nonvoice.

He wades through the stream of teenage waste. She composes her-self, then takes a step back so they'll be out of ear- and eyeshot.

"What the hell is going on out there?" she says in a loud whisper.

"Nothing," he says. "We're just dancing."

Oh, his beautiful eyes. Just like Gary's. Where *is* he anyway? She has a hard time reprimanding this child—Jake has always repeated her admonishments from the time he was two. "Oh, I not listening? I was bad? I'm sorry." Damn him.

"But, what kind of dancing? Did you tell everyone to dance this way, or—"

"We're just dancing. It's how people dance." He holds up his arms as if preparing to box, makes a kissy face, and moves his hips.

"Stop that," she whisper-hisses. "Why is everyone dressed that way?"

"What way?"

"You know what way. Like—" Oh, boy. She tries again: "Why aren't they dressed the same as they were when they first walked into this house?"

"Because it's a hood party," Jake says.

"A what? A what? A what-the-shit-did-you-just-say party?"

He covers his mouth and laughs because she just said *shit*, which is so minor right now. She could say all sorts of things and it wouldn't matter.

"A hood party," he says, like it's no thang. "Like we're people in the hood having a party. It's something everyone does now."

"Oh my God," she says. "Oh, my flapping God." She's not sure what's worse—that they're doing it here or that it's something everyone does now. *What the big balls is wrong with everyone?*

She looks up the stairs, swats Jake to the side, then peeks around the wall. A girl dances, looking over her left shoulder, then her right. Barrett sees Maggie's son by the flat screen eating a piece of fried chicken.

"Oh, my God!" She presses her back against the wall. She thinks of the mothers talking about her on the SFMC forum or the whole night being filmed by some sleuth kid, the footage going to the school, the news, *Dateline, Primetime,* YouTube! *A disturbing new trend among white, suburban teens. Are parents promoting racism at private schools?* The NCAA would sue them, there would be death threats, the cereal would pull its ad—wait. Is it NCAA? That doesn't sound right. Isn't it A something? Oh, fuck it. *Some* organization is going to beat her ass.

Jake's forehead is gleaming with sweat. He smells a little. She has never noticed that before. He's starting to smell like a boy.

"It's fun," Jake says. "What's wrong?"

"No," Barrett says. "I don't think so. This is not fun. This needs to stop. God, Jake!"

"What?"

"Just. I won't make a scene. But turn the music down, suggest a game, or a movie, or cake! I bought a cake. Have at it. All you can eat. Please come up and have cake. You guys can do whatever with it. Do shots of cake! I'm cool."

Her son looks back at the scene with longing, then at her with desperation and hatred, as if his life hinges on the ability to thrust and do the Pissing Dog.

"Find a segue, Jake," she says. "Make a natural transition into some other activity. You're smart. You can pull it off. But I've got two mothers up there, and if you don't put a stop to this I'll come back down here and I won't be nice about it. I'll make a scene. You know how I do. And I want everyone's normal clothes back on."

"But why?" he asks. "Why is it wrong? Jay and Cassie are here. They're black and they're doing it."

"They're rich! Strike that—it's just wrong! On so many levels."

"But why?"

Perhaps he really doesn't know. Perhaps she doesn't know either.

She remembers when she and her sister wanted to get those big gum balls in the machines at Safeway. They asked a girl their age if they could borrow two quarters. She could write down her address and they'd pay her back, which they would have done. The girls' mother came out of the store, witnessed the transaction, and completely freaked out.

"Shame on you," she said. "How could you take advantage of her like that? Shame on you."

The girl had Down syndrome, but Barrett and her sister didn't take this into consideration. They just needed two quarters and she was a kid like them and she was there. They would have asked any kid who was there.

These kids in her den—aren't they still innocent? Do they really know what they're doing? Or are they imitating what they see on television, the music videos? They aren't like frat boys, blatantly making fun, but it's just too hard to explain.

"It's wrong because I have a feeling it's wrong," she says. "That's why. I'm going with my gut. You're ridiculing. You're enforcing bad stereotypes."

Barrett listens to the music in the background, a new song: *I got hoes, you got hoes. Let's call the whole thing off.*

"We aren't ridiculing anyone," Jake says.

"Then it's appropriation or something," she says.

"What does that mean?"

"It's just bad, okay? I have to get back up there. Find a transition, okay? Redirect. Hell, spin the bottle for all I care. Do Seven Minutes in Heaven."

"What's that?"

Barrett walks back up the stairs. "Just stop," she yell-whispers. Her heart is pounding; it's gyrating. She takes a deep breath at the top of the stairs and looks back to see if Jake is gone. He's still standing there, but facing away from her. She can see his profile. He looks stricken and confused, but she continues on despite the strange feeling that she's abandoning him.

She's relieved to see Christine and Maggie in the kitchen. Everything is normal. Everything's okay.

"This looks fantastic," Christine says.

"I know. I can't believe you cooked this," Maggie says. "I never cook."

"Never," Christine says.

Well, how nice for you, Barrett thinks. To save money she doesn't even buy presliced cheese or snack-size anything. *Snack-size* means you are paying someone extra to put less food into a smaller container.

"How were they down there?" Maggie asks.

"Great!" Barrett says. "They're having some dinner, too. Some . . . chicken, and they're listening to music, but they're going to come up soon and have some cake. Sing 'Happy Birthday.'"

"It's so hard to plan a party," Maggie says. "It's like they don't want the cake and the song, but you have to have the cake and singing to make it a birthday! Matt just had his thirteenth and they did the same thing—went right downstairs and blared Lil Wayne, Lil' Kim, Little Richard, God only knows."

Du dum dum chi. God only knows how often she repeated that joke. Barrett puts some food on her plate, torn over what to do. She supposes she can tell these moms what's going on, tell them what the kids are really doing downstairs, and not just at her house, she's sure, but in basements all over San Francisco. It's crucial these parents know about this activity, yet does it have to be at her house? She needs to sell real estate. She needs to get to know other mothers at Jake's school.

Most of all she doesn't want to hurt her son's social life. He has just been given a portal she isn't about to block.

"It's such a hard age. They're embarrassed by us now!" Christine says. "So you just have to back off."

"I know," Barrett says, resolved to aid and abet. She thinks of the girls' behinds pressed against the boys' crotches. "It's a very hard age."

The fish is excellent, and Barrett believes more needs to be said about this. The fish. How excellent it is. Maggie is well on her way to becoming trashed. She's trying to hide it, but her eyes are all glassy and googly. Barrett likes her better this way. She always finds herself liking people more if they drink a lot, even though it means they'll be driving their children home buzzed. It is one of those moral dilemmas she doesn't really know how to get around.

In the living room she fake-laughs at the things Maggie and Christine find to be funny. Maggie insists her son loves Frank Sinatra. Christine insists her daughter loves foie gras.

"It's the weirdest thing," she says, "but she loves it."

Like they know, Barrett thinks, smugly. Their kids are downstairs pretending they're in Compton and these chicks are telling me what their kids love. I mean, blow me. She doesn't know everything either, of course, obviously, yet accepts this as part of life. She won't be familiar with supersize pieces of her son's world. How sad, she thinks. How very sad.

"I love this table!" Maggie says. A bit of wine sloshes over the rim of her glass and onto her beige sweater. "Damn it," she says. "I always do that. I can't go through one day, not one day, without spilling something or another on my shirt. It's ridiculous. I'm like a walking wet T-shirt contest. Hello! I'm surprised I don't get dollar bills from strangers . . ."

Barrett waits patiently. She wonders where Maggie's going with all of this and if she'll get out okay.

". . . Yoo-hoo! Mommy gone wild. Oh, it's absurd. Ab. Surd."

Barrett dares to look up. Christine looks worried and eager, as if she's watching someone do hurdles with a sprained ankle. When Maggie appears to be done, Christine shakes her head. "I know, I know," she says, but Barrett prefers to let Maggie feel like an idiot and says nothing.

Finally. What she's been waiting for all night. The sound of children coming up the stairs.

"I'll get the cake!" she says and jumps up so fast you'd have thought she'd been zapped. She goes to the kitchen to light each candle with a long match. Thirteen candles, thirteen years. Her boy, her love bug. A skateboard on the chocolate cake, resting against a tree. It is really quite lovely, and cake is something you can never outgrow.

She turns the lights low so the candles burn brightly and walks toward the dining room table. She launches into the birthday song, realizing she's in a fairly low register and it sounds like she's moaning, but the kids join in, their voices surprisingly soft so the whole moment feels like a séance, a plea to some ghost, an elegy to childhood and times you once fiercely knew. She watches Jake through the candlelight, his sweet face, his awkward stature with its latent hunkiness. He looks exactly the same as he did when he was four years old, shyly watching his friends singing to him, watching his mother moving toward him with a lump of pride in her throat. Exactly the same look. But not the same, of course. Not exactly. Not at all.

She stands in front of him. She doesn't need to bend down anymore. Jake blows out the candles.

Everyone claps. The boys whoop, and then she hears that sound she loves. The door opening. Gary and Tara finally coming home.

"Gary!" she says, a tremor in her voice.

*   *   *

Later that night, after everyone has gone, Gary tells her about the funeral for the baby whose name was Thomas. Every time his name was spoken during the service Tara yelled, "Thomas? Thomas! Thomas the Train!"

"I said, 'Shhh.' I said, 'No, not the train. He's a boy. A boy.' Then Tara said, 'Thomas the boy,' but kept yelling his name."

"That's horrible," Barrett says.

Tara walks to Gary, who is sitting cross-legged on the floor, waiting for the assigned book. Tara hands him her choice, then plops down onto his lap. Instead of cleaning up, Barrett sits beside them and listens to the story about the green sheep. She wants to tell Gary about tonight, but doesn't know how. It could be a funny story. It could be worrisome, horrific. It could be nothing. It is nothing compared to the funeral.

"Here is the moon sheep. And here is the star sheep," Gary reads. "But where is the green sheep? Where IS that green sheep?"

"Where is Thomas?" Tara asks.

The question brings tears to Barrett's eyes, and she and Gary exchange glances. What do they say? When do you start telling your children the truth?

"Oh, sweetie," she says. "Thomas had to go."

Tara looks at Barrett with her mouth open. "Oh, he had to go?"

"He had to go," she says.

"He's okay," Gary says.

"Yes, sweetie," she says. "He's okay. He'll be okay."

There are a lot of women who look like Dora at San Francisco playgrounds because . . .

A hood party is racist because . . .

Thomas is dead because . . .

Her boy is growing up. He will become . . .

She can't fill in the blanks.

Tara turns the page, and there's their answer. The mystery is solved.

"Turn the page quietly," Gary says. "Let's take a peep. Here is our green sheep, fast asleep."

Barrett and Mele push their daughters on the swings, both secretly wishing there was a swing button they could press. Ellie leans back in her bucket seat, splayed as though on a zip line. She looks up, in love with the show in the sky.

"Did the moms ever find out about the party?" Mele asks.

"God, no," Barrett says.

Mele thinks about the toons, the princesses that make Ellie so happy. Who cares if she's playing with plastic toys and reading books that aren't about biracial eagles with two proud fathers? Who cares! There's a show up there in the sky!

She tells Barrett she's thinking about chicken wings, corn on the cob, maybe some play on hot dogs.

"*Haute* dogs," she says.

"Haute *dawgs*," Barrett says.

"Maybe some kind of coleslaw."

"With cartoons in it so the kids will eat it."

"Dora Slaw," Mele says.

"And don't forget the cake."

Mele wonders: funny, sad, light, heavy. What approach do you take? Do I dare do chicken? Do I dare eat a peach? Thomas, birth, death, children. Birthday parties, times you once fiercely knew.

"Why did Tara go to the funeral?" Mele asks.

"The parents wanted children there. They wanted a lot of life there."

She wonders when Ellie will stop being entranced by a crowd singing "Happy Birthday" to her. When the awe of oneself begins to diminish, when you don't think celebrating your existence is justified.

Mele will create a recipe for an irresistible cake that makes even teenagers line up like toddlers, giving in to their childish selves. She'll create a bulimic's fantasy, an anorexic's nightmare, a stoner's wet dream. The cake demands loud singing and seconds. A campfire s'mores ice-cream cake.

"Did you still want to look at dresses?" Barrett asks.

"Sure," Mele says, backing out of asking directly where she stands. She can't get a read on what Barrett thinks of her going to the wedding, but she must be somewhat supportive if she's willing to let her shop her closet.

They are both standing with their arms crossed, overlooking the playground as if it's their kingdom.

"Have you spoken to him lately?" Barrett asks.

Mele's always embarrassed by this question, so rare is it that she and Bobby talk. He usually texts: *Need anything?* Or, *All OK?* the kinds of general questions that you're supposed to answer no and yes to. You can't say: *I need love and eggs.* You can't say, *Yes, all is okay except when it isn't.*

"Yeah," Mele says. "We check in. He's been busy with the . . . wedding and all."

Barrett nods, and Mele knows she doesn't believe it. When is a man busy with the wedding? It's then she reads Barrett clearly. She doesn't think Mele should go. She needs to hand Ellie over for the wedding and pick her up when it is over. She could even wait in the car, bring a book.

"Is it okay still? To come look at dresses." *Is it okay to go to the wedding?*

"Stay for dinner," Barrett says and gives Tara a push. She's a friend that makes you live with your thoughts.

How do you help your child make good food choices?

I don't know. Sometimes I do, sometimes I don't. Sometimes I cook up boxed mac and cheese and call it a night. I rarely have the motivation to sculpt food into "magic pinwheels" or "giggly goblins" or whatever. I have all the time in the world, but when I attempted to make a face out of apples, raisins, and squiggles of bread Ellie looked at it and said, "What the hell is that supposed to be?" or at least it seemed she was saying this, especially since my Picassowich ended up on the floor and in the buckle of her high chair.

After hearing about Barrett's son's birthday party, I came up with Insert-Your-Favorite-Toon Slaw. Dora, Barbie, Caillou (such a pussy of a boy), Diego, Handy Manny—you just pick a character and stick it in for incentive. Barrett told me a story that reminded me that pop culture affects the palate. Sometimes it's all in a name. Cinderella Salad, you could call it. Or Belle's Beauty Slaw. Or Jasmine's (the token minority) Magic Confetti. I use the characters to help me. I think of them as my bitches.

Tonight needed no such supports. We went to Barrett's for dinner, and Tara eats like a sumo wrestler and Ellie likes to copy everything Tara does, out of fear most likely.

Tonight, Tara, newly four, asked me at the dinner table what I would do if someone asked me to show them my penis.

"Um, well, I don't have a penis," I said, looking at her parents. They both continued to chew, unfazed—they'd obviously been through this before.

"I mean, your she-she part," Tara said. "If someone asked you to show them your she-she part."

"You mean my vagina?"

Gary coughed.

"What?" I said. "If she's going to know *penis*, she should know *vagina*, right? Why should we get the stupid nickname? Oh, shit. Have I crossed the line?"

"No, no," Gary said. "It's fine."

"What would you do if someone asked to see your verchina?" Tara said, but before I could answer she yelled, "You tell a teacher!"

"That's right," I said.

"You tell a teacher!" Ellie mimicked.

"What if the teacher's the one who asks?" Gary said.

This confused the shit out of Tara.

"You tell Mommy and Daddy," he said, all proud 'cause he knew the answer.

"Daddy, what would you do if someone asked you to show your penis?" Tara asked.

I smiled politely, trying not to look down at his lap.

"I'd tell a teacher," he said. "Unless it was Mommy. Then I'd look up in the sky to see if any pigs were flying around."

Further confusion.

"I can't believe teachers are talking about this stuff already," Barrett said. "I tried to help her put her panties on and she said her body was sacred."

"Your body is sacred," Gary said, and Barrett rolled her eyes.

"We didn't talk about sex until fifth grade," I said, remembering when Ms. Lum (who wore this cool multicolored eye shadow) asked the class to think of all the slang terms for *vagina* and say them out loud: *pussy, snatch, box, oyster, choach, coochie, cunt, slit, stink hole, punani, tuna, va.* Then we did the penis beginning with the meats: *sausage, wiener,* and *frank,* then *dick, rod, prick, schlong, dong, dipstick, tubesteak.* As we got comfortable, everyone started to yell the obscenities with a crazed glee. Ms. Lum wrote our responses on the chalkboard, then asked how these words made us feel. We looked at the dizzying array of bad words written out in her petite cursive. Good! I thought. They make us feel good!

"So you ready for the big day?" Gary asked and promptly got elbowed by Barrett.

"Seriously?" she said.

"What? You ladies were looking at dresses. I thought it was out in the open."

"It's not *her* big day, idiot," Barrett said.

"It's fine," I said. I loved being with Barrett and Gary. They were so cozy and adult. I wanted them to adopt me. I looked across the table at Gary and could imagine being so endeared and annoyed by him, like a real husband.

Ellie and Tara got up from the table to play with Tara's new tool bench.

"If Barrett remarried would you go to the wedding?" I asked. "If Tara were the flower girl?"

"I don't see Tara as a flower girl," Gary said. "She'd be a flower killer. Maybe your sister's kid though. She's obedient."

"So you'd go?" I asked.

"Hard to say," Gary said. He leaned back and sipped his wine. God, he's great. As a single person you know what the best trait in another person's husband is? When they don't flirt with you! Gary didn't flirt!

"Did she cheat on me?" he asked, and rubbed Barrett's head. She lurched away. "Or did I cheat on her? If I cheated on her, then I'd go. I'd support you, hon."

"You'd never cheat on me," Barrett said. "You'd be the worst." She looked at him like she wanted to either kill him or hug him.

"So, Gary, you could possibly be supportive and show that you're okay with your life. You could show that you're mature—that you're not threatened?" I took a bite of sweet potato.

"Show Barrett I'm mature?" Gary laughed. "If she were getting married, I don't think she'd notice me." Barrett made eye contact with me, maybe hoping I'd get his message. I'd be caught up with how I was perceived, what I was proving, whereas Bobby wouldn't even notice I was there. I needed to actually *feel* self-assured and not just pretend I was.

"I'd bring a date," Gary said. "For sure."

"But I'd know she was a fake date," Barrett said. "With fake boobs."

"Ho ho!" he laughed. "You'd be so pissed! But how would you know she was a fake date?" he said, becoming contemplative. "She could be the love of my life."

They were getting off topic. "Do you think it's ridiculous that I'm going?" I asked.

They both looked down and moved some food around.

"Not ridiculous," Barrett said. "It just seems like it would hurt."

"But maybe you'd go and it wouldn't hurt," Gary said.

I thought about this, the wedding like a thermometer.

"Knowing what he's like, would you want him back in your life?" Gary asked. "Would you want to marry him?"

"No," I said, surprising myself. "Lately, no."

"Time heals all wounds," Barrett said.

Indeed, but it's the sense of possibility that has soothed me. The slight change of focus. And perhaps, the wedding would just be an experience. Something to write about. That's what I like about writing—I can look on coldly: observing, hearing, and feeling, knowing all of life can be used on my own terms. Even when I was young I'd experience life this way. Always noting, always writing in my head, narrating my own steps. I can walk into that wedding with my mental pen and paper.

Beautiful white doves were released above the newlyweds. One pooped on the bride's soft and loose updo. Mele assured the bride that no one noticed

175

and that it blended right in to her shit-colored hair, then she danced with her date under the stars. She could feel him—

"Has it been enough time?" Barrett asked.

"I don't know," I said. "I think so." I took a sip of wine. "Henry mentioned maybe coming with me."

Barrett raised her eyebrows. "His wife's okay with that?"

"Well, yeah. I mean, you know. They're not even speaking to each other. Plus, we're friends. I'd be like a charity case. It would be like if I went with Gary."

Gary gave me a look like I wasn't making a very good case.

"I don't know," I said. "I kind of told Bobby I had a date." Admitting this seemed to confirm everything Barrett was thinking: that I wasn't psychologically ready, that I was hurting myself.

I left their house without a dress.

After a night with Tara and her tools, Ellie was craving princess books. I tried my best to not skip ahead or comment on all the extraneous adverbs, but with the nuptials creeping in like a tide, I couldn't help but ask Ellie some questions. In regard to the prince whisking off these chicks with their shy laughter and porn bodies, I asked: "How does she know she'll even like him? They never even spoke to each other. He could be a total loser. He could be like, 'Hi, wanna ride my horse.'"

"I want to ride his horse," she said and pulled the covers up to her chin.

"But why would she go off with a stranger who did nothing more than kiss her? I mean, is he stable? Does he work, or just live off his parents? What are his table manners like? His taste in music? His morals?"

"He likes silly music, I bet, and Bob Marley." She yawned, then said: "I'm not tired."

"Are you excited to be in a wedding?" I asked.

"Yes!" she said, holding her fists together.

"Would you be okay if Mommy wasn't there?" I didn't know if I wanted to hear the answer.

"Yeah," she said as if it was no big deal.

"Well, I might go," I said.

"Okay," she said, and then I had to stop myself with my petty baits and lures. *I wonder why Daddy didn't want to marry me? I wonder why Daddy doesn't spend more time with you?* Depressing, confusing questions from a depressed mom.

This was why Barrett and Annie thought I shouldn't go. They wanted me to cut ties, let Ellie have her own memory of the event, not pollute it with my needs.

I needed to let Ellie love what she wanted to love.

I closed the book. "Did you love the story?"

"I loved the story pretty much," she said.

I kissed her on the forehead. "Good night. Love you."

"Love you more," she said.

"Love you more." I stood and walked away, slowly to hear her shout: "Love you more!"

Each time this happens, I imagine her in the bed, mouth still open from yelling, hands gripping the sheet. She's expectant and wondering if there'll be one more answer from me or if that was all. Eyes wide open, waiting; the suspense coming from knowing the result and enduring. Every night the same thing for both of us, and yet still the hope from her that it's not over, the satisfaction for me to fulfill this wish. We've got this. The two of us. We've had another day together.

"Love you so much," I said, and then, softly she said: "Love you."

I don't always make good food choices for my child. Or parenting choices. I could have this all wrong, but as far as bedtime goes, I'm awfully proud to have created this routine.

Don't tell the admissions director she looks like a young Sophia Loren. She knows she doesn't. Julianne did this and the director was all "We don't use pop culture references here. And we frown upon character backpacks."

Don't send gift baskets from Neiman's or offer your Truckee condo. All of them have been bribed.

Don't give directors the first degree, especially during a tour with other parents. Ask them questions that will make them shine.

Definitely write a thank-you note to the admissions director after the tour. And write the head of the school. But don't go overboard. Maeve wrote a thank-you to the janitor for opening a door. That was noted. It completely ruined her.

—Advice given to a mother on getting her child into preschool. Overheard at Cow Hollow Playground

At this moment what scares you the most about raising your child?

I try not to bother with fear and hysteria, but I do have concerns. I'm concerned she may feel rejected by her father, but I was rejected by my father and I put it to good use. I'm concerned I won't be able to give her everything she wants, but you know? Tough shit, Ellie belly.

At this moment if I had to be afraid of something tangible, then I'd say I'm scared that she won't get into preschool. Yes, it's driving me a bit batty. I've done my research and have applied mainly to the ones that didn't require a visitor's fee. A *visitor's fee*—like the school is some kind of museum of stick-figure art. I also applied to co-ops, not knowing how I'll afford the seventeen-thousand-dollar tuition that most of these schools seem to ask for. How will we make it out of this city alive? That scares me: poverty. And I'm not, like, a poverty type of person. Sometimes I see the suburbs beckoning, but I won't look them in the eye. I'm not ready, I tell them. Let me try.

So I've been proactive, going on tours. My first was a co-op in the Outer Sunset, Way Outer. It seemed like a school for the last kids on earth who survived an epidemic. The parents formed a line outside, and I found myself counting them, figuring one of every three had hep C. I don't know why, the thought merely came to me, perhaps inspired by the sight of blond dreadlocks. I won't apologize for that. One can't control one's thoughts, only one's words, and I didn't say shit out loud.

So we walked around looking at preschool stuff, my thoughts drifting toward venereal diseases, when I felt something on the back of my upper thigh. Was it swollen? Did I bump into something? Have I already caught a human papilloma virus in this wretched place? I touched the spot, surprised by the softness, and then I felt the bump move—it began to slide a little toward my calf. When it reached the back of my knee I realized what was happening. What was happening was that I had to get my daughter into preschool in San Francisco, which is like trying to find a feminist in a polygamist community, and having dirty underwear balled up into the leg of my jeans wasn't a good start, because that's what the bump was—dirty underwear—and it was slinking toward my ankle.

"This is the climbing wall," the director said. "Volunteers worked all weekend to put it up, and the kids are just crazy about it."

I prayed my panties wouldn't make it down to my ankle, especially since I was wearing cropped jeans. I wondered if they were granny panties or lacy, sexy panties, and which would be less awkward to have fall out of my pants. The tour began to move from the climbing wall, and I tried to keep up with an inconspicuous slow walk, but I'm sure I looked like I was trying to scratch an itch in an unfortunate, private place. Joke's on me for thinking bad thoughts about the others, meanwhile they all probably thought I had a yeast infection. The whole situation of trying to keep my panties in my pants reminded me of when I used to pad my bra with those silicone falsies and sometimes my bra would come unlatched and I'd have to use my biceps and elbows to keep the fake boobs in place until the situation could be corrected. Once at a club, one of the boobs popped out on the dance floor and a guy picked it up and said, "What's this!" I snatched it from his hands like I was CIA and the booby was top-secret, like a bomb or the womb of an alien. "It's nothing," I said. "Just move along and get crunk."

I managed to creep forward. The tour came to a halt outside. I looked around for dogs, worried that one would come up and sniff my leg. Or a child with sensory spectrum disorder. The tour director smiled at me, and I tried to look as goony-eyed as the rest of the mothers there.

"I've been talking a lot," the director said. "Do you have any questions?"

"What do you do about the child's emotions?" one mother asked. She had gray hair, which is sort of rude, I thought. I mean, why can't she dye it? I'm very short, and so I always wear heels as an act of courtesy. I didn't understand the mother's question—"What do you do about a child's emotions?"

"What the hell are you talking about?" I asked. No—I didn't really. Apparently the director knew exactly what ol' Granny meant, because she nodded and immediately said, "We respect them. We respect all emotions. Even anger. If someone is angry, we'll say, 'Hey, when I'm angry, I like to throw a ball in an area where other children can't be harmed. When I'm angry'—and here she enacted anger, which made her look like she was reading very fine print—'I just want to pick up a ball and throw it as far as I can, after first checking my space.' Great question."

The questioner nodded and seemed very satisfied, as did everyone around me.

I felt like I could go. I had the pamphlet. The director just reiterated everything in it. It was like the first day of school, when the teacher just reads the syllabus. Plus, I don't really understand the intricacies of schools' philosophies—Waldorf, Montessori, Reggia Emilio. "We're play-based," they all say, and they all claim to provide a supportive and enriching environment. They value imagination and a child's uniqueness. Some value economic diversity, which seems to mean that they value extremely wealthy people so that they can let in a few poor kids and then write in their brochures, "We value economic diversity." They all purport that the children will thrive and grow, as opposed to rotting and receding like in those other preschools.

"What about separation anxiety?" another woman asked. I glared at her. Enough questions. Annie was watching Ellie, and I didn't want to be a bother. Plus, I'm a very quick person—quick to shop, make choices, quick to judge. My workday is quick, I read quickly, write quickly, and talk quickly, using very few words. When things don't happen quickly, I get very anxious and expect everyone else to sense this somehow, that I'm in a rush to go and get something else over with. I sighed, tapped my foot, then stopped, not wanting to trigger a panty avalanche. I looked around for someone who looked bored or impatient, but all I saw was sincerity. A mom with a buzz cut popped some sort of breath mint and chewed it with her front teeth like a rat. She offered one to her neighbor, a tall woman who slouched. She took the mint, which grossed me out.

"Some children experience sadness because they miss their parents and so they wear pictures of their mommies and daddies around their necks so when they get sad they can just look down," the director said.

I pictured Ellie wearing me, Bobby, and her cheesy stepmom around her neck.

After everyone's questions were answered and I thought I could finally go and take my panties out, we were led to the snack area, where a mom was placing grapes into tiny paper cups. I hobbled along.

"We take turns bringing a snack for the class," the director said. "But we're a nut-free facility." I looked around the room. One of the volunteer moms was dancing in the playroom to "Beat It." Nut-free? Sure you are.

"Also, your snack day is your day to clean the bathroom."

She smiled at everyone around her, and I chuckled along with the other parents, but then realized she was serious. I would actually have to clean a bathroom. Are you kidding me? I spend all week cleaning and cooking, and now I'd have to clean a school restroom? It also occurred to me that I'd have to interact with kids once a week, like teach them how to make something out of pipe cleaners and a milk carton, or dance around to Michael Jackson's "Beat It," which is a tad inappropriate at a preschool.

"We are a family here," the director said.

A writing instructor once told me to never use the word *beam* as a verb, but this woman was beaming at all of us, radiating groovy, nut-free love. I didn't want her in my family. I no longer cared if my underwear fell down. I wanted them to fall down and land on my foot. Then I'd kick my leg and the underwear would fly up and I'd catch it in my mouth. I didn't want to go to this preschool. I told Georgia I'd look at the co-ops she recommended—it would be nice to save some money, meet other parents, and see Ellie at school, but I didn't want to meet these kinds of parents. They were too happy with themselves, or something. I wouldn't fit in. I guess it would be like a real family.

All the parents stayed back to kiss ass. This whole process feels like we're trying to get into the hottest club in town. I left, not even taking an application. I was taking a risk, but hell, I guess I'm like all the other mothers in the San Francisco Mother's Club that I make fun of. I want my child to go to a school that doesn't return your phone calls, but expects you to check in every month to inquire about your position on the waiting list. I wanted a school that had kids who were vaccinated.

When I got to the street I crushed the flyer in my hand, then reached up my jeans for my underwear. The green silky ones with white polka dots. I walked to the car. It was like being back at college again, doing the walk of shame with my underwear in my pocket, vowing *never again*.

What will I do if she doesn't get in anywhere? I hear about this all the time, moms and their kids slumped at their windows, watching the neighbor kids skip to school. Something fierce pops up in a mom if she sees her child being shorted.

The next one wasn't any better, and it required I pay the seventy-five-dollar application fee before seeing the school and knowing whether or not I even wanted to apply.

Another co-op, but this one was in Laurel Hill. I got there early so I could walk in exactly on time. I needed to step up my game, even at the co-op "safety schools," and I'd heard great things about this one. Kids who go here go on to kindergartens I've never heard of, but that must be good because the brochure lists the schools proudly like they're celebrities. I had high hopes and envisioned the working parents sitting on beanbags and drinking coffee and talking about real estate.

This time I wore sensible shoes and checked my pants for balled-up underwear. I also did some research. I learned from my SFMC chat group that I needed to smile and ask good questions that gave the directors a platform to ramble on about their schools' unique qualities. They loved questions that weren't really questions, but more like little diving boards they could do cannonballs from.

This director had neat, cropped hair, and the parents on the tour seemed much more synthetic, which was great. We all walked around—the space was very nice and open with lots of room inside and out. I saw two girls playing together in the outdoor sandbox and was reminded of an old friendship. I was very sick one day at school and barfed on my friend Elena, and then Elena barfed in the sink so I wouldn't be alone. "See, I barfed a little, too," she said. I've always remembered that.

The memory was wonderfully timed because the director looked over and thought I was smiling at the girls and not my past. Five minutes into the tour and I basically knew everything I needed to, but the tour kept going. And going. We kept being marched along, the pleasant little tricycles and sandboxes and artwork beginning to feel like purgatory.

The director led us to the "Tree Room." Kids playing. Noted. Then on to the next room, where we had to pass an open bathroom. A row of low toilets led out to another open door. A little girl was standing in front of a toilet naked, and we all watched her reach around to wipe her butt. She looked at the toilet paper after she wiped, then dropped it into the toilet, flushed, then headed to the sink to wash her hands.

"Good job, Lily," the director said. "We let the children go naked if they want to." She held her hands together in front of her chest like she was in a choir.

Wait. What?

"It's a safe and protected place, and if it's something they choose to do then we follow their will."

One mom looked ecstatic. Another, afraid. I was very hesitant. I mean, there are countless pictures of my young self running around naked. My daughter loves to be naked and barefoot. My mom never slept with underwear on because she wanted to "let it breathe," which always made me think of a vagina inhaling and exhaling and snoring a little. But it was cold out! And there could be pervs with telescopes! What if the children wanted to douse themselves in Sunny D, then roll around in tuna fish? Follow their will?

We walked outside and I hugged my shoulders. Two boys yelled, "glug glug glug," and made airplane wings with their arms and crashed into each other. I pretended it was endearing. The worker parent looked at them, or through them, and I wondered what she was thinking about—probably groceries. That's what I do most of the time.

"As you can see," the director said. "Our parents are on the periphery. They don't instruct or guide, or interact. They are here only to make sure the children are safe. They keep their bodies safe and their feelings safe."

"So, we don't have to teach crafts or anything?" I asked.

"No. We do not expect you to teach in any way, and at our meetings we will equip you with the know-how to keep the kids safe, to do dispute resolution in a way that lets the kids solve problems for themselves. The meetings will be informative, and they'll give you the chance to meet, since you don't really have any contact with each other at school. We are here for the children."

Great. There goes my time to read magazines with other moms and talk about restaurants.

"These meetings are two Tuesdays a month, and you are expected to attend every one."

I quickly scanned my brain to think of what TV shows were on Tuesday night. It was a slow night, thank God, but then I thought of spring. *American Idol* auditions! All those deluded children!

"So, they just roam around from room to room doing whatever they please?" a mother asked, the one who looked worried about nakedness.

"Yes," the director said. "We're all about free will, free choice. The children decide what they want to do with their time. At circle time, they can come to the circle or they can elect not to."

I didn't like that one bit, but I pretended to be down. We walked back toward the entrance and the mother kept wondering out loud if this was the place for her son, who was having trouble focusing.

"I just think he needs structure, and with so much free choice and free play he may not function."

I envisioned a robotlike boy looking around at all his options and just sputtering and smoking and going in circles, saying in a scary android voice, "Too much data. Too much data."

This woman wasn't going to get in. Why was she expressing her concerns out loud in front of the director? Apparently she hadn't read the articles I'd read, which remind parents that they're being watched, not their children. They're the ones applying, and the directors are assessing if we'll be good volunteers, if we're rich, black, Asian, Mexican, gay, divorced. Your best bet is to be a gay, black, starving artist who has adopted kids. Try to be that.

I took an application, out of fear. I didn't want my daughter to go to this hippie naked school, but I was scared for her life, especially when I imagined Betts and the old playgroup, their rancid children all going to the best schools, where they'd learn to play golf and guffaw and turn green acreage into condo developments. Ellie deserved the same.

Which led me to a private school in Lower Pacific Heights. This was the one I want and the one I can't afford. It's purportedly one of the best preschools in San Francisco, the one Henry sent his children to.

I went with Barrett. We met in front and walked in together.

"If it's a guy doing the tour, should we unbutton our shirts a little?" Barrett asked.

"Sure," I said.

"I heard you're supposed to let the school officials know you can build a new playground, but have a friend mention it."

"I can't build a new playground," I said. "I can build a sand castle."

We walked in, put on name tags, and then about ten of us were led to a small room where we were given a speech by the director. I coached myself beforehand to pretend I was at a poetry reading: look like you understand, smile knowingly. I was going to try to pay attention because I always tuned out. Immediately I found myself lost in thought as the director spoke about the school's values: She's not wearing any makeup. No foundation, concealer, mascara. Look at those lashes. Like dandelions.

I tuned back in to hear her talking about things called "interfacing," "decompressing," and the "gross-motor room." She talked for about half an hour longer, and Barrett and I were really struggling. We were rolling our eyes and nudging each other, and holding back laughs. There's nothing better than to have a fellow eye roller, and Barrett was also a note passer. On one she drew a monkey sniffing his finger, and the thought of her taking the time to draw this made my chest and throat hurt. I could barely contain a burgeoning barking laugh, and I eventually had to cough to mask my snorting.

We were finally let out of that torture chamber, then split up into small groups. We were to go from classroom to classroom for "observance" and instructed not to talk to the kids and to sit only in the adult chairs. This was very important.

We walked quietly into the first room and sat and watched the kids doing the usual things: playing, talking. We just sat there like scientists watching apes. I leaned over intending to say to the mom next to me, "How long do we have to do this?" but noticed her scribbling copious notes and stopped myself in time. What did her notes say? *Kids are playing! Playing here and there, everywhere!*

"I cannot stress how boring this is," I whispered to Barrett.

"We watch our own kids do this every day," Barrett said. "What in the world are we supposed to be learning here?"

We did this in four more classrooms. I walked into the art classroom and watched the kids there. Exhausted, I sat down.

"Please sit in an adult chair!" a teacher said.

"Oh," I said. "Okay!"

"Jesus Christ," Barrett said. "You got verbally spanked."

I sat in a goddamn adult chair and watched the smocked kids paint. Big frickin' deal. Barrett kept shifting in her adult chair and picking at herself.

"What's wrong with you?"

"I have a vaginal wedgie," she whispered. "A veggie."

"Did you make that up?"

"On the spot."

"Quiet please," the teacher said.

I let out a loud yawn.

After "observance" we all came together to watch a class have a meeting in which they talked about yesterday's walk in the Presidio and the consequences of cutting in line; then the director took us to the outdoor play area and spent time talking about each and every play structure.

"These are the bikes," she said. "The children ride these in this area here. These are the bars that the children hang from."

Barrett and I did the stop, look, and roll.

"We're always looking for ways to improve this area," the director said.

"Are parents allowed to finance improvements?" a woman asked. We snapped our heads toward her. She had smooth brown hair and Tory Burch–like clothes. She looked like Bobby's fiancée—that same glossy perfection. I could just envision her on Instagram, looking down, laughing at a puddle.

"The school appreciates all contributions, especially since so many of our kids are on scholarship. We love help from parents!" The director laughed. The woman laughed. Ha ha ha! Ha ha! Ha ha!

"I told you," Barrett said. "She basically just promised a new playground. She's in."

I looked at the woman's tribal, leather handbag, alongside her hip. Did it just flip me off? I believe it did.

We then went through another of those inane lengthy question-and-answer sessions, and finally, two hours later, we were released. On our way out I noticed Ms. Philanthropist talking to the director.

"I have some tips," Barrett said. "Don't worry."

We picked up our girls up from Annie's, then went to my place to fill out our applications.

I'm always a little nervous when the kids are together. This makes things a little uncomfortable for me around Barrett. I don't know the etiquette for telling a friend's child to please stop fucking with mine. Fortunately the girls were doing well, painting at opposite ends of the table.

I took my time filling out the application, using my neatest hand-writing.

"After you mail this you need to call them every month." Barrett pointed her pen at me. "Start a relationship, a friendship. Show them how enthusiastic you are."

"Henry says I need to tell them I'm an ethnic writer."

"He's right."

I tried to imagine how I'd work in all of this information: "Hi, this is Mele Bart, a slightly ethnic, aspiring writer, and I'm calling to check on my status because I'm very enthusiastic about your school."

"I write a food blog," I said. "And I haven't published anything yet. And I'm just a little Hawaiian and a little Chinese."

"You're writing a cookbook," Barrett said. "So for ethnicity just double the recipe."

I looked at my daughter, Ms. Minority. Her skin is like my sheets: Oatmeal Linen. Her hair is wispy, thin, and straight, the color of straw, but on paper she'll be a brown girl with roots from afar. Polynesia, China.

"Have you asked Henry to the wedding yet?" Barrett asked.

"No," I said. I hadn't seen him in over a week. "It was a stupid idea."

She didn't disagree.

"What are your tricks?" I asked.

She was writing quickly, then stopped and looked up. "Tara is African American," Barrett said, then continued filling out her form.

"You're not really putting that, are you?"

"Of course I am. I did that National Geographic DNA thing. They said my ancestors were originally from Kenya."

"They can find that out?"

"Apparently."

"Yes, but all of our ancestors were from someplace like that."

"Then she's African American, too," Barrett said, tilting her head toward Ellie.

"I don't think the school means what is their nationality traced back thousands of years."

"Well, they don't specify."

I gestured to blond-haired, blue-eyed Tara. "I think they'll be a bit confused when they meet their new black student."

"It will be good for them. Teach them more understanding."

"Sister, I'm not sure about this," I said. "And I'm usually pretty immoral."

Barrett sighed. "Look. My daughter is unique and intelligent. She's diverse; she's a fuckin' sundry, and if this city is going to make it impossible for our kids to get into schools, then I'm going to match wits and beat 'em at their own game. Now, you say you're part Hawaiian? Hawaiians don't count for shit. They weren't totally persecuted. They're not living on reservations. They didn't have to sit in the back of the bus. They are, however, native to Hawaii. Hawaii is in America. And thus, your daughter is a Native American. You see how it works?"

"I can paint!" Ellie said. "I paint all of it all up." She put the paintbrush to her face. I didn't stop her. I remembered at carnivals getting my face painted, the cold, wet paint, the soft bristles of the brush.

"You see!" Barrett said, laughing. "One Who Paints on Face!"

I looked down at the ethnicity box (that would be a good band name). I sometimes picked Pacific Islander for Ellie and myself, but knew deep down that this wasn't really given much credit. When they saw this box checked, admissions officials most likely envisioned coconuts and hula dancers, an idyllic, balmy existence, before stamping ENTRANCE DENIED over Keolani Miller, or whomever.

"Her name doesn't sound Native American," I said.

"Doesn't matter," Barrett said. "Names get changed. Look at Ellis Island. Your last name could have been Wolfe Range, but your great-grandfather changed it to avoid persecution, or had it changed by some conformist boss. Tara's grandpappy could be Suge Knight for all they know. They can't question you."

"You're out of control," I said.

"Out of control," Ellie said.

Tara glared at Ellie and held her paintbrush tightly to her chest. "Mines!"

"You have to pay an application fee to even see some of these schools," Barrett said. "Some charge seventeen thousand dollars a semester. For preschool! Henry paid for that art room you saw. If you want to get in, you need to either build a new gross-motor decompression room or check the right box, and don't feel bad about it. Do it!"

I had filled in everything but the ethnicity box. My essay was two pages long. It had a thesis, body, and conclusion. It stressed how much time I had on my hands to volunteer.

"Did you do this for Jake?" I asked.

"Jake? No. And it took me three tries to get him into his old elementary school, so he entered late and he had no friends. He wouldn't listen or focus. He hit kids. He smelled everything, like obsessively. We thought he was on the spectrum for a while there. I'm not putting Tara through that rejection."

She looked at me with intensity. It was as if we were in the trenches and she was building me up to make a run for it. "Just do it," she said. "Do you want her to have no friends like my son?"

I thought of Betts enrolling Bella when she was still in the womb. I thought of that woman today, implying that she'd pay for a new play area. I thought of all the moms who had hired preschool consultants and of the school tours, the boredom, the time, the cost of applying, the effort to keep my knickers concealed.

"Do it," Barrett said. "This city is a battlefield. And we are warriors."

I looked at the black paint on my daughter's face and held my pen. Native American. Check.

*　*　*

So that's what scares me the most—not just preschool but the choices we make that herd us toward a certain point, making the other points and places fall away. I'm scared of my choices. I'm scared of what I'm capable of doing for my child, I'm afraid I've already taken too many bad turns and she'll look back at the map and say, "Why didn't you go here? Why did you turn there?" and *"Why can't we go back?"*

I know we're not supposed to use this forum to advertise our own business, but there have been so many posts on potty training that I thought it would help to let you know about the company I founded, Poop in the Potty Forever, LLC, which provides private education services and potty boot camps. My process involves interviews, observations, educating your children about their bladder and bowels, and devising a customized plan for your little learner. Contact me if I can help!

—Consultant Linda York, MA

I wanted to warn everyone about a business called We Fix Doors. I had an appointment with them, but found another company who could do it for a better rate. When I called to cancel, the repairperson hung up on me. I called back and he answered the phone saying, "F— you in the ass. F— you in the ass, you cheap bitch." And so I would not recommend We Fix Doors.

—Email response to a mother asking SFMC for garage-door repair recommendations

Mele finishes her post on saffron-roasted cauliflower. How she loves roasting cauliflower! It's like taming a shrew.

Ellie comes to the kitchen in her fourth outfit of the day. "Make it happen," she says.

Mele doesn't know where that came from, probably Michael, the boy from her daycare who has a head shaped like a football. She had heard his mom say to him one day, "Make today your best day," so figures it's one of his family's platitudes. Maybe she could have Ellie pass one along to Michael. He could go home saying, "Live like you'll die tomorrow" or "I don't sweat, I sparkle."

Mele grabs the Pirate's Booty and fills a baggie with carrots. "Are you sure you don't need to go potty?"

"I'm sure," Ellie says and lifts up her dress.

"Then we're off." Another afternoon doing the mom thing. Park, bath, dinner, bed, repeat, repeat, repeat. They are making it happen.

"Henry!" she says when she sees him at a picnic table. She exaggerates her enthusiasm, like they are buddies and everything is all g and normal and her heart isn't racing, her body not aflutter. It's so strange when you land upon the idea, the fact, that you're attracted to a friend.

It's like discovering something that was there the whole time. Like money in your pocket, or something in your purse you didn't miss but are so happy to find. Henry! It feels wonderful to want something, to be charged by something, to let her know she isn't dead down there. Mele had been beginning to accept a nunlike kind of living, but at the sight of him, she's thinking, *See ya, sisters, I'm dropping you like a bad habit.*

She walks in, closing the gate behind her. For the first time she feels single and happy about it. Married parents can't realize the significance of this simple thought and the healthy rise you get from believing it.

"Hey," Henry says, almost standing up. They give one another awkward high fives. He always looks so nice, though not overly styled. He wears Ray-Bans, a collared shirt, and jeans.

"We've missed you guys," she says, looking at Tommy.

"We went camping," Tommy says. "We camped a lot. We ate marshmallows, we had a wagon. It was my wagon."

"We went camping, too," Ellie says. "We built a fort."

Tommy stands with his hand on his hip, assessing if he is going to let this fly. Mele can read him. *Did she really go camping? That makes my camping less significant. How should I define myself?*

"Want to go down the pole?" Ellie says. "Only I can do it so."

"I can, too," Tommy says, seeing an opportunity to reinstate his masculinity, and they walk off. Mele looks after them, imaging them as siblings, then quickly pulls in the reins. How did it go from friendly attraction to stepmom? There seems to be little difference between young crushes and adult crushes: at both ages you are willing to compromise so much of yourself. Mele remembers during her freshman year in high school, she quit dance, something she loved, something she was so good at, just so she wouldn't miss Jared Terra's call. Cell phones must be changing young love lives.

"Sorry," Henry says. "I didn't let you know."

"About what?"

"Camping," he says.

She laughs and crosses her arms and sits down next to him. "Why would you need to let me know?"

She doesn't trust herself to look at him or to move. She would be so devastated if she is reading him wrong. He's like a hot drink. She has to go slow.

"We had dinner that night and I forgot to mention we'd be gone all week."

"You don't need to check in with me," she says. Her voice breaks a little, like she's gotten teary! How awful. She clears her throat. "Was it fun?" God, now her voice is husky. She pulls the zipper on her sweater up to her neck.

"I needed to get the kids out," he says. "Outside, not thinking about things. She's been with the guy for a year." He gazes out at the playground. "How was your week?"

She doesn't answer. Who knows what her voice would sound like? He turns his head. "What did you do?"

Okay then. She won't address the yearlong affair. They can always circle back. "I did preschool tours. They're horrible."

"I wouldn't know, to be honest," he says. He puts his ankle on his opposite knee, grazing her leg. "Kate just enrolled the first kid and the rest followed."

This is the opportunity. On the application she didn't end up saying that Ellie was Native American. Barrett chickened out, too, after Gary asked if she was all right in the head.

"Could I ask a favor?"

"Shoot." His face opens up and relaxes as though this is a relief to him.

"I visited Tommy's preschool and I really loved it. You must get asked all the time, and I don't know—"

"I'll call Ms. Eldridge tomorrow morning," he says and takes out his phone, perhaps writing it in his calendar.

She restrains herself from saying anything but "thank you." This is how the world works.

"Did you finish your book?" he asks.

"I got everyone's stories," she says.

"Yeah?" He looks over at her, genuinely enthusiastic.

"Yeah," she says, his energy affecting her.

"You should come over sometime, cook some of the recipes. For all of us," he adds. "Georgia, Annie, Barrett. The gang."

"Sure," she says. "Sounds good."

They stay for a long time that day. Tommy and Ellie hang from the bars, cross the wooden bridge, slide, and sit on stumps. There's an older boy near them, kicking sand and sucking a Popsicle. He wears shorts and has fresh wounds on his legs. He has long, dirty hair, and the skin around his mouth is stained red. He looks like Faye Dunaway in *Mommie Dearest* when she gets all crazy with the makeup. He puts his mouth around the Popsicle. In college, Mele knew some guys who were so afraid of seeming gay that they wouldn't suck on Popsicles or eat bananas.

"Too many babies here," he says to another boy who walks over. Henry and Mele exchange looks.

"You want to know a place that's baby-free?" the other boy says. He has khaki pants, longish black hair, and sad eyes.

"Where?"

"Under there." Mele looks under the wooden ramp that leads up to the hutch. "You know why?"

"Why?"

"Babies can't dig."

"That makes no sense," she says to Henry.

"If anything they can dig," he says. "These boys seem old to be here. They should be playing basketball or smoking or something."

"Is your mom here?" they hear the tough boy ask.

The boy in the khaki pants points to the bench. "She's over there."

Mele looks at a woman in the distance sitting on the green bench. She loves listening to kid conversations.

"But she's not my mom. She's my babysitter. I have two babysitters."

"Why?"

"'Cause I was adopted."

"Oh," the tough boy says. "How do you know?"

"My second mom told me."

"How come you were adopted?"

"I don't know. Someone needed money."

The boys walk off, leaving Henry and Mele a bit bewildered.

"That was something," Henry says. "I love stuff like that."

"Me, too," Mele says. "How old do you think they are?"

"Around nine," Henry says without hesitation. She guesses it's because he's known that age before. She can't imagine Ellie as a nine-year-old. What will that look like? Maybe a parenting trick is to look at your child and think to yourself: *You will be five years older than you are right now.* This age will be over and you will rejoice and you will mourn.

Ellie comes over and smiles at Henry and pats his knees. Henry swoops her up, kisses her head, then hands her to her mother. It feels like the most intimate thing in the world.

"We better get going," Mele says, standing up.

"No!" Ellie says and sprints toward Tommy by the ladder.

"Have you ever been to Nopa?" Henry asks. "Right down the street. We could walk with the kids."

"They'd love that," she says and thinks of Courtney talking for her baby. Parents use their kids all the time. "Ellie needs a nap" often means "I'm dying to get out of here."

"They're so cute together," she says, watching Tommy push Ellie's butt so she can reach the next rung.

"They can have their second date," he says.

Wine, dinner, company. No bath, dinner, repeat. She's warmed by what life can do sometimes, and by the second glass of cabernet.

The children share the pappardelle, recalling *Lady and the Tramp*. She and Henry share the asparagus with duck egg and fried leeks, the avocado toast with pickled jalapeño and smoked cheddar, and when the kids are still content, still civilized and users of inside voices, they continue on to the porchetta and halibut.

Mele tells him the story about momentarily stealing the belt.

"I know every one of them," he says. "My wife's friends."

She looks down, avoiding commentary. She imagines Kate is like Betts, an expensive though minuscule appetizer. When it arrives you know it's valuable, but you're still like, "What am I supposed to do with that?"

Henry circles back to Kate, though he uses code names and code words, so Mele feels like a spy. Kate is "Karl." Divorce is "Diabetes."

"Karl said that God brought them together," Henry says. "Karl and this other man. He has a bumper sticker on his car that says KITE SURFING IS REALITY."

"Well," she says. "Maybe it's better than JOGGING or BIRD WATCHING IS REALITY." God, was that lame? She puts her hair up in a ponytail. If only guys knew girls fidget with their hair when they find them attractive.

"So she said she couldn't ignore this gift of love from God."

"What did you say to that?" She bites into a trumpet mushroom and tastes basil, pine nuts, and hope.

Henry grins and blinks, recollecting some private moment. "I said, 'Jesus Christ,' then made the sign of the cross with my middle finger."

His teeth are tinted with red wine. It conjures the image of Bobby, coming home late at night, purple teeth, a smoky T-shirt. She sees Henry doing the same, stumbling home with secrets. What is Kate's side of the story? Henry places his hand on his son's head, his grin falling away, and Mele feels suddenly self-conscious sitting across from him. She must look so small and unkempt compared to his wife. She wipes her mouth with her napkin.

"I can't believe she's friends with those ladies from my old playgroup. We could have been in the same group." She laughs and looks down. "I didn't quite fit there."

Ellie and Tommy are going through their fourth bread basket.

Henry leans forward. "They're older, that's all," he says but looks away, knowing that wasn't all. He seems to be giving up on something. "You'll find your way."

She thinks of him in his kitchen, advising his son and his friends, and she feels a bit like a student. She wonders then if that's how he sees her, as a friend he is looking out for, himself as a mentor—someone who can help her along. She likes the idea of that, but it takes her down to a lower groove.

"Thank goodness you didn't fit in," Henry says. "We wouldn't have met."

"Yeah!" she says. "And what would these guys do without each other?" Ellie and Tommy are poking holes in the bread and putting them up to their faces to see out of.

Her heart races. She takes her hair out of the ponytail, then puts it into a low bun. Her leg touches his under the table.

"Sorry," she says.

"I don't mind," he says.

This just isn't a good idea. They are friends. It is healthy. Right now nothing has happened. She can ignore the innocent flirtation and they can split the check and call it a night. He's married. He's rebounding. Who's to say he isn't just like Bobby?

He's not like Bobby, though. Deep down, she knew who Bobby was and what he was capable of when they first met. Bobby was a trend. Henry is a staple. Henry is an evolved ham and cheese sandwich, what you long to come home to when you slip out of your dress and into a big T-shirt.

Mele takes a deep breath, feeling a tightening, a sweet heat, and moves her leg back next to his.

What are your goals for this book?

I'm not dead down there! I want to have sex! I masturbated for the first time in maybe a year! Seriously, this is huge!

That isn't the goal for this book, but I have to say that maybe writing this has led to something, which is why I embarked upon this hogwash in the first place—to lead to something, to simultaneously take me away and bring me back. I'm such a better parent when I'm happy. I have a sense of humor! But not a sarcastic humor. A Barney-ish one. I'm a Barney!

So. Today I got my hair done—up there and down there, too, just because. I'm feeling like a woman again, and I really wanted to get all girly and smooth, and I even danced a little naked in front of the mirror, making sexy faces, my hair blown out, my privates all porno, and I have to say, when Ellie went down for a nap, I gave a little somethin' somethin' back to myself—again! I haven't thought about sex in so long. I felt like a twenty-two-year-old! Kinda sad, but besides Bobby I never really had adult relationships, just youthful encounters that filled me with dread.

I remember enduring conversations like this:

Guy: Take off that skirt, girl. They call me the plumber 'cause
    I can fix it.
Me: I'm not wearing a skirt.

Or this:

Dude: Look at that. My mojo is rising.
Me: Wow.

Or this:

Boy: Have you ever done it wheelbarrow style?
Me: No.
Boy: What about tractor?

I tried to envision this, but couldn't. "No. But I've done it big-rig style," I lied, having no idea what I was talking about.

Last:

Drunk Man: Do you want to sit in the cockpit?
Me: That's so lame. (Bottle of wine later) Ready for takeoff,
    Captain.

I could fill a book with romance. I never thought I wanted to add to this book; I thought I was okay being done with the chapters on sex and wannabe love, but something is bubbling all right, and yes, Henry is the catalyst, but it's the concept of him, the belief that I can move forward that brightens my day and my vagina. It's not like I'm expecting something to happen with him, but the flirtation is enlivening, like a cool night and the sight of stars.

Tonight, I made Pad Ma Coeur just like the last time when I got my wax, but now it has such better connotations. A Brazilian no longer equals Bobby, loneliness, and humiliation. It no longer harkens to Ellie and our insulation. A Brazilian wax equals hope, happiness, and possibilities, and just maybe it equals Henry Hale.

So, the goals for the cookbook. Of course I hope that the dishes turn out well. I hope they make you happy. My goal is that you like the food, and that you like us, I guess. My playgroup. Here we are—family-style.

My goal is to reduce our lives into something tangible, edible. How can we bake our joys and complications into something someone will want to pick up and put in their mouth? Eat me. That's what I'm saying with this book. Bite and savor me.

There's something else, too. This happened months ago and I hate thinking about it. I was so angry with my Ellie. I don't remember why. She ran away when I was trying to leave Annie's house. She made it impossible to leave. Something small that seemed big at the time. Yelling always makes it worse, but sometimes I just give in to the anger because it's exhilarating to feel. She cried in the car, rattling me into a tizzy, and this awful adrenaline was electrifying me. I reached back and slapped her hand. Then I told her I was going away and wouldn't come back. She started to cry, and a part of me was so satisfied, so happy that the thought of my leaving was making her sad. It's the worst thing I have ever done to her. But hours later, blank slate. She ran to me after her nap, hugging my legs. "Mommy."

Whenever I have a hard time with her, whenever I feel sorry for myself that I'm going at it alone, I think, This time right now will be over. Gone. She used to wrap her legs around me and do a little humping motion on my hip. Gone. She used to sit in her high chair and screech, then look around as if she didn't know where the sound was coming from. Gone. She used to sleep with her arms up like a football goal. Gone.

Maybe my objective is to have this book as a keepsake, knowing that this time will disappear like today and yesterday. Like handprints on a cold glass window. Here's some proof that she was my little baby, my little girl. Here's evidence that I had these friends that kept me company and let me get to know them. Here are these friends, and one night I fed them at Henry's house.

What is your proudest moment?

The day I gave birth. No, not really. I'm sure everyone is going to say that, but when I gave birth I didn't feel proud. I was scared shitless. I wasn't sure how to hold her, and she made my boobs hurt so bad. The pain was worse than the actual birth. Why doesn't anyone tell you that you need a goddamn epidural to breast-feed? Each tug that gives your baby sustenance makes you cry in agony. No husband holding my hand and feeding me ice chips. Bobby was at work for most of the labor. No parents holding my hand or a mirror so I could see the birth. I held the mirror myself and was not proud of what I saw in the reflection. And then when she was out and placed on my deflated belly I still wasn't proud, necessarily. I'm sorry, Ellie. You are beautiful, but when I first held you, you were slimy, red, and wet and you mewed like a kitten.

But the epidural—that was amazing. I want one right now. There's nothing worse than those moms who brag about their epidural-free childbirths. They're probably the same ones who get molds of their bellies or have professional photos taken of them while they're pregnant strolling down the beach in translucent skirts, using their fingers to make the shape of a heart around their belly buttons, totally blissed out when really they're probably passing gas and thinking about pork rinds.

Last night I made my friends a few of the dishes inspired by them, and I guess I was proud that I pulled it off.

It was the first time any of us had seen Henry's house.

Annie and I arrived at the same time.

"This is insane," said Annie, who has a gorgeous home in her own right, but this was a bit beyond. This was a freestanding home on a quiet, wide street, with the city at its feet. The home had a brick facade, a deep portico entry, and in the front swath of lawn there was a towering sculpture of a cheetah on its hind legs, water spouting from its mouth into a birdbath. I sort of thought it was a disclaimer saying, "Yes, this house is huge, but we're not like our parents. We have money, but we're ironic!" I remember Henry once told me that on their block, the neighbors fought via yard art.

We hobbled up the path to the front door, both of us sore from yesterday's workout. Annie has recruited me to the Bar Method. She has found a babysitter with a pierced nose, vocal fry, and who calls Max "bro" and "M-dog," so she's happy. The class is ridiculous—you just move your pelvis back and forth and do pliés, and by the end you're groaning and your legs shake rapidly like a wet Chihuahua's. Then you lie on your back and basically hump the sky while listening to elevator rap.

Henry opened the door. There was that wide smile and expression that seemed to be holding back laughter.

"Ladies," he said. "Welcome. Come on in."

We came on in, walked through a wide hall, and past a staircase. "Rooms," he said, pointing up. "Kitchen," he said, pointing to the right as if that was all there was to see.

The home was beautiful, carefully curated, but warm and lively with colorful furniture and artwork. He didn't give us a tour, thank God. One, because it would take so long, and two, there's something awkward about tours, being led from room to room and feeling obligated to comment on everything.

He got Annie a glass of wine, then led me to the kitchen.

"Can I help?" he asked.

"You just go enjoy yourself," I said, but he stayed anyway, orientating me. He'd step out to talk to the others, then come back to check on me. It felt like we were hosting a party together. It was more intimate than our legs touching under the table. When I was done he carried out one of the dishes: Blue Cheese Greens, inspired by him.

"Serve immediately before your marriage is over," he said.

I found myself smiling long after he was gone. I was so comfortable in the kitchen, so cool, dark, and clean. White kitchens are the trend, but I like the ones that harken back. I like the grays and browns, the stone and beams. I filled another bowl with salad. This used to be a favorite of Bobby's as well, back when he cooked for me. God, I thought he was so dick-napped back then, so whipped you could spread him on toast, but of course he was. I was a mistress, a secret. I know I need to watch out with Henry. It's possible that both of us aren't seeing very clearly. We're responding to something, flying like pinballs and colliding into one another. I don't care though. I'm in a place where I need to collide and make mistakes and masturbate. I won't know if it's a mistake until I try.

When I walked into Henry's living room, I stood back for a moment, observing everyone talking in front of the huge arched windows with views of the terrace and beyond that, the bay, Golden Gate Bridge, and Alcatraz. Barrett and Annie were eating the Sloppy Joe trumpet mushroom sliders. The kids were swarming over the s'mores cake. It was the blue hour of night, where everything was hushed and vivid, the bay a dark sheet between us and the lights from Belvedere. His house was spectacular, but it was more spectacular seeing Henry in it, as opposed to the Panhandle, and how he fit both settings. Both were his realm.

Georgia and Chris, her older son, were in the corner of the room, sitting on cushions in front of a low circular table. They were eating the artichoke dish, inspired by her story of his stint in jail. I walked over to them, and they were laughing at something.

"What's funny?" I asked.

"The artichokes," Chris said. "My mom and I ate at this lookout once and she thought the artichoke gang was coming to take us down. Effing classic."

Georgia looked at me, with a funny grin, a closed smile that ran horizontally. Chris had no idea he was eating his story.

Barrett's son, Jake, walked over to Chris with a piece of the s'mores cake. He was so cute, I couldn't imagine him getting all o.g. in the basement. Chris looked at the huge piece of cake. "That's my kind of salad," he said.

"I love this," Georgia said, holding up the hors d'oeuvre.

And I loved that disappointment had become an adventure. Her son's mess was now an artichoke, and a moment in a beautiful living room with his mother. If nothing else went right this week, this year even, there was always this. Georgia picking something from his hair, Chris cringing, then seeing what it was. I felt like I was watching a most unimportant moment that was somehow momentous.

Barrett saw me watching everyone. It was weird that I knew all the backstories to the dishes; the others knew only theirs, and only their versions.

"Supergood, Mele," Barrett said. I walked toward her. "We're rooting for you."

"Thank you," I said, taking that to mean more than the competition. They were rooting for me to succeed as a mother, a writer, and a woman who wanted so many things.

At the end of the party I told Henry I'd clean up even though he said someone was coming in the morning. I rolled my eyes and went to the kitchen, putting leftovers into Tupperware. When I came out, he was on the couch with Tommy and Ellie.

"We should get going," I said.

He got up and walked us to the front door. Ellie almost escaped me to run up the staircase, but I caught her. I did not want to see bedrooms.

"Come on," I said and held her hand. "Stay the course."

There wasn't any evidence of children. Everything was put away, sort of like at Betts's house. The entry was spare and modern with herringbone floors, two iron sculptures framing the front door. I could imagine a designer telling Kate to step out of her comfort zone and embrace bold neutrals. I never wanted to leave.

"Thanks so much for doing this," I said.

Henry stood close. "Thank *you*," he said. "I liked my salad. And my sandwich, good God. It's exactly what I wanted. What I want every time I go out." He tucked a strand of hair behind my ear.

Oh, how I wanted a nanny right then to whisk the children away.

Then I heard a door from the kitchen opening, the splash of keys on a counter. It wasn't my fairy nanny—it was Henry's wife.

She came into the hall and looked me over. "Oh. Hello," she said.

She turned to Henry and leaned in for what looked like a staged kiss, or maybe it was real. Had God told her to come back to him? I felt both protective and naïve.

I noticed Tommy stayed by his dad, holding his leg.

"So you're the one in my parking spot," Kate said and laughed.

"Oh sorry, I . . ." I felt spotlit like one of the sculptures.

"It's totally fine," she said. "I forgot your playdate thing was today. I'm Kate. Are you the chef?"

"Of sorts. This is Ellie. I'm Mele. Nice to meet you."

"Molly?"

"Mele," I said. "Like . . . Mele. Not to be confused with Melee, though that suits me, I guess. I'm a state of tumultuous confusion. Anyway. It's Mele. Hawaiian for 'song.' Rhymes with Pele, the goddess? Or the soccer player?" I cleared my throat. "Molly works too."

She smiled and hum-laughed.

I kind of really hated her immediately. Her hair was sandy and warm, her eyes, a cold blue. She wore a blouse that could be hideous on someone else, but on her looked like art. Half of it was white, the other half was like a Rothko. Her pants were black, fitted; heels, black with gold cube studs.

Ellie was doing the pee-pee bounce, and I wanted to get out of there before she said anything. I did not want to ask this woman to use her bathroom.

"Say, hon," Kate said, touching Henry's hand. "We need to get going. Starts in half an hour. Tommy, Desiree is in the kitchen with your dinner."

"I already ate," Tommy said.

"Well, go on and say hello to Desiree."

Tommy slumped toward the kitchen.

Henry gave me a look I couldn't really interpret. "Thanks again." He opened the door for me, patting my back when I was outside.

I couldn't look at him. "Bye, Mr. Henry!" Ellie said. I let her do the farewell for me. We walked down the steps to the garden. There were frickin' flowers everywhere. It smelled so good. This stand-alone-house thing was killing me. I thought of my mom, leaving my slacker dad to go find a ladder to climb up. Go for it, I thought. I mean, what the hell.

Whoops. I realize I was relating my proudest moment story and not my story of abashment. I guess I was proud for leaving with my head held high. Or fairly high. If you were looking at me from the back, I personified aplomb. I was aplomb shell. When Ellie started to exclaim she really, really had to pee, I did not go back to the castle and beg for plumbing. I told her to squat next to the cheetah.

If you could construct an interview for yourself, what questions would you want to be asked?

How do you keep in such great shape?

This isn't a question, but I just wanted to say how slamming you are. You don't look like a mother. I mean you could be in *Maxim*'s Hot 100.

Oh, thanks. That's so sweet.

And one more question: Where did you get that beautiful belt?

Henry called yesterday, and asked me to meet at the park.

"The skate park," he clarified. "In Pacifica."

Ellie and I set off, and it was good to do something new. We wound down to the coast, the dark sea with its raging whitecaps, such a different ocean than the one I was used to with its saccharine blues, the visible reefs and sand on the ocean floor. But I liked this Pacific, too, the moodiness of it, the dark mystery.

"You excited to see Tommy on his skateboard?" I asked E.

"Yeah," she said. "I like Bob Marley music, too, sometimes."

It was what we were listening to. She heard "Redemption Song" on the radio once. I told her who sang it, and now she demanded Bob Marley all the time.

"How come you like Bob Marley?" I asked.

"Because . . ." I looked at her in the rearview, watching her think—it's so neat that she thinks, she considers and reflects.

"Because I like Bob Marley music sometimes," she said.

"Me, too," I said.

We pulled into the lot and saw Henry leaning against the gate. He was wearing a trucker hat, jeans, and a T-shirt, and had a skateboard, which made me laugh.

"What's funny?" Ellie said.

"Nothing," I said. "Look at Mr. Henry. He looks like a kid."

We walked in the gate to the big cement bowl. I love the sound of wheels rolling over cement. The last time I was at a skate park was in Woodland Park, Colorado, watching my boyfriend and trying the little half-pipe myself when no one was looking. It was my senior year of college, and I was young enough to believe that fathers didn't skate. There was a very clear line between a kid and a grown-up, and maybe I assumed you crossed this line in an instant, leaving youth behind. It would be like going through customs. But there was Henry, a forty-five-year-old socialite dropping into a cement pool. *Socialite* is the wrong word. Man. He was a man who smuggled his youth past customs.

I was angry when I left his house the other day, but then I thought it was a good reality check. There was nothing, really, to be mad at. If Ellie hadn't been born, it would have been my obsession—how he felt, what was happening, were he and Kate back together? But now, with my daughter, my life wasn't hinging on him.

I heard Henry yell, "Ow," and then he trudged out of the pool with his board, Tommy following behind with a wide smile.

"Do you need a Band-Aid?" Ellie asked.

"I need a younger body," he said.

"I'll get a Band-Aid." She began to run off, but I stopped her. There were too many places to fall and who knew when a skater or a board would erupt out of the pool. It upsets her so much when I thwart her missions. "I just have to um, um, um," she said. "I just need to get a Band-Aid!"

Henry distracted her with his board. He helped her onto it, held her hands, and slid her back and forth. She looked like she was walking for the first time, grinning like she couldn't understand who was moving her legs. And then she got off, bored, and moved to a corner curb, where she began chattering away, playing school, telling the imaginary children to crisscross applesauce.

"So," Henry said.

"So," I said.

"Sorry it was awkward the other night."

"It wasn't awkward," I lied.

"Tommy!" he called. "Stay on this side. Let the big kids go on that side."

More people were starting to show up, and ironically they were all men, not boys. Thirty-five-, forty-year-old guys.

"I mean, it was awkward," I said. "But I'm not sure why. It wouldn't have been awkward if . . ."

"If . . ."

"If there was something . . . we're friends," I said, cringing at the word.

"We had a school conference," he said. "That's why she was over."

"Cool," I said. "You don't need to explain."

A boy slid up and out of the bowl, catching his board and eyeing Henry. He looked about eight years old.

"You better wear helmets," he said to us. "Or the cops will bust you."

"They'll bust us for not wearing helmets?" Henry asked.

"No, they'll bust you for being gay."

Henry and I looked at one another and then at this kid. "What?" Henry said.

The boy had rusty blond hair and a shirt with holes in it.

"Why would they do that?" Henry asked.

"I don't know," the kid said.

"All right, dude," Henry said. The kid shoved off.

"Kids are so weird," I said. "Remember those two the other day?"

"Yeah. They're such weirdos." He crinkled his nose and looked out toward the ocean. "We like each other," he said. "We always have. But now it's something more. That's why it was awkward."

I looked out at the sea, the grays and deep blues, the seagulls diving, then being lifted by the wind.

213

"I like you?" I said.

"Yeah. You like me." He tilted his head down and looked up at me with an expression that was both confident and inquiring.

"Do you want to go to a wedding with me?" I asked.

"I like weddings," he said.

Ellie had recruited Tommy into her school. He sat on his skateboard and listened to her many rules.

"Are we just pinging off our disasters?" I asked, regretting how dramatic that sounded. But this, potentially, was dramatic stuff. This was children and marriage and lust and love and friendship. In our own spheres this mattered.

"We're always bouncing off something," he said. "Let's go to this wedding. We'll take it from there. Actually, let's go to lunch first. Take it from there."

We walked to our cars, planning to meet at the Tipsy Pig. As Ellie and I were backing up, he knocked on my window. I put it down, and he handed me an orange box wrapped with dark brown ribbon. An Hermès box. I knew that inside I would find a belt.

"What's this for?" I asked.

"It will help keep your pants up."

We both cringed at the same time.

"That was horrible," he said.

"So wrong," I said.

At Nopa he had listened to my story about my belt theft, then gone out and tried to buy me the very same belt. He was listening to me, then later, thinking of me. It was more than Bobby had ever done. There's such magic in the simple act of attending. I couldn't wait to open the box. It would be like opening him, opening a memory, opening the thought of his absurd and touching act.

"Thank you," I said. Thank you so much.

* * *

Some days I can't stand San Francisco. You can never get a cab and it's cold in the summers. I get irritated by the urine-scented sidewalks, moving the car with Ellie on street-cleaning days, finding parking far away and carrying all the accoutrements of children. The Haight street kids asking for change—I want to tell them to get a job or dip into their trust funds. Then in SoMa the young dudes and girls walking fast, talking into their headsets, the bicyclists, the protest signs—NO WAR FOR OIL, always simplistic, and I mean, if there ever was a reason to go to war . . . and then the parades and fun runs, the naked men with withered genitalia, the paint on the homes—green, blue, pink, orange. The pushy moms, pushy kids. It's like being in the Willy Wonka factory.

Other times, like now, I see sparkling buildings underneath puffs of fairy-tale fog. I see impossible bridges and streets that feel like roller coasters. I see vast parks, sharp cliffs, an endless, cryptic ocean. A place that finally feels like home.

Has my tone changed since I began this questionnaire? I feel a bit mushy, soft-serve versus hard-packed.

How does that make you feel?

It makes me feel like slow-cooking. Something warm and nourishing. Something to share, taste, and inhale, a phenomenon to mark the end of these blues. It makes me feel like I'm ready to take on more than just this cookbook. I'm ready to write a story, and I'm ready to turn the page.

We are looking for housekeeper referrals. Ours is continuously misrepresenting her work. When I asked her about the fireplace mantels, baby changing table, LR, DR, and Kitch, at first she lied and said she did clean them, but then backtracked when she saw my finger pick up dust in all these places. When I asked about the mopping, she claimed to have wiped down all the floors by hand with a wet rag, which I might have believed if she'd gotten the sticky spot in the hallway where my daughter spilled yogurt yesterday. Another lie. Can anyone recommend an honest worker?

—Gina C.

Can anyone recommend a good spoon to gag myself with?

—A.L., West Portal

PERFECT GUESTS

Before the wedding that afternoon, Mele has Barrett and Annie over to look at Bobby and Eugenia Avansino's website. She never said her name aloud before, even in her head, but now she is letting it replace variations on *cheese*. She has a name that guarantees a stylish life—an editor at *Vogue*, a noted tastemaker, or what she is: the founder of Avansino Creamery and the soon-to-be-wife of Bobby Morton. Georgia and Chris drove Ellie out to the wedding this morning, the kindest favor, from both of them, though Mele has a feeling Georgia and Chris like the excuse to take long drives together.

In Mele's bedroom, Barrett reads the wedding story from their webpage out loud with a neutral, melodic voice.

"It all began with the wedding announcements, which were simple and clean, with a touch of boho style. We introduced our colors: sun-kissed shades of lemon and orange, and our signature flower, the African daisy, which personifies our over-the-top playfulness."

"Bobby's playful all right," Mele says. "While she was picking the signature flower he was playing with my boobs."

"Shhh!" Annie says. "No bitter Betty, remember? You're healing. You're impenetrable."

And so Mele continues flat-ironing her hair while listening to the engagement story, how he popped the question and a bottle of champagne on the balcony of their hotel in Positano, the silky Tyrrhenian waters and Lattari Mountains their only witnesses. She listens, and it's okay. In fact, she feels a little bad for Eugenia, who had to work so hard to edit the story. In her adaptation there is no baby, no other woman, no deceitful fiancé. There are just lemon and orange trees, sunsets on the Amalfi Coast, fishing boats and such. Then back to reality—juggling schedules—burgeoning companies, new restaurants, living long distance, delays due to "unexpected success in the workplace," planning a wedding that would be stunning, stirring, yet understated, and the delightful addition to their family: Ellie.

Mele checks her temperature. It's a little high, but she'll survive. If they want to pretend Ellie materialized like a fairy, so be it. Mele is surprisingly even.

"Sorry about the cookbook," Annie says, though she looks like she's trying to hold back laughter.

"It's okay," Mele says, and it is okay. If she was going to publish a book, it wouldn't have its seeds in SFMC, and she likes her final product even if the judges did not. She had no way of knowing Courtney, Kate's best friend, was on the steering committee and read every word. Courtney, whose baby Mele said either resembled John Madden or looked like she was on Klonopin. Probably both. Courtney, whose belt she left on the hot, pissy sidewalk. Courtney, whom she may have called a catty-scanning, festival-ready bee-atch. Courtney did not appreciate her writing.

Mele will stick to fiction.

And now, an hour later, a knock on the door.

"He's here!" Barrett and Annie say in unison and run to the door.

Mele feels both embarrassed and bolstered by their enthusiasm. They would never run to the door if their husbands were behind it, but this is sport to them. She should have made them some hot dogs.

Mele gets her clutch and ducks into the bathroom to take a last look. She hears them in the entryway. "Henry, you look so dapper!"

"Wasn't expecting a cheer squad, ladies," he says. "I love it."

She looks in the mirror, and you know? Her reflection is quite nice—there she is, this person she's been for so long. This person, constant and dynamic. She sees Ellie's hazel eyes, the light spray of freckles on her cheekbones. It's not often that they're apart for an entire day, and seeing pieces of her daughter in this reflection is more sustaining than love from any man or any friend. Her DNA is in Mele, just as Mele's is in her. They're apart and always together.

She straightens the Dora-sticker potty chart next to the mirror, checks her teeth, and prepares to walk out to Henry. She laughs to herself at these actions—straightening a sticker chart to walk out to a man who's accompanying her to Bobby's wedding. Time not only lessens pain and recolors it; time reveals life's abundance, its ability to astonish, give, and take away. She turns off the light and walks out to the front door.

"Ready," she says, looking up and smiling, mouth closed, at Henry, who looks, for the first time, slightly shy. "You look great," she says. She knew he would, but this is just right. He looks handsome in a suit with an unexpected gray and white aloha shirt beneath. Dapper, with a touch of humor, a subtle nod.

Her friends step away and she feels self-conscious, like they're her ladies-in-waiting retreating, heads bowed.

"Hi," he says and kisses her on the cheek, then immediately opens the door, ushering her out.

"Bye, ladies," he says.

Mele can tell they want more—they have more to say, more to fuss about.

"Good luck!" Barrett says.

"Bye," she says.

"Text us!" Annie says, and he closes the door. Then he stands facing her, taking in her gold and cream Alice and Olivia dress. It's fitted on top—a bit like a bustier, then from there flows to the ground. Her hair is down, natural, loose. She knows then that he didn't expect her friends to be there and didn't want to chat and banter with the girls. This isn't a playdate. He is here just for her.

"You look beautiful," he says.

"I clean up?"

He doesn't joke back. He smiles, almost sadly, but in that way where wistfulness and optimism are bound so forcefully. At least that's how she feels as he puts his hand on her lower back and pushes her forward.

Forward to Bobby's wedding, this union that she and her pregnancy delayed for more than a year; this event that has tormented her for so long. Henry seems to detect her nervousness during the ceremony. He is a presence beside her, a quiet one that she doesn't need to speak to or entertain. He is just there with her. She uses her skills, pretending to be a social diarist, coldly watching a couple she doesn't really know at all:

The country estate is elegant, the signature colors well represented on the floral centerpieces, cupcakes, and pedestals upon which violinists sit.

The bride and maid of honor arrive with panache in an MG, one of the bride's dad's classic cars. The bride wears a chic and understated gown. Her breasts look amazing and most likely, always will. Her hair is in an intricate updo that no dove has soiled.

Ellie is glorious, walking down the aisle with her basket, and throwing her African daisies. She doesn't scatter or sprinkle or float the flowers. She really chucks them at the ground like she's flicking mud off her hand. Mele Bart is so proud.

And then the I dos, the rings, the laughter, the kiss (Mele doesn't look away), a hip, exit song, and it's over. Done.

Mele ditches her remote surveillance—"Let's get a drink," she says—and decides to fully attend the party.

"That was nice," Henry says as they walk across the lawn toward the bar.

"Lovely," she says, and they look at one another and laugh. What else is there to do? To say?

She drinks Veuve and eats crab legs and oysters from a table sculpted of ice. She walks out toward the kids to party with her little Ellie, who is buzzed on chocolates and cake and sparkling apple cider. She watches her run, unleashed, with the other children, who are all being supervised by the provided babysitters on the sprawling lawn. They are like free-range chickens. An older couple sits at the edge of the tent away from the adults, watching the kids, and she wonders if one of them is their grandchild or if they're just here to avoid socializing. She does that sometimes, excuses herself to check on the children just to watch them play and be in her own thoughts.

"One of yours out there?" the man asks. He's tall and very thin, his legs crossed at the ankles, revealing fantastic, orange socks.

"Yes," she says. "Ellie. She's almost three."

"Are you a friend of Eugenia?" the woman asks. Her outfit is finely put together—pearl earrings, long green dress, a bold gold necklace—except for an old white scarf she wears around her shoulders. Mele's grandmother Eleanor was the same way, carefully coiffed in a good-spirited versus fussy way, and always with her a white shawl, in her purse, or on her shoulders, or later, on the back of her wheelchair—it didn't matter if it matched. It was a staple, a comfort, like a child's blanket.

"I'm an old friend of the groom's," Mele says, finding warmth in this couple, the way they remind her of her grandparents, both dead, both missed, both loved.

"Ah," the woman says, biting her lower lip. "I was one of those once."

Mele laughs out loud, then glances back toward the party to find Henry, who is already looking right at her. It's a new feeling, this. When she was with Bobby she always scanned the room for him, finally finding him laughing with a pack of guys, or girls, always occupied, never the one looking. She checks to see what Ellie's doing—jumping in the air with the other kids, clapping bubbles like little seals. Her girl is just fine. Mele says good-bye to the couple and walks toward him.

She and Henry mingle with guests. He outshines Bobby, in her opinion, and he seems to know many of the people there. There are so many guests that she can be anonymous and avoid awkward conversations. She is simply an old friend of the groom. Henry introduces her as "his dear friend, Mele," which she likes very much.

There is one snag. After the first dance—how boring to watch one couple dance—no one likes this—they are talking to a group of guys, their wives huddled nearby. Ellie walks up to her with one of the hired "child entertainers."

"I'm taking the kids to the outdoor movie screen," the girl says. "Okay if she joins us?"

"Of course," Mele says, grateful for this child-watch luxury. "Have fun, sweetie." She swoops Ellie up for a hug. "Proud of you."

When Ellie leaves, she feels the women's eyes on her.

"That's *her*," one of them says. She has glossy auburn hair and sweat on her upper lip. She says to her girlfriend, "What was he thinking?"

222

Mele can't help herself. She touches Henry's shoulder, excusing herself, then walks toward the bar, pausing by the women: "I believe he was thinking about a last hurrah," she says. "And that my pussy was like the Jaws of Life. Cheers."

Besides that, she was a perfect guest.

"You did it," Henry says.

They are on the dance floor under the tent draped with lights that look like stars. The violinists have been replaced with a live jazz band. His hand is on the base of her back, her hands rest on his shoulders. Dancing is such a brilliant idea. How else would they have an excuse to be this close so quickly?

"I did it," she says. "It wasn't that hard." His eyes are a darker green at night, with faint lines like whiskers in the corners. "I was distracted."

"By what?" he says, his expression jokingly bemused.

"The prawns," she says.

"And all that cheese," he says. "A sea of cheese."

"Ewe," she says.

He laughs; his smile is so broad. He takes her hands and moves her out then back in again, and she can see it—the witty—or not so witty—remark that's about to roll off his tongue. It's what they are doing these days and tonight, a toying repartee. They are dabbling, sipping slowly, and while she likes their carefulness and coquetry, it has become procrastination.

She puts a hand on the back of his neck, drawing his face toward her, kisses him gently, crossing that line into an unfamiliar and unexpected place, which feels exactly where they're supposed to be.

They will take it from there.

ACKNOWLEDGMENTS

I started this book when my daughter was a toddler, and now she is taller than me. Thank you David Forrer and Kim Witherspoon, my agents at Inkwell Management, for being with me the whole way through.

Whenever I read the notes, critiques, and suggestions from Marysue Rucci, I immediately return to my manuscript with inspiration and energy. I don't know what more I could possibly ask from an editor. Thank you so much for making me love to write and rewrite.

And thank you to the real playgroup—Jen Murdin, Sara Starr, Michelle Delen, Yeli Yoo, Lindsay Hunter, and Christina Amail, as well as many other San Francisco mothers who made parenting a lot less lonely and a lot more fun. I loved partying with you.

ABOUT THE AUTHOR

Kaui Hart Hemmings is the author of the story collection *House of Thieves* and the novels *Juniors, The Possibilities,* and *The Descendants,* a *New York Times* bestseller and an Oscar-winning film. She has degrees from Colorado College and Sarah Lawrence and was a Stegner Fellow at Stanford University. A one-time resident of San Francisco, she now lives in Hawaii.

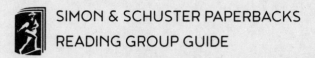

This reading group guide for *How to Party With an Infant* includes an introduction, discussion questions, ideas for enhancing your book club, and a Q&A with author Kaui Hart Hemmings. The suggested questions are intended to help your reading group find new and interesting angles and topics for your discussion. We hope that these ideas will enrich your conversation and increase your enjoyment of the book.

INTRODUCTION

Two years after being blindsided by her (surprise!) engaged-to-someone-else boyfriend and subsequently dumped while pregnant, Mele Bart is a thirty-year-old single mother who spends most days sitting in various San Francisco sandboxes with her daughter, Ellie. While she's been lucky enough to have found fellow parents who become her de facto family, what Mele doesn't have is much in the way of professional drive or romance—but all that changes when her ex invites her to his perfect Napa wedding to his perfect cheesemaker fiancée, with little Ellie to play the role of flower girl.

Aimless and dateless, Mele decides to occupy her mind in the months prior to the wedding by entering a cookbook contest sponsored by the San Francisco Mother's Club. Mele begins to listen to her friends' revealing, honest, and often hilarious stories—tales of babysitter envy and teenage delinquency, cheating spouses, over-sexualized tweens, and super-rich mommies whose idea of charity is donating their lightly-used Hermes belts to the less fortunate—and transform their memories into rich, evocative meals. In the process of writing her cookbook, Mele, too, begins to transform in ways that she never sees coming as she opens her mind to love and a life that consists of more than just simply living. Laugh-out-loud funny, insightful, and real, *How to Party With an Infant* explores motherhood, relationships, and food from a unique and timely perspective.

TOPICS & QUESTIONS FOR DISCUSSION

1. Why does Mele decide to enter the cookbook competition in the first place? What does she mean when she says, "It's comforting to be able to explain yourself, or to be asked anything at all"? In what ways do the questionnaire and the cookbook become Mele's diary? How do you think Mele would feel actually to win the competition? Is this even her goal?

2. What do you think about the unconventional format of the novel, from Mele's revealing first-person responses to the questionnaire and her friends' stories to the Greek-chorus-style emails from the SFMC listserv interjected throughout? How does this creative structure contribute to your understanding of the plot and characters of the novel?

3. Talk about the concepts of "the mommy wars" and "helicopter parenting," and how they come to play out in this novel. Have you ever found yourself the victim of judgment over choices you have made, whether pertaining to parenting or otherwise? How does the author satirize modern parenting in San Francisco?

4. Discuss the crucial role that class plays in the novel; think about specific scenes such as Mele's first SFMC playgroup with the rich mommies, Annie's obsession with Tabor Boyard, and Henry's embarrassment over his friends' reaction to his home. How and why do certain characters feel defined by and defensive about their wealth (or lack thereof)? Why does social class become such a key part of the relationships and interactions in the novel?

5. The core of the novel is Mele—the careful observer and frustrated writer—listening to the wide-ranging stories of her friends and reimagining their varied experiences as recipes. Of all the stories she hears, whose did you relate to the most and why? Which character would you like to hear more stories from? (And which meal would you most like to eat?)

6. Georgia tells Mele about the night she bailed Chris out of jail and ends up spinning a web of lies for her teenage son—that she was a model, a cocaine addict, and a yogi in India. Why does Georgia lie to her son? What does she stand to gain from the story she tells him? How does her tall tale impact her relationship with her son in the short term, and what does their one unplanned day— when "she's not on a playground bench staring into space, when she's not at home watching other people on television making love"—do for Georgia?

7. Why doesn't Mele confess that she's taken the Hermes belt from the charity giveaway pile at the Betts's house? What does the belt symbolize and why does Mele ultimately leave it on the curb?

8. While Annie and Mele have only very young children, Henry, Georgia, and Barrett all have tween and teenage children in addition to their younger children. How do each of these characters' stories highlight the increasingly complex challenges facing parents of teenagers? What fears about raising children to adulthood do each of these parents reveal in their stories? What can Mele learn about raising Ellie from her friends' (often cautionary) tales?

9. Despite the fact that Henry's wife cheats on him and Annie's husband is constantly travelling for work, Mele is the only one of her

friends who is definitely single. What challenges and judgments does Mele face as a single mother? Georgia says that she envies Mele and that she is "free." Do you think that Mele is indeed free, or is it more complicated than that?

10. "Ellie wasn't a baby anymore, and I was still reacting versus living." How does becoming a mother change Mele? What does she miss about her life before Ellie, and how does she set out to change her approach to her life over the course of the novel? Do you think that she successfully reaches a place where she is in fact living versus reacting? If you are a parent, can you relate to Mele's sentiment?

11. Discuss how Mele and Bobby's relationship changes and develops over the course of the novel. Do you think that Mele should ask more of Bobby as a father to Ellie? Why does she decide to attend the wedding? What do you think the future holds for her, Bobby, and the cheesemaker wife?

12. Were you surprised by the end of the novel? What do you think happens next with Mele and Henry?

ENHANCE YOUR BOOK CLUB

1. In writing her cookbook, Mele sets out to listen to her friends and "take moments from their everyday lives—moments that define their issues somehow, and come up with the food equivalents" and "make a difficult moment in their lives a little more palatable." Talk about a significant memory or moment from your life and what meal you would serve to make the memory more palatable. If you're feeling ambitious, have a book club dinner party where you all bring your dish along with recipe cards to compile a book club cookbook!

2. Select a few questions from the SFMC questionnaire and tailor them for your book club to answer together. For example: What was the last thing you ate? How have your friendships from your book club changed your life? What is your proudest moment? If you could construct an interview for yourself, what questions would you want to be asked?

3. If you could write a cookbook, what would the title be, and what would some sample recipes be? Would you want to insert stories from your life into the cookbook?

It was so fun and refreshing to read a novel with such an unconventional, unique structure! How did you come up with the idea of the SFMC cookbook questionnaire?

When you publish a book the publisher's marketing team sends you an Author Questionnaire, asking questions like, "How did you come up with the idea for your book?" Years ago I wrote an essay/story entitled "Author Questionnaire" that I really enjoyed writing—the structure allowed for a kind of ad lib narrative. So, I decided to implement that structure in a novel form.

Would you ever enter a cookbook competition? If you had to enter a contest, what type of cookbook would you want to write and what would be three signature recipes?

Sure, I'd enter. I love that we no longer look to the experts anymore. I get so many recipes from friends or blogs, written by women who aren't chefs. They just love to cook. Signature recipes? Sukiyaki, roasted cauliflower with this walnut sauce I make, and chicken marbella (though I often make brussels sprouts marbella). I love cooking with vegetables and I love throwing things together with whatever's around.

Your debut novel, *The Descendants*, was turned into a movie starring George Clooney and Shailene Woodley. If this book gets made into a movie, who would be your dream cast?

My favorite funny ladies—Amy Schumer, Kristin Wiig, Maya Rudolph, Reese Witherspoon. Throw in Michael Fassbinder—why not? For Mele, someone who doesn't fit that "mother's club" role and who'd be the elephant in the Pacific Heights living room. Zoë Kravitz? Selena Gomez? It would be nice to have a multiracial leading lady.

As a Brooklyn mom, I really identified with all the scenes and observations in the novel about the Bay Area mommy wars, from the breastfeeding debates to the preschool obsession. Did you have to do any research to get these details so right, or were you able to draw from your personal experiences of when you lived in San Francisco?

Fortunately (or unfortunately) no research was needed. I was part of a mother's club in San Francisco and many of the things said (and all of the quotes before chapters) were right out of the mothers' mouths. And yet, I don't like the term *mommy wars*. We are all moms with opinions, insecurities, and sometimes rigid beliefs, but we're all just trying to connect, do our best, and get it right. And party.

I loved how Mele's San Francisco friends truly became her family and her support system. Did any of your own friendships inform or inspire Mele's friendships? Why did you choose to have Mele be so independent from her own parents and from her previous life in Hawaii?

My friends in San Francisco (whom I met through the mother's club) inspired a lot of the sentiments about friendships formed as a mom. We never would have met in any other way, and sometimes a forced bond turns into a real one.

Parenting is hard. Parenting without family is even harder, which is why I chose the distance. Unlike myself, Mele was more than physically distant from her family. I wanted to write about a young woman trying to forge her own path, a coming of age, but with the heroine strapped with an infant and who should already have come of age.

Which character's story was the most difficult to write and which was the easiest? Which character do you relate to the most?

I relate to Mele's struggle to find her people in San Francisco. I was twenty-seven, living in a small apartment on the Panhandle and wasn't planning on having a baby. I related to her desire to fit in and yet be herself. I related to the way she observed the world around her, how life—the good, the bad, and the ugly—could be her material. This also made her character harder to write because I don't like writing about myself, so I had to use my experiences and yet allow myself to get out of character. Henry was easiest for me. For some reason I'm at home being a middle-aged man.

If you had to pick one moment from your life and one meal to serve alongside your story of that memory, what would it be, and why? When I gave birth to my daughter I remember first returning home from the hospital and looking back at her in the car seat, swaddled and tiny—she was like a little hors d'oeuvre. It was crazy to see a baby in the car, and yet, like that, you adapt. I thought to myself, with no fear or apprehension, and yet no certainty as to what lay ahead: Okay. This is my life now. With my son it was similar, even though we first met him at the adoption agency in Ethiopia. We were led to his crib and he peeked over, grinning and swaying back and forth, and I thought: This is incredible, this is crazy, and okay, this is my life now. I'm not sure what to do with these gifts, but let's go ahead and unwrap them. The meal to accompany these memories would have to be lau lau, a Hawaiian dish, typically made by wrapping pork, fat, sweet potatoes, and fish in layers of luau leaves (like spinach). Once it's swaddled, it's then wrapped and held together with ti leaves that seal in the flavors. It's then steamed, or put into an imu, an underground oven. It's both simple, ingredient wise, and yet complex and laborious and rooted in history. It's a beautifully presented gift that requires unwrapping. A lot has gone into it, time and care, lessons from and connections to the past, yet while eating, you're fully in the present—delving into the layers, trying to figure it out.

What do you think happens next with Mele and Henry? Do you think you'll return to any of these characters in the future?

They live happily ever after, with complications from Henry's divorce, adapting to stepchildren, a new (much larger) home. They live happily and unhappily depending on what went down that day. Like Mele I also write "something bad" into my daily calendar so I won't be surprised. My son hit the substitute teacher today—well—it's in the calendar! I don't know if I'd return to them or not. I always love when novels leave various possibilities. A *How to Party* cookbook would be fun though.

What are you working on now?

A young adult novel, an adult novel, a screenplay, a kindergartener, a sixth grader, a crazy puppy. I'm working on trying to convince my husband that we need a mini horse. I'm working on skateboarding since my son loves it and doing dance tutorials on YouTube with my daughter.

Also by
KAUI HART HEMMINGS

Pick up or download your copy today!